PRAISE FOR
THE SOUTHERN QUILTING MYSTERIES

Knot What It Seams

"Craig laces this puzzler with a plausible plot, a wealth of quirky characters, and rich local color as Beatrice and her friends try to restore peace for the piecers." —*Richmond Times-Dispatch*

"Elizabeth Craig has created a charming world of quilting, friendship, and intrigue with this series, and *Knot What It Seams* is a fun, fast-paced, and intriguing tale." —Sharon's Garden of Book Reviews

"[Will] entice any quilt lover to put down their needle and sit a spell and read." —The Mystery Reader

"Interesting and intriguing." —Fresh Fiction

Quilt or Innocence

"A delightful new series as warm and cozy as a favorite quilt. Elizabeth Craig captures Southern life at its best, and her characters are as vibrant and colorful as the quilts they sew."
—Krista Davis, national bestselling author of the Domestic Diva Mysteries

"Sparkles with Craig's cleverness and plenty of Carolina charm." —*Richmond Times-Dispatch*

continued . . .

Also by Elizabeth Craig

Quilt or Innocence
Knot What It Seams

QUILT TRIP

A SOUTHERN QUILTING MYSTERY

Elizabeth Craig

AN OBSIDIAN MYSTERY

OBSIDIAN
Published by the Penguin Group
Penguin Group (USA) LLC, 375 Hudson Street,
New York, New York 10014

USA | Canada | UK | Ireland | Australia | New Zealand | India | South Africa | China
penguin.com
A Penguin Random House Company

First published by Obsidian, an imprint of New American Library,
a division of Penguin Group (USA) LLC

First Printing, December 2013

Copyright © Elizabeth Craig, 2013

ISBN 978-0-451-24063-7

Printed in the United States of America
10 9 8 7 6 5 4 3 2

For Mama and Daddy, with thanks and love.

ACKNOWLEDGMENTS

Thanks to my family for all the ways they support me. Thanks to Mary Spann Peterson, Henry Spann, and Beth Spann for being thoughtful beta readers. Thanks to Sandra Harding for her skillful editing and always-sound story vision. Thanks to my agent, Ellen Pepus. Many thanks to my friends for their encouragement and for the writing community in general. And thanks to the mystery writers who have written before me for the inspiration they've provided me.

Chapter One

Beatrice Coleman looked in horror at her neighbor
Meadow Downey. "You mean we're not even invited? We're gate-crashing?"

They were in Meadow's aging green van and
Meadow was speedily driving them to a home just
slightly outside their town of Dappled Hills, North
Carolina. Beatrice felt a bit dizzy as they wound up
the curving road and sped through wooded hills.
She hoped the van was up for the trip—the high-
pitched whirring of the engine hardly inspired confidence. Beatrice always felt slightly self-conscious
when riding in her friend's van—she must have
stuck at least fifteen bumper stickers on it, all es-
pousing a variety of unusual philosophies.

Meadow chortled. "Gate-crashing?" she said. "You
can't gate-crash a Special Quilt Guild Meeting, Beatrice. It's completely impossible. Gate-crashing is

for parties. What we're doing is dropping in without calling first."

"What we're really doing," said Beatrice gloomily, "is trying to persuade a sick, elderly woman that we're the best candidates to chair a quilting scholarship committee." She peered again out the van window as the scenery flew by. "Meadow, I think it's going to snow. The sky is that odd mottled gray. I'm getting a really bad feeling about all of this. We should turn around now and go back home."

Meadow glanced away from the road to give Beatrice a reassuring grin, although the result was anything but. Meadow had that fervent expression that she had whenever she was all geared up for quilting. Her eyes behind her red glasses were full of fire. She'd tried to tame her long gray hair into its customary braid, but must have been distracted because it escaped in wisps. The overall effect was rather maniacal, Beatrice decided.

"We can't go back, Beatrice. This is the perfect opportunity for the Village Quilters. If old Mrs. Starnes wants to create a foundation and award scholarships to ensure the longevity of the quilting craft, I can't think of a better guild than ours to distribute them. I already have a recipient in mind. Apparently, Mrs. Starnes is even going to delegate funds for the guild that administers the scholarship—to get them out in the surrounding communities and schools to demonstrate the craft and encourage it. The Village Quilters are perfect!"

"But, Meadow—the weather. Can't we just send

Mrs. Starnes or whoever she is an e-mail in which we express our qualifications?" asked Beatrice.

Meadow vehemently shook her head. "No. Mrs. Starnes doesn't have electronics in her house. She's an old, eccentric woman, Beatrice."

Beatrice bit her tongue to keep from pointing out that there was an old, eccentric woman sitting right next to her.

"Besides, I'm sure she would have invited us if she'd remembered. She probably simply forgot about getting a representative from the Village Quilters guild. We're helping her out," Meadow said in a righteous voice.

"We're foisting ourselves on her under the guise of being helpful," muttered Beatrice. "Look— It's sleeting."

"Pooh. Who cares about a little sleet?"

Clearly not Meadow. Actually, it looked like a combination of sleet and freezing rain. And as Meadow pulled the van into the driveway, the ominous sky gave Beatrice the feeling they were embarking on an adventure.

Dappled Hills was a small, picturesque mountain town full of steep hills, and Beatrice was accustomed to rather treacherous driveways. But the driveway Meadow was currently scaling put all the rest to shame.

"Where are the switchbacks?" Beatrice asked. "We're going straight up. Shouldn't there be switchbacks to keep us at a safe, gradual ascent?"

"This house and driveway are so old that there

probably weren't a lot of people using switchbacks back when it was built," said Meadow airily. "We'll be fine."

The driveway was a narrow, potholed dirt road stretching through dense trees straight up the side of a mountain. At the crest sat a dilapidated old Victorian house complete with a turret, cupola, dormer windows, a wraparound porch, and a steep roof. Its white paint was peeling off and its gingerbread trim had a bad case of rot.

"Southern gothic," Beatrice said under her breath.

Several other cars were parked at the top of the driveway. "See?" said Meadow. "It's not as if we're interrupting a huge party or anything. There are probably five or six other people here. Besides, I come bearing food and quilts! Who's going to turn that down?"

Beatrice had a feeling that old Muriel Starnes likely had gobs of quilts in her eroding Victorian mansion. But she'd agree with Meadow on the food. Meadow was a fantastic cook and Beatrice had been enjoying the aroma of whatever wonderful food she'd cooked all the way from home. She couldn't wait to dig into it. "What did you bring?"

"Hot bacon and artichoke dip. Doesn't it smell delicious? Could you help me with these quilts, Beatrice?"

Beatrice clucked over the way Meadow had flung the quilts into the back of her messy van. "Meadow, these quilts are getting wrinkled and dirty! You didn't bring hangers for them, or a garment bag or something?"

Meadow waved her hand dismissively. "Oh, no. Quilts are made to be used, Beatrice. Who cares if they have a little bit of dirt on them? That's life! Quilts aren't merely an art form, although I know that's usually how you view them."

Beatrice was a retired art curator who'd moved from Atlanta to the tiny town of Dappled Hills to spend more time with her grown daughter. Meadow was right—Beatrice saw quilts through the eyes of a curator. She always saw the artistic merit—or lack of it—in them first, then thought of ways to best display and preserve the quilts.

Meadow trotted brazenly up the warped wooden steps onto the wraparound porch. The front door had apparently originally been black, but now most of its paint was peeled off. She lifted the heavy brass door knocker and rapped authoritatively.

A breeze blew up and Beatrice shivered from the chill, pulling her full-length black wool coat around her.

A dour, bald older man wearing an immaculate suit and a frown opened the door. He raised his eyebrows at Meadow's wildly colorful appearance. Meadow was solidly constructed and tall, but had never shied away from wearing large prints and bright colors. Her long gray braid hung to her waist and the twinkling eyes behind her red glasses were mischievous. The man seemed somewhat more comforted when he studied Beatrice in her no-nonsense coat, black ribbed turtleneck, khaki pants, and silvery blond hair. "Are we expecting you?" he asked doubtfully.

"Mrs. Starnes *should* be expecting us," said Meadow breezily—meaning, of course, that Mrs. Starnes should have invited them but hadn't. Beatrice's head started pounding.

"I brought hot dip and chips," said Meadow with a big smile, as if that would guarantee her entry.

The man opened his mouth to inquire further, but snapped it shut again and frowned as he squinted at the dirt driveway.

Another car was approaching. As the man crossed his arms as if planning to offer a roadblock to anybody trying to enter the house, the car came into view.

"It's Posy!" said Meadow delightedly. She explained to the grim man, "It's Posy Beck, owner of the Patchwork Cottage shop in Dappled Hills. She's in our quilting guild."

Beatrice groaned softly. "Look who's with her."

"It's Miss Sissy!" crowed Meadow, who didn't appear to understand that a crazy old woman wasn't going to make it any easier for them to get into this gathering. The sleet mixed with freezing rain fell harder.

"Meadow, I'm thinking we need to leave," Beatrice said. "We're clearly not being encouraged to come inside, and the weather is getting worse. How will we get out of here if the ice starts accumulating? We're on top of a mountain with a steep driveway."

There was a cough behind them and an old woman hunched over a walker gazed steadily at them from hooded eyes. The man exclaimed with concern and reached to assist her, but she waved him off with irritation. "I'm fine," she grated. "Let these women in, Colton. It's pouring down rain—or something—out here."

Colton still seemed reluctant. "Do you know them, Muriel?"

"I know they're quilters because they're holding quilts," she said dryly. "It seems as though that other car holds more quilters. They're all welcome here."

Colton tightened his lips, trying to keep himself from arguing, then stepped aside to let Meadow and Beatrice in.

"I have hot dip!" Meadow said brightly to Muriel Starnes.

Muriel gave a close-lipped smile and hobbled in with them. "We're all sitting in the library," she said

Meadow was unfortunately, and as usual, in a very chatty mood. She'd made any number of inane statements before reaching the library and, once there, didn't seem affected whatsoever by the general atmosphere in the room.

But Beatrice was. The library was a large room, and a cold one. In fact, the entire house was cold. Beatrice shivered and decided to leave her coat on. A stone fireplace held several shards of wood that were quickly burning out. The sight of books usually had a cheering effect on Beatrice, but these books had a depressing never-read look about them. The room was full of dusty, heavy furniture in dark-colored woods. Actually, the entire house was full of dust, and her nose tickled as she saw some floating in an anemic sunbeam from the library window. Beatrice sniffed delicately. There was definitely a scent of decay and mold in the room. The only inviting spot was the bay window seat.

The gathering of quilters was fairly subdued. In fact, they were completely mute. They nodded a greeting in response to Meadow's over-the-top hello, then took to gazing around the room or staring at their quilts or their hands. The women were of various ages. No one else had brought anything to eat or drink and Muriel Starnes didn't appear inclined to offer anything. Everyone appeared to be waiting for a speech or an official welcome of some kind.

Colton came in with Posy and Miss Sissy. His expression was one of disdain. Posy, fluffy as usual in a pastel cardigan and beagle brooch, beamed at everyone and was completely innocuous, so Beatrice had to assume that it was Miss Sissy who was responsible for Colton's dismay. She was looking even wilder than Meadow—most of her hair had pulled out of her bun and she wore a long floral dress that had seen better days.

"Wickedness!" proclaimed Miss Sissy, hissing the word as she glared suspiciously around the room.

Posy and Beatrice exchanged glances. Apparently, this wasn't one of Miss Sissy's good days.

Muriel Starnes walked over to a large leather armchair and carefully sat down, keeping her walker in front of her. "Thanks to everyone for coming," she said in a voice that was weak but still had remnants of authority in it. "It's certainly a tribute to the quilting craft that I have had such a good turnout. Perhaps even"—she studied Meadow, Beatrice, and Miss Sissy—"more of a turnout than I anticipated."

Beatrice felt herself blush. Meadow seemed unconcerned.

"I'm going to let my lawyer, Colton Bradshaw, explain the general setup of the foundation I'm creating and give you more information about it," said Muriel, leaning back wearily in her chair.

"Lawyer?" said Meadow, chortling. "I thought he was your butler!"

Colton gave her an icy glare and stood up stiffly, holding several papers that he appeared to be planning to read from. Beatrice sighed. Judging from that script of his, they might be trapped here for hours.

"Thanks to Muriel Starnes's generosity, the assembled are gathered here today to offer insight and input on finding and vetting qualified and worthy recipients for the quilting scholarships," he intoned.

Beatrice sighed again. His delivery wasn't very good, either. She decided to tune out Colton and spend her time watching the other women in the room. It was an odd group. Most of the women were watching Colton seriously. One or two of them appeared almost suspicious, and another looked anxious. Meadow, on the other hand, was like a wriggling puppy. She could barely stand to wait for Colton to finish so she could enthusiastically give her thoughts on the scholarships.

Two of the older quilters had unreadable expressions on their faces. One of the women looked fairly sour and the other was blankly watching Colton read his prepared statement. It seemed that everyone should have been as enthusiastic and excited as Meadow was. Weren't they supposed to be selling themselves as good candidates to administer the scholarships?

Muriel didn't appear to be listening to a word Colton was saying, but then, she'd surely already been familiar with his little speech. Her hooded eyes watched the other women closely. Sometimes the quilters caught her staring and glanced away.

Miss Sissy was ravenously gobbling down all the crackers, having apparently decided that she didn't care for a component of the bacon and artichoke dip.

Colton finally concluded his speech. Or maybe he was only pausing to catch his breath. Meadow jumped in while she had the chance. "I'll speak for all of us, I'm sure, when I say that I'm absolutely thrilled that you're helping ensure the longevity of the quilting craft through your foundation. And I want to explain how the Village Quilters guild is perfect for administering this scholarship. You see, our guild's amazing history—"

"Thank you, Colton," Muriel Starnes interrupted as seamlessly as if Meadow hadn't said a word. "And now I have a confession to make. I haven't been completely honest with you about the reason you're all here."

There was suddenly a great, snapping *Pow!* outside the window and the lights went out.

Chapter Two

There wasn't nearly as much natural light inside the library as there should have been, Beatrice thought. After all, it was still daytime. But the heavy cloud cover outside meant that there wasn't much sunlight to be had.

Added to the darkness, it was a little unsettling to have Miss Sissy, her mouth still full of snacks, shrieking, "Murder! Murder!" and shaking her arthritic fists.

Beatrice tried peering out the bay window but couldn't see anything, so she hurried out to the front door. Several other quilters and Colton Bradshaw followed.

A tremendous tree had lost a huge limb, which was now completely blocking the driveway.

"Thank goodness it didn't hit our cars," gasped Meadow, always one to look on the bright side.

"Except now we're trapped," said Beatrice. "Our cars aren't much good if we can't get past that limb."

Meadow squinted at the limb. "We can move it, Beatrice."

"Speak for yourself! I'm pretty sure I don't have the strength to move it. I'm over sixty years old." Beatrice glanced over at the lawyer standing next to her. She was fairly sure he wouldn't have the strength, either. He was evidently even older than she was.

"Odd. It appears the limb didn't fall on the power lines," said Colton, frowning. "But they're down as well."

"They snapped," said Beatrice, pointing at the lines. "When ice builds up on a power line, the weight of the ice brings them down."

Meadow said, "I still say we can heave that branch out of the way."

Nature's response to this statement was to split an entire tree farther down the mountain, causing it to fall at another point of the driveway.

"Never mind," Meadow said with a laugh.

One of the younger quilters, who appeared to be about fifty, said hesitantly, "We could walk down the driveway and find help."

"I think you'll find that's quite impossible," Colton said. "The driveway will soon be a sheet of ice, if it isn't already. Even if you reached the bottom, the nearest house is two miles down the mountain. Very treacherous."

Beatrice sighed. "There is such an invention as the telephone. Let's go inside and call the power company to report the outage. Then we can phone someone to come as close as they safely can and we can meet them at that point."

Meadow winked at her. "Will you be calling Wyatt, Beatrice?" She fluttered her lashes at Beatrice.

Wyatt was a local minister with whom Beatrice had a warm friendship. At this point, it hadn't yet blossomed into anything else. Not that Meadow believed it.

"Or Ramsay," Beatrice replied. Ramsay was Meadow's husband and chief of police.

Meadow shook her head. "Ramsay's off on his hunting and fishing trip out West with his college buddy. Remember? I told you about it in the car on the way over."

It must have been one of those moments when Beatrice had desperately tuned out the babble.

Muriel Starnes spoke from behind them. "Unfortunately, it doesn't matter whom you'd contact, because the phone lines are down. I've checked."

Now they were standing there in the freezing rain, gawking in dismay at Muriel.

"Stuck here?" asked Meadow. "With no toothbrush?"

"We do have cell phones," Beatrice said. "I'll just run in and grab mine from my purse."

"I think you'll find," Muriel said steadily, "that there will be no cell phone reception here. The nearest tower is quite some distance away and this entire area banded together to block the carrier from clearcutting trees to build a tower on this mountain."

Beatrice was already walking inside to check her

phone, but heard the quilters who had their phones on them muttering over the lack of reception.

She pulled her phone from her pocketbook. Nothing. No signal at all. Beatrice dropped her phone back in her bag and sank into a chair in the dark library. The ominous feeling from earlier grew stronger. Something was wrong here . . . something besides the storm.

Posy joined her. "No reception?" she asked, an anxious frown on her features.

Beatrice shook her head. "I'm afraid not. And Piper is in California visiting Meadow's son. I don't have anyone who'll even notice that I'm missing right now—and neither does Meadow, since Ramsay is away. What about your husband, Posy?"

"Oh, Cork will notice I'm gone," she said. "He'll be wondering where his supper is when he gets home from work."

Beatrice relaxed a little. "Well, thank goodness for that. Maybe he can bring a small team of people up here to help get us out."

Posy knit her brows. "But, Beatrice, he didn't know I was coming here. Cork doesn't take much interest in the guild meetings and all. I didn't even write it on our wall calendar in the kitchen. It was sort of a last-minute thing. Meadow called the shop yesterday and asked if I could come here with her. She thought I might be able to host special community outreach programs and that we could convince Muriel that the Village Quilters would be the right guild to help her with her foundation. So . . . Cork knows nothing about this."

"Murder!" offered Miss Sissy, who had followed Posy back into the library and was scraping together the crumbs that were all that remained of the crackers.

"I'm afraid we're stuck," said Posy with a sigh. "I guess at some point they'll either figure out where we are or else the phone company will repair the line and we'll be able to call out."

"Or the ice will melt," said Meadow. She was still remarkably upbeat, which irritated Beatrice.

"Being stuck in a decaying mansion isn't exactly my idea of fun," said Beatrice. Then she groaned. "I took Noo-noo to the groomers today to get her nails trimmed and have her undercoat brushed out. They're going to think I deserted her!"

Now Meadow was serious. "And my Boris is alone. With a self-feeding dog bowl, though."

Beatrice put her hand over her mouth. "Your house! It's going to be a doggy restroom. Oh—no, you've got a dog door, don't you?"

Meadow nodded.

Posy said, "I'm sure Cork will figure out soon that I'm with the two of you. He'd have checked with one of you first to see if you knew where I was. Once he realizes we're all gone, he'll be sure to see after the dogs. He's as much of an animal lover as I am."

Beatrice said, "I'm still going to keep trying to get a signal to call out with my cell phone. Maybe after it stops raining I can walk outside and see if I can get reception somewhere."

The other quilters joined them in the library. A fiftyish quilter with an aquiline nose and black hair with several streaks of white said, "No one has cell phone service. We've all checked. And some of us use different carriers."

"It's just the way it is," said Muriel Starnes with a shrug. She dropped into her armchair, exhausted.

"That's fine for you, Mother," snapped the black-haired woman furiously. "You don't have anything to do but sit around up here on top of your mountain. Some of us have other plans."

Mother? Meadow and Beatrice blinked at each other.

Muriel noticed their surprise. She sighed. "Since it appears as though we're going to be spending time together, I suppose that introductions are in order. As you've already gathered, this is my daughter, Alexandra Starnes."

Alexandra gave them a condescending smile that didn't reach her cool blue eyes.

Muriel waved a thin hand at the red-haired quilter, who seemed to be fifty, although her freckles and sweet expression made her appear younger. "This is Holly Weaver. Librarian by day, quilter by night." Holly's eyes crinkled in a smile and her dimples flashed.

"This," said Muriel, gesturing to a woman in her seventies with sharp features and reading glasses hanging from a silver chain around her neck, "is

Winnie Tyson. She's a friend of mine who quilts and teaches school."

"Former friend," said Winnie in harsh voice.

Muriel ignored the correction and nodded toward the last of the quilters, a hefty woman wearing a T-shirt with an American flag on it. "And this is Dot Giles. A fine quilter."

Dot grinned. "A compliment? From you, Muriel? I may have to take to my bed."

The introductions appeared to be taking a lot out of Muriel. "Could the rest of you introduce yourselves? I'm not even exactly sure who you all are." Muriel frowned at Miss Sissy, who glared back at her.

Posy hastily said, "I'm Posy Beck and I own the Patchwork Cottage shop in Dappled Hills. Miss Sissy here . . . well, she spends a lot of time at the shop. She didn't really have anything to do today, so I brought her along." She nervously fingered the buttons on her fluffy cardigan.

Meadow launched into what sounded more like an introduction at a personal motivation conference. "I'm Meadow Downey and I'm here to tell everyone how wonderful my guild, the Village Quilters, is! I'm planning to explain how the Village Quilters can play a part in building the future of quilting."

Beatrice was pleased that she was able to keep from wincing at Meadow's little speech. "I'm Beatrice Coleman. I'm a former art museum curator and new resident in Dappled Hills. I'm interested in the artistic side of quilting and the historical element of it, as well. I'm in the Village Quilters guild and

Meadow persuaded me to come along today." She smiled through gritted teeth.

The library became quiet—a loud sort of quiet that drew attention to itself. Finally, Muriel broke it. "As I was mentioning before the power went off, I haven't been entirely honest with you all. Yes, I'm creating a special foundation to promote the longevity of the craft I love. Husbands, friends, and family have come and gone in my life, but quilting has always been here. I'd like to do my part in making sure the next generation picks up the art."

She leaned forward. "But that's not the only reason I brought you here today. I'm personally connected to everyone in this room. Well, nearly everyone. The people who I'm connected to are angry with me. Angry because I've let them down in some respect." She took out an old embroidered handkerchief and blotted her face with it. She was beginning to look even more tired.

She took a sip of water, then continued. "As you can see, I'm having health difficulties. Unfortunately, the doctors have determined that I'm in the advanced stages of cancer and am not expected to live more than the next few weeks."

There was a murmur in the room. Beatrice was struck, however, that the only people who were remotely concerned or sympathetic were the Village Quilters group, and perhaps the younger quilter, Holly Weaver. Muriel's daughter's eyes were hard as flint, although she said, "Poor Mother," rather unconvincingly.

"What I'm trying to accomplish today, in addition to ensuring the future of the quilting craft in our area, is to make amends. I've hurt people in my time and I want to formally apologize and set things right with them before I meet my Maker." A fleeting expression of fear flashed through her eyes, surprising Beatrice. Muriel Starnes genuinely seemed afraid of entering the hereafter. What could she have done to make her so worried about the status of her soul?

Muriel leaned back in her armchair again, slumping. "I knew that some of you wouldn't bother coming if I issued an invitation merely asking for a visit. That's another reason why I created this foundation. If this was about quilting, I knew you'd come." Her gaze circled the room, resting on each of the quilters in turn.

She appeared to have completely run out of steam. "So, to all of you," she said, not singling out individual names, "I wanted to express my deep apologies and regrets for any wrongs I may have done you in the past. It was thoughtless of me and I truly hope you'll offer me your forgiveness."

Her words sounded sincere. Beatrice thought they sounded practiced, too. It was interesting how she gazed at a spot in the air behind them all. And how extraordinary of her to bring this up now, with regular quilters in attendance as well as people she didn't even know. And why choose to make this impersonal, blanket apology? Why not try to speak to everyone in private, later on?

The other quilters stared at her. Muriel's daughter,

Alexandra, had a cynical expression on her face and looked as if she might be trying not to say something cutting. Holly Weaver just seemed confused. Winnie and Dot had calculating looks on their faces, as if trying to gauge what Muriel's speech really meant to them.

"And now that that's done, I'd like to hear you all pitch why your guild would be best to serve in an advisory position for the foundation. I can't have you all do it—too many cooks spoil the stew, you know. We'll go around the room. I've gotten the gist of Meadow Downey's thoughts on the matter." She gave Meadow a squelching frown, and Meadow sighed. She'd be biting her tongue while everyone else spoke.

Everyone briefly talked about their guild, the history of it, its connection to the community, and its ideas about outreach. Sometimes Muriel appeared to be dozing, but Beatrice had the feeling that she was wide awake and listening intently. This was the kind of woman who would want to give the impression that she was less alert than she really was, simply to gain an advantage.

When the quilters had finished speaking, she nodded. Then Muriel said, "Unfortunately, it appears as if everyone is marooned here, at least for tonight. I was unprepared for this, of course, but I'll do my best to make you all comfortable. It may be a challenge."

Beatrice said, "While there's still a little light in the house to see by, we should find candles or flashlights. If you tell me where to find them, I'll gather them together."

Muriel gave her a measuring glance. "Good thinking. Perhaps you should have been the one to speak on behalf of the Village Quilters. I don't have many candles, I'm afraid. Getting more supplies for the winter was on my list of things to do, but once I got my diagnosis, it all seemed rather pointless. If you go to the dining room, there's a sideboard there. The bottom drawer should have candles and matches in it."

"And flashlights?" asked Beatrice.

"There are a few," said Muriel with a shrug. "The closest is on the floor of the kitchen pantry,."

Beatrice walked through the dark hall to the dining room, where there sat a tarnished silver tea service and a brassy pitcher on a sideboard. Spiderwebs stretched across the corners of the room. These weren't the tentative, gossamer-like webs that Beatrice quickly dismantled in her own cottage. These were architectural wonders—thick, corded webs of active spiders. Beatrice shivered again.

When she opened the sideboard drawer, she saw candles and a matchbook. She picked them up and headed to the kitchen. Beatrice raised her eyebrows when she opened the pantry door. There wasn't much food in there. Maybe enough for a dying woman living on her own, but definitely not enough for houseguests. She found the flashlight on the floor and turned it on. It put out an anemic bit of light with a sputtering beam. It was going to be a dark night.

Beatrice returned to the library. "This is all I found," she said, putting the candles and flashlight onto a heavy mahogany table. "Do you think there are any other candles or flashlights or matches anywhere else?"

Muriel shrugged her shoulders.

Posy shivered, which reminded Beatrice of another point. "I see a lot of radiators around. I know it's going to be a cold night. Do the radiators work?"

"They used to work," said Muriel in a cool voice. "About twenty-five years ago. Since then I've used firewood. But it was time to place my order for more last week and it simply didn't seem important, with everything else I had on my mind. So I'm afraid there isn't much firewood. Well, there should be enough for several days, but that's it."

"I'm sure everything is going to work out fine," said Meadow with a sunny smile. "We certainly won't be here any longer than a couple of days. I bet by tomorrow morning this will all be melted. Or else Cork will have figured out where we are and have called the cavalry."

Beatrice distinctly remembered a brutally cold forecast, but she didn't want to be the pessimist in the group.

"There are plenty of bedrooms here," said Muriel, "if that's any consolation. And they're all made up, although the rooms and bedding might be rather dusty. I'm feeling very tired, so I think I'm going to lie down in mine. . . . It's the bedroom at the very end of the upstairs hall. You're all welcome to whatever rooms you find. Let's see—there are nine of you. I believe I have six other bedrooms. Some of you will need to bunk together."

The Village Quilters decided to share rooms—Beatrice with Meadow and Posy with Miss Sissy. And quilters Holly Weaver and Dot Giles offered to share with each other, too. Muriel suggested that the Village Quilters use the adjoining set of bedrooms, and then directed Holly and Dot to the other bedroom with twin beds.

"After I put my feet up," said Muriel, "I'll figure out what we'll eat for supper. Not to worry—there's plenty of food. We just won't all be eating the same thing," she said with a short laugh.

Chapter Three

The cold air and the darkness in the house made everyone sleepy and most of the quilters headed upstairs for a nap. Portraits of long-dead Starnes ancestors lined the staircase and their eyes seemed to watch the quilters' ascent.

"It's almost like a set from a horror movie," muttered Beatrice to Meadow. "All we need is a suit of armor in the hallway upstairs and pipe organ music."

"You said Southern gothic before," reminded Meadow. "I don't think you can put a suit of armor and a pipe organ into a Southern gothic set."

"This house does have that gothic feel to it, though," said Beatrice. "A crumbling mansion, complete with turrets and rotting cupolas, and the heavy, dark atmosphere inside."

"Don't you have to have dead bodies and jilted spinsters for a Southern gothic?" asked Meadow thoughtfully. "So that rules our situation out. Muriel was married several times that I know of."

There was no suit of armor upstairs, but that unreal feeling persisted. Beatrice and Meadow peeked through various doors until they found a room with twin beds; it adjoined another room where Posy and Miss Sissy would stay.

"Well," said Meadow, hands on her hips as she surveyed their room. "Well."

The room felt drafty, making Beatrice shiver as she walked in. There were faded heavy velvet curtains at the windows. The same heavy dust pervaded the room. There was a chunky walnut desk holding yellowed black-and-white photographs of what Beatrice supposed were Muriel's grim relatives. A rickety chair that needed to be caned stood next to the desk. The twin beds were covered in bedspreads that had seen better days. The woolen Oriental rug was moth-eaten and there was the head of a startled moose on the wall.

"I won't be able to sleep a wink with that awful creature gawking at us. Not a wink!" exclaimed Meadow.

But Meadow was soon snoring loudly in one of the room's twin beds. Beatrice sighed. She wished she had something to read. But then, who'd have guessed that she'd need a book tonight?

After an hour had gone by, Beatrice heard the sounds of arguing. One of the voices sounded male—Colton Bradshaw, presumably. She couldn't make out who the other voice belonged to. Meadow continued her enthusiastic snoring, so Beatrice moved quietly to the door and opened it.

Beatrice saw Muriel's daughter, Alexandra, standing at the top of the steep staircase, eyes narrowed, listening intently to the voices below. Dot and Holly's door was open, and they didn't appear to be in the room. Winnie Tyson stood outside her door, away from the stairs.

With her door open, Beatrice could make out the voices easier. It was Muriel talking with Colton Bradshaw. "Regardless, I want to go ahead and make the changes in my will. It's the whole reason you're here, Colton."

"It's most irregular. Especially with heirs here."

"What difference does that make? We'd planned on making the change this afternoon after the meeting. Once the ice melts, you're heading back to work hours away. I'm *dying*, as I mentioned to you before. I don't know if I'll be available to sign a revised will later on when it's convenient for you to return here," said Muriel, exasperated.

"There's no expectation of privacy here. I won't do it tonight. Let's try for tomorrow afternoon, Muriel. Perhaps the ice will have melted by midafternoon and this impromptu house party will be over." Colton sounded as though he was not particularly pleased about the gathering of quilters—and least of all being included in it.

"You're being stubborn. Lucky for you that I'm so tired or I'd put up more of a fight. I suppose we can work on it tomorrow afternoon. But we're changing it tomorrow, no matter what. If the ice is still trapping us here, then we're going to go to a quiet room to get this done," said Muriel.

"And aren't you going to have that private conversation?" asked Colton. "I thought that was part of your plan for this afternoon."

"Well, as you pointed out, this hasn't been the best time to have a private conversation," Muriel said. "I'll talk with her after supper."

Supper looked to be a do-it-yourself affair until Meadow and Posy took the reins. "Everybody stop messing in the pantry," said Meadow. "Posy and I will put a meal together. I think it would be best if we could avoid opening the fridge for as long as possible, so we'll try to make something from the pantry."

Beatrice said, "Muriel, if you have a cooler, I'll put the food from the fridge outside. It's so cold out there that it will obviously keep better there than in here. Just in case the power doesn't come back on soon."

Muriel did have an ice chest, so Beatrice busied herself with transferring food outdoors while Meadow and Posy worked on supper.

And somehow they came up with a perfectly decent meal. They cut up apples for everyone, and found peanut butter and bread and made sandwiches.

They sat in a tremendously large and dusty dining room with vast, dark Victorian furniture and tarnished silver with elaborate patterns. Since they were being careful to preserve the supplies, their food was lit by one meager candle flickering bravely in the gloom.

Meadow was as bubbly as usual. "Now I call this an adventure!" she proclaimed several times, attacking her supper with gusto. Posy smiled gently at her friend.

Miss Sissy quickly gobbled up her sandwich and apples and stared greedily at everyone's plates as if prepared to pounce if anyone lost their appetite.

Alexandra Starnes gave Meadow a coldly calculating smile, as if she was searching for ways to burst Meadow's bubble. "That's the spirit. Hopefully you can hang on to that attitude through the night. It's going to be a cold one and we won't have any heat, since Mother's heat pump runs on electricity."

Muriel gave her daughter a thoughtful gaze. "That's true, Alexandra. But we do have plenty of quilts. Every closet in this house is full of them. Each person here could load fifteen quilts on their bed and we still wouldn't use up all the quilts. This family has been involved in the craft for generations, and I've finished quite a few quilts myself. Ordinarily, a heat pump is an energy-efficient method of heating and cooling in this mild climate. This is only a minor, temporary setback."

This positive note appeared to squelch Alexandra, who picked at her food in irritation.

Yet somehow the negative mood spread. The quilter who'd been introduced as Winnie spoke up. "At least you have a place you can call your own, no matter how hard it is to keep it up."

The bitterness in her voice made Beatrice raise her eyebrows. This must be one of the quilters Muriel Starnes had been referring to when she'd talked about doing people wrong.

Muriel looked sharply at her. "That's true. Although living in a drafty mausoleum isn't as pleasant as you're making it sound."

"Still, it would be nice to have a home you couldn't get evicted from. That's a luxury—believe me," said Winnie.

"Life doesn't actually owe you anything," said Alexandra, rolling her eyes. "If you want stability, make your own."

"It's better to be independent, instead of depending on others for money," said Muriel with a meaningful frown at Alexandra.

"You think I haven't worked?" asked Winnie bitterly, turning to face Alexandra. "I'll have you know I work hard every single day, despite my age. But teachers aren't paid what they're worth. It's easy to be smug about being independent when you've always had money to fall back on."

Holly Weaver anxiously wound a strand of red hair around her finger as she listened. The quiet librarian finally couldn't wait to smooth everything over and jumped in. "I think they're both equally important—striving for independence and also trusting and relying on others."

"An interesting position for you to take, since you

grew up in foster care," said Muriel, tilting her head to one side. "And by the way, Holly, I was wondering if I could have a word with you after supper."

"Of course," murmured Holly, knitting her brows in confusion.

This was greeted by silence until Dot Giles said in her jolly voice, "You're right, Holly. They're both important. As for jobs—they sure are tough, aren't they, Winnie? And nobody is grateful for your service. Yessiree, it used to be that you could work for the same company for thirty years and get the gold watch at your retirement party. Sure isn't the same, is it? No loyalty these days." She clicked her tongue. "Such a pity!"

Beatrice got the distinct impression that Dot was making a point of some kind.

Meadow took a big bite of her sandwich, apparently not picking up on any of the negative vibes at the table. Miss Sissy glared balefully at her empty plate, and then peered hopefully at Colton Bradshaw's. He had been picking at his food throughout the meal and had eaten only a few bites.

Unlike Meadow, Posy was sensitive to the tension in the air. She sighed with relief when supper was finally declared over and they retired to their rooms for the night.

"Well, it's a little musty in here, but it's home," said Meadow, turning down her covers. "Do you think we should open the windows for a few minutes to air out the room?"

"Meadow, we'll freeze to death if we do. It's cold enough in this room already," said Beatrice.

"Once we pile all the quilts on, we'll be nice and cozy," said Meadow firmly. "Our room alone has almost ten quilts in it . . . plenty to keep us warm. Did you see this quilt? Isn't it lovely?"

All the quilts were lovely, actually. Muriel was clearly an adept quilter and apparently came from a long line of gifted quilters. The quilt that Meadow was pointing out was an excellent example. Although the colors were faded from time, red strawberries still popped on a creamy background. The fruit waved on delicate green stems.

Meadow was continuing. "Yessiree, I think we're in fine shape in this room. Except for that moose head on the wall over there. I'm thinking about throwing a quilt over the thing so it will stop gawking at me."

"At least we ended up with a flashlight. Even though it's a pretty pitiful excuse for a flashlight."

"What's nice about having a flashlight is that we can turn it on and off at a moment's notice," said Meadow. "We don't have to fumble around with matches first."

"I hope it doesn't immediately run out of batteries," said Beatrice. And with that, the flashlight sputtered into darkness.

Beatrice sighed. "Shoot. I should have knocked on wood."

"Yes, you should have. Heaven knows there's plenty of heavy Victorian furniture to knock on. Oh, well. We were about to turn in anyway. Maybe we'll win the lottery for the candles tomorrow night," said Meadow.

"I'm hoping we'll be out of here by then!" Beatrice hesitated. "I think I should go to the bathroom once more before I go to sleep. I can feel my way out."

"Well, be careful. This is no time to break a hip."

No, it wasn't. Beatrice carefully felt her way to the door and opened it to head for the small hall bathroom.

As she stepped into the hall, she heard sobbing coming from downstairs, but she couldn't see who was crying. Beatrice heard a steady-sounding Muriel saying, "Are you all right, Holly?"

And finally Holly was able to stutter out, "No. No, I'm really not. Look, I need to turn in and get some sleep."

Muriel gave a dry laugh. "I'm tired, too, but I haven't slept for weeks. I'm sure tonight won't be any better with a houseful of guests. But I do have a sleeping pill that the doctor prescribed for me for when I really need to have a night's sleep. I'll take that tonight."

They both began to head up the stairs. Beatrice quickly stepped into the bathroom to avoid an uncomfortable encounter.

Beatrice slept harder than she thought she would. Meadow's snoring made for a white noise, while the cold air in the room and the stress of the day set the stage for a deep sleep.

The sound of a creaking door—all the doors on the second floor had that annoying trait—woke her up briefly. Beatrice made an attempt to read her watch in the dark before finally giving up. If it was pitch black outside, then clearly it wasn't time to wake up yet. She rolled over and went back to sleep.

The next time Beatrice woke up, the sun was just starting to light up the room. She and Meadow had left the heavy curtains open, hoping a small amount of moonlight would illuminate their room overnight. Now the sun was lighting the room up quickly. She got up, feeling the cold floor on her feet, and walked to the window. Although it wasn't as cloudy as it had been the day before, the landscape outside the window was completely iced over. There would be no leaving until that sheet of ice melted.

They hadn't made plans for breakfast since no one was particularly excited about their ordeal. It would probably be oatmeal and cornflakes—and there might not be enough milk to go around. And the meal would quite possibly be accompanied by arguing or drama. Muriel Starnes was the kind of person who stirred up the passions of people around her while remaining unaffected herself.

Beatrice turned her cell phone on to see whether she had better reception upstairs than she'd had downstairs. There were no signal bars on her phone, though, and she saw to her dismay that she only had about twenty-five percent charge remaining. She quickly turned the phone back off.

Beatrice heard signs of stirring out in the hall, so

she smoothed down her clothes—which *did* look as if she'd slept in them—and walked downstairs to the kitchen. There she saw Winnie, trying out an older-model cell phone and making a face.

"Nothing?" asked Beatrice.

Winnie shook her head and glared at her phone. "I was hoping that maybe I could get a signal, but we're really in a bad spot here. I really want to get out of here."

Beatrice wondered over that a little. She could understand wanting to get out of there—she wanted to leave, too. It was inconvenient, it was cold, there were no changes of clothes, meals required a good deal of creativity, and the tension in the house was strange and strong. But the sheer desperation in Winnie's voice was perplexing.

"I knew I shouldn't have come here," Winnie continued with frustration in her voice. "But my guild really pushed me to come to make a pitch for us to be in charge of that scholarship. Muriel had sent an invitation directly to me. I knew I should have thrown it in the trash."

Beatrice frowned. "I wonder how she knew who to contact in each guild? Muriel seems so isolated here."

"She probably has a computer of some kind here," Winnie said with a shrug. "She's a sharp business-woman and probably manages her own stocks and things like that. It helps if you have a computer."

"Why isn't Muriel keeping up her house better, then? If she is so successful and has such good business sense?" asked Beatrice.

Winnie gave her an irritated scowl. "Who knows? And I, for one, don't care. If I had to guess, I'd say that she simply doesn't care about the house. If she cares about something, she'll pour money into it. Or maybe she's just too cheap to put money into an old house."

The possibility of a computer was good news, at any rate. Hadn't Meadow said that Muriel didn't have any electronics in the house? "Let's track the computer down, then! We can e-mail the police department or our friends and get out of here."

"No power, remember?" Winnie reminded her in a gloomy tone.

No power. It was very easy to forget that, when you were so used to having it.

Dot Giles joined them, along with Holly Weaver. "What are y'all thinking about for breakfast?" Dot asked, pulling open the pantry doors. "My tummy is starting to really growl at me. Hmm. If we want traditional breakfast food, it looks like there is cereal. Or we could have bread with butter . . . No toast, though, obviously. Otherwise, we're going to start getting into cold canned soup."

Holly laughed. "I'm hungry, too, but the thought of having cold chicken noodle soup at eight thirty in the morning isn't doing anything for me."

"Well, there is milk in the ice chest outside. And maybe Muriel will have other ideas for breakfast foods," suggested Beatrice. "Has anyone heard her up and about this morning?"

Alexandra Starnes entered the kitchen and raised

her eyebrows when she heard Beatrice's question. "Mother isn't up yet? Age must finally be getting to her. She was always up with the chickens. Used to drive me nuts."

Beatrice suddenly felt uneasy. "Alexandra, maybe you'd better check on her."

"That's not necessary, is it?" Alexandra said. "She's an old, sick woman and she said herself that she was very tired yesterday."

"Then I'll check on her," said Beatrice. Alexandra's attitude made her furious. She couldn't imagine having a daughter like her. Her Piper had always been loving and caring. She was in California, visiting Meadow's son, but Beatrice knew that as soon as Piper tried calling her and couldn't reach her she'd start frantically calling around. She hated putting her daughter through that.

The unspoken criticism stung Alexandra and she moved quickly to the kitchen door. "Never mind. I'll do it."

By this time, the rest of the quilters and Colton Bradshaw had come downstairs.

"Good morning, everyone!" Meadow said cheerfully. "It's a beautiful morning, isn't it?"

Winnie groused, "Beautiful and cold. I don't think we'll get much melting this morning."

"Did anyone get a signal on their phone?" asked Posy, an anxious frown creasing her brow. "I'm sure Cork must be beside himself with worry now. I hope my sub from yesterday will run the shop today so the quilters can buy their supplies."

"I tried but couldn't get a signal," said Beatrice. "What's more, my phone's battery is about to die now."

They talked a little about how long it would take their close friends and family to wonder where they were, but were interrupted by a pale-faced Alexandra. She stood stiffly in front of them, mindlessly twisting her watch around her wrist.

"Mother's dead," she said quietly.

Chapter Four

The group gave a collective gasp.

"But she was fine last night!" said Meadow. "Tired, but healthy enough. Are you sure?"

"I think I can tell when someone's not breathing," said Alexandra haughtily. Beatrice was struck again by her lack of emotion. Yes, she appeared surprised or concerned, but hardly grief-stricken.

Colton Bradshaw seemed more like he'd been dealt a blow. "I don't believe you. I'm going up to see for myself."

Alexandra shrugged. "Suit yourself."

Beatrice jumped up and hurried to catch up with Colton, who was already halfway up the stairs.

"It can't be. It would be too convenient," muttered Colton, almost to himself. "Her dying like this. With all of us here. And under the circumstances."

Beatrice frowned. "What do you mean, 'under the

circumstances'? My understanding was that Muriel suffered from a terminal illness."

But Colton tightened his lips and moved faster toward Muriel's room.

Alexandra had left the door ajar and Colton pushed it the rest of the way open. The room was huge and so was Muriel's bed. Although she hadn't been a small woman and was very imposing when she spoke, she seemed tiny in the massive canopied bed with the heavy curtain, tremendous headboard, and thickly columned bedposts.

For all his hurrying before, Colton now hung back in the doorway, so Beatrice walked up to Muriel. The bedsheets covered her smoothly, as if she'd been carefully tucked in, and her face was calmly at peace, as if she were sleeping. Beatrice couldn't resist double-checking for a pulse, but quickly dropped her hand after a moment, not finding one. There was a small glass and a bottle of pills beside the bed. Beatrice read the label and saw they were sleeping pills. Muriel had mentioned she was planning to take one and it looked as if she'd followed through.

Beatrice took a tissue from a nearby box and carefully opened the bottle of pills. The bottle was nearly full. She read the label. The prescription had recently been refilled.

Colton said, "I can't imagine she would . . . she didn't . . ."

"No," said Beatrice. "The bottle is full."

Colton released his breath in a relieved sigh. "I

couldn't believe she would. She had such strength of character." There was real admiration in his tone.

Beatrice carefully studied Muriel, very gingerly lifting an eyelid. "Colton, I hate to say this, but I don't think her death was natural." Her voice shook a little as she spoke.

"You don't?" He didn't sound surprised at all and Beatrice gave him a sharp look.

"No. I know that Muriel was desperately ill, but we can't assume that's the reason she's passed away. I've actually run across this before—there was another murder investigation I was close to and there were signs of suffocation . . . bloodshot eyes, a whiteness around the mouth. Muriel has those same signs," said Beatrice. "And if she took a sleeping pill, she was likely sleeping very soundly, making it even easier for the murderer."

Colton shifted uneasily, then took his carefully ironed handkerchief out of his suit pocket to dab the beads of perspiration from his face.

Beatrice glanced around the room, trying to see if anything appeared out of place. But everything seemed very much in order. Besides the bed, there was a heavy walnut-colored armchair with an ottoman, a large mahogany desk, a bookcase full of dusty books, a couple of chests of drawers with mirrors . . . Nothing appeared remotely odd or out of place.

Posy and Meadow appeared in the bedroom doorway. "Was it . . . ?" Posy asked, clutching her cardigan around her neck as if she felt a chill.

"Murder? I'm afraid so," said Beatrice.

Meadow's mouth dropped open, and for once she wasn't making lemonade out of lemons. "Are you sure, Beatrice? After all, she was a very sick lady. Couldn't she have simply died in her sleep?"

"It certainly doesn't look that way. Unfortunately, there are indications that she may have been suffocated," Beatrice said grimly.

"What are we going to do? So we're stuck here with no way out—with a murderer?" asked Meadow.

Colton shook his head. "Muriel Starnes was targeted. I don't think we're in some horror movie situation where a crazed killer is trying to eliminate everyone. There was a reason she was murdered."

Beatrice shivered. Reason or not, it was a very unsettling thing to discover.

"We haven't even had breakfast," spat out Meadow indignantly. "This is unforgivable!"

Posy looked anxiously at Beatrice. "What happens now?"

"Well, we've all tried our phones this morning and they don't work. We have to wait for the ice to melt or for someone to find us here." She stared at the still figure in the massive bed. "We should also preserve this space as a crime scene. Is there a way to lock this door from the inside and pull it shut behind us?"

"In this room, there is," Colton said. "Unfortunately, the doors on our own bedrooms can't be secured. Well, I believe some of the doors have locks, but the locks would be easy to pick open."

Meadow's eyes grew even wider. "We can't lock

our doors tonight to keep out the homicidal maniac? Beatrice, are you a light sleeper?"

Beatrice ignored her and shepherded everyone out, taking the tissue again to turn the glass lock on the door, then pulling it shut behind her. She tested it on the other side. It had locked.

They rejoined everyone downstairs.

Holly asked in a small voice, "It's true, then? She's dead?"

Alexandra rolled her eyes.

"I'm afraid so," said Beatrice quietly.

They were quiet for a few moments. Then Dot said, "Well, good riddance." She blinked at the scowls directed at her from the others. "Y'all will have to excuse me if I don't boohoo over Muriel's death. I can't stand to be fake. Muriel wasn't the nicest person sometimes—I say, what goes around comes around."

"You knew her before yesterday?" asked Posy.

"Oh, yes. I think all of us knew her before yesterday. We're all involved with the quilting community, yes, but that wasn't the only reason we were here. You heard Muriel's 'apology' last night. It wasn't much of one, just a kind of blanket apology to all of us who knew her. That's because she was rotten," said Dot, without any animosity in her voice.

Holly sniffed a few times and Beatrice was surprised to see that she was genuinely affected by Muriel Starnes's death. "Well, I didn't know her before yesterday. And I wish I'd known her better," she said in a soft voice.

Winnie Tyson snorted. "You're the only one," she said.

"There's more, I'm afraid," said Beatrice. "I'm positive that Muriel Starnes's death wasn't natural."

They all stared at her. Finally, Winnie said, "What do you mean, 'not natural'? Of course it's natural. She told us herself that she was terminally ill."

"It's clear that she's been smothered," said Beatrice briskly. "The signs are all there. I've locked up her bedroom and we'll leave everything intact for the investigators to study."

"I don't believe it," Dot said roundly. "Not a word! I think you've been hitting the brandy . . . Beatrice, is it? There was a sick old woman and she died. End of story."

"Not the end of the story." Beatrice's voice was quiet and firm. "Most of the people here have a past that features Muriel Starnes. It's obvious that no one liked her." Seeing Holly splutter, she quickly added, "Except, perhaps, for Holly. Who may not have known her very well. Now, I don't know what's up and I'm drawing conclusions about her death, it's true. But I do know that with the suspicions I have, the police would want us not to disturb the body and to keep her room blocked off. That's what I've done."

Miss Sissy suddenly erupted. "Murder! Wickedness!"

Winnie closed her eyes briefly at Miss Sissy's interruption. "So what you're saying," she stated in her dour voice, "is that someone here, obviously, killed Muriel Starnes. And we're trapped in here with a murderer."

"Evil!" offered Miss Sissy.

"I'm suggesting that there were reasons why someone might have wanted to murder Muriel, that there was opportunity to do so, and that the suspects are limited to the people here in this house, yes," said Beatrice.

"I nominate Beatrice," said Meadow stoutly.

Now everyone was staring blankly at Meadow instead of Beatrice.

"For what?" scoffed Winnie. "Most likely to be delusional?"

"For investigating the case, of course. For finding out who killed Muriel Starnes. Then we can lock this person up somehow until we get rescued," said Meadow calmly.

"Wickedness!" hollered Miss Sissy.

"There, there, Miss Sissy," said Posy soothingly. "We're working everything out to make us all safe. And," she said in her sweet voice, "I second the nomination. Beatrice could act as a temporary law enforcement officer."

"And then we could report the results of her investigation to my husband," said Meadow. "He happens to be the police chief of Dappled Hills."

"This *isn't* Dappled Hills," Winnie pointed out in a grouchy voice. "The sheriff would be the one to make any arrests."

"Whatever," said Meadow airily. "I don't worry over details."

"It would certainly make me feel a lot more secure," said Posy with a slight shiver. "Beatrice has such wonderful sense. I'm sure she could get to the bottom of all this. Or at least help us feel like we're doing something. What an awful thing to have happened!"

Colton Bradshaw said slowly, "It does make sense for us to delve deeper into this event while our movements are still fresh in our minds. Perhaps Beatrice can log the interviews in a notebook for the police."

"Beatrice can solve it!" said Meadow. It sounded like a rallying battle cry.

"I don't know why Beatrice is such a perfect choice," Winnie said in a peevish tone.

"For one thing, she's solved cases before. She has a real knack for it," said Meadow, looking down her nose at Winnie. "She's solved cases that my husband, the police chief, couldn't solve."

"I'm sure he would have eventually," said Beatrice quickly.

"And for another, she's very, very clever," continued Meadow.

Beatrice sighed.

"Besides, she's not at all involved with this mess. She'd never met Muriel Starnes before yesterday and I had to drag her over here with me."

That, at any rate, was true.

"For heaven's sake," Alexandra said with twitchy exasperation. "Let the woman poke around, if it will make her happy and make Meadow shut up."

"Well!" Meadow said coldly.

"I think I will, actually," said Beatrice. "I do like figuring things out, and there is a safety issue to consider with this particular problem and our close proximity." Besides, Beatrice was already feeling a monstrous case of cabin fever stirring up. She had a tendency to be restless and knew it was already setting in with a vengeance.

Meadow was pleased. "Now that that's settled, let's have breakfast." She put her hand over her mouth, chagrined. "Sorry. Did that come across as callous? Y'all knew her, after all. Should we have a moment of silent reflection?" A faint blush crept up Meadow's cheeks.

"I think your idea to have breakfast is perfectly reasonable," said Alexandra, moving toward the pantry. "Mother would have wanted us to eat, after all."

After a breakfast of cold cereal, Colton cleared his throat. "I was thinking that Muriel's study might be a good place for you to conduct your interviews, Beatrice. It's a smaller space than the library and would be easier to heat. You should go ahead and get started while we all still clearly remember our movements last night."

Alexandra sighed. "I can't believe we're really going through with this farce of an investigation."

Beatrice ignored her. "Good point. And I wondered if I could talk to you first, Alexandra. To get a fuller picture of your mother, since I wasn't long acquainted with her."

Alexandra had a sour expression as she followed Beatrice to the study behind the library. Colton took a couple of pieces of wood from a small stack in the kitchen and started a fire there. This smaller room was a good deal more cheerful than the library, and Beatrice had the feeling that Muriel spent a lot of time here. There was a well-worn toile armchair that proved it. There were floor-to-ceiling bookshelves on several of the walls, but these books were more modern and seemed to have been read. She didn't see signs of the industrious spiders in here—no webs in the corners. There were small oil paintings crammed in between the built-in bookshelves, and a lovely crown molding adorned the room. Over-stuffed armchairs covered with frayed fabrics and scattered with old needlepoint pillows filled the space. It was very cozy.

"How are we with wood?" asked Beatrice, frowning. Colton was trying to conserve the firewood.

"There's more wood in a stack near the back door," Colton said as he poked at the fire with a poker. "I think we should have enough for a few days if we conserve it. But the wood by the back door isn't covered."

Beatrice groaned. "So it's sopping-wet wood, then. That's not going to help us out much."

"I'll go out there in a minute and bring in another stack," said Colton. "That way it can at least start drying out and perhaps we can use it sometime to-morrow."

"Tomorrow?" Alexandra frowned. "I'm planning

to break out of here tomorrow if the weather hasn't changed. One way or another. I'll go absolutely nuts if I'm still stuck here then."

Colton tightened his lips together as if editing what he was about to say, then said in a quiet voice, "I think I might find it a challenge just getting the wood that's right beside the back door. You might have more trouble than you think if you attempt to walk down that steep driveway."

Alexandra snorted but looked away, as if acknowledging the point.

After Colton ensured the small fire wasn't going to go out, he left the study to head out the door for the wood. Alexandra sighed. "If only this place had a gas stove. I'd kill for hot coffee, even instant. But we're stuck with electric."

Beatrice couldn't imagine a caffeinated Alexandra. The woman was already twitchy and restless—traits Beatrice understood and was usually sympathetic toward. But she couldn't warm to Alexandra—her frosty reaction to her mother's death really bothered Beatrice. In contrast, Beatrice knew how worried and upset Piper would be as soon as she was unable to *reach* Beatrice, let alone if she'd abruptly passed away.

Beatrice managed a smile. It wouldn't do to alienate Alexandra this early. "Has your mother lived here long?"

Alexandra nodded. "I grew up here. She lived in this house even before I was born. Her father owned several huge mills in the area. Mother took them over when he died and made them even more profitable."

"So she was a talented businesswoman." Beatrice made a few notes in the small notebook that Colton had dug out of the desk for her.

"Talented . . . or ruthless," said Alexandra with a shrug of a thin shoulder. "Her ruthlessness served her well in the business world. She'd make drastic cuts in staff and was rewarded in profit. It made her rich, but it didn't make her popular."

Beatrice hesitated, then asked delicately, "Did your mother lose her money perhaps? Bad investments, maybe? I'm only asking because the house is in such poor condition."

"No," Alexandra said. "She hasn't lost a dime as far as I know. But Mother was always a fairly stingy person and she became quite miserly in the last five or six years. She couldn't care less about the house . . . She wasn't the kind of person who really went in for material things. What she liked was the power that money provided."

"What was your relationship with your mother like?" Beatrice asked. "Would you say you were close?"

Alexandra laughed shortly. "No, I would *not* say we were close. Not at all. I would say that we had an indifferent relationship with each other."

That would explain her reaction to her mother's death. "And your father? Sorry for being nosy."

Alexandra studied the fire. "I never knew my father. His name was Ernest and he wasn't a healthy man at all, apparently. He died when I was a baby and my mother never saw a reason to divulge much information about him. He was a good deal older than Mother was, I believe. At least, he appears much older in the pictures I have of him."

Beatrice said slowly, "If you and your mother had a sort of distant relationship, don't you find it surprising that she invited you here?"

"Not particularly," Alexandra said impatiently. "Lately, it seems like Mother was trying to find any excuse to try to get me to come over here. In fact, I wondered briefly if the whole quilting foundation thing was simply an excuse to lure me over."

"It obviously worked," said Beatrice.

"Well, I do love quilting. That's the one thing that Mother and I actually did have in common. Somehow she managed to pass her love of quilting down to me, and her ability."

"I can't really picture this stern, cold businesswoman you've described as a quilter," said Beatrice.

"There are all kinds of quilters," said Alexandra. "Don't believe the stereotype. She was very good at it. Quilting was a creative outlet for her and she found it very rewarding. I do, too, and I'm an accountant. I'm sure that accountants don't fit in your vision of the traditional quilter, either."

Not particularly, but Beatrice could see how the restless Alexandra would always want to keep busy with something. Quilting probably filled that need.

"So you believe that she really did want you here to help her plan this quilting foundation."

"No, I don't. I think it had more to do with that sort of blanket apology that she made to everyone here. It sounded very much like something a politician would be forced by his PR person to say. Didn't it? 'If I've given offense to anyone, please accept my apologies.' All without admitting fault," said Alexandra bitterly.

"What do you think she was offering her blanket apology to you for? I mean, what transgressions do you suppose she thought it covered?"

"Being a hands-off, uncaring mother, I suppose," said Alexandra, rolling her eyes.

"Obviously, she had a personal connection with other people here in the house. Do you know what those connections were and what she might be apologizing to them for?" Beatrice asked as she jotted down notes.

Alexandra blew out a breath. "Well, you're the investigator, Beatrice. I think that's something you'll have to investigate." She gave Beatrice a smug expression and Beatrice studied her steadily until she said, "All right, I guess I could get you pointed in the right direction at least. Winnie Tyson was one of my mother's friends. Once upon a time. They had a falling out, though—clearly."

"Anyone else?"

"Colton wasn't merely my mother's attorney," said Alexandra in a suggestive tone.

Beatrice raised her eyebrows. "Can you elaborate?"

Alexandra said mock-coyly, "Oh, I think Colton is

more qualified to address that topic than I am, so I won't say any more about it."

Beatrice kept making notes. "And what were your movements last night?"

Alexandra was looking bored again. "I had that miserable dinner with all of you. Then I was tired and went upstairs to bed. I put a bunch of quilts on my bed and went right to sleep from pure exhaustion."

Beatrice somehow got the feeling that wasn't the full story. "You didn't see or hear anything?"

"I thought I heard Winnie Tyson's voice at one point. Having an argument with my mother. It didn't surprise me at all, which is why I went right back to sleep. After all, they had plenty to argue about. You'll find out when you talk to Winnie, I'm sure."

Chapter Five

After Alexandra left the study, Colton tapped gently on the door. "I've put more wood in to dry in the library, since that's one of the rooms we're heating."

Beatrice hid a smile when she noticed Colton had gathered wood with his suit on. Shouldn't he have at least removed that spotless jacket? "Good," she said. "I'd hate to think we couldn't warm up during the day at all. But you shouldn't be the only person doing that—I'll try to remember to bring some in, too."

"Just be very careful," Colton said solemnly. "There were a few times that I slipped, and once I fell onto one knee. It's a sheet of ice out there." He hesitated. "I should probably talk to you now. While last night is still fresh in my mind. Although my own activities were rather dull."

Beatrice turned to a new page in her notebook. Colton closed the door behind him and pulled up a chair close to the fire as if he had a chill.

"I had supper downstairs with everyone. I did have a conversation with Muriel where I sharply disagreed with her on a particular business issue. I'm afraid that this argument made me leave in a bit of a huff, so I went upstairs and didn't come down again until morning." Colton watched the fire as he spoke.

"An argument?" Beatrice asked innocently, although she'd heard part of it herself.

"Yes. I was concerned for several reasons about what Muriel was doing. She was determined to bring this particular group of women here because she perceived she'd somehow maligned them in the past. She wanted to tell them she was sorry before her terminal illness took its toll." He tightened his lips together in disapproval.

"And you thought this was a bad idea?"

"Well, of course it was. It's all very noble to want to do something like that, but the reality is very different. For one thing, Muriel Starnes was excellent at a good number of things. Apologizing wasn't one of them. Besides, even if she *were* good at apologizing, she was approaching this task in a very naive way. She wasn't, clearly, a naive woman ordinarily, but she didn't understand much about how people worked. If you hurt people badly enough, they will hold grudges. A blanket apology isn't going to wipe away years of hard feelings. Muriel didn't seem to understand this." Colton let out a small sigh.

"Did she even really want to set up a quilting foundation at all?" Beatrice asked, thinking about

Meadow's wasted efforts to commandeer the foundation.

"She did. Muriel loved quilting and wanted to encourage it as an art form." Colton cleared his throat. "Unfortunately, she died before she was able to incorporate this idea into her will. She has left money to various quilting organizations and guilds, but her will wasn't amended to incorporate the foundation. Actually, there were several amendments she wanted for this new will—that was the primary reason I was here yesterday. But with the development of the bad weather, we didn't end up making the changes."

Beatrice remembered the argument she'd heard between Colton and Muriel. "You, in fact, discouraged her from making the new will, didn't you?"

Colton tightened his lips again. "I thought it would be better for us to conduct our business in private. And despite the size of this house, it's difficult to create a private moment when people are actively trying to listen in on a will's provisions."

Beatrice raised her eyebrows. "That seems directed at Alexandra. I'd imagine she'd be the only heir in the house."

Colton gave her a cagey look and didn't answer.

Beatrice studied her notebook for a moment, then said, "Alexandra told me something interesting before. She mentioned that your relationship with Muriel Starnes wasn't strictly business related."

Colton flushed. "That was unkind of Alexandra. She knows that whatever Muriel and I had is in the past. It was, actually, all on my side anyway. Once upon a time I had a fondness for Muriel in my heart. It's gone now." There was an emptiness in his eyes as he spoke.

After Colton left the study, there was a tap at the door and Posy stuck her head around it. "Is it all right if Miss Sissy and I come in for a few minutes? We thought you might be ready to take a short break."

Beatrice smiled with relief. "Yes, I think I need rescuing. I'm ending up with lots of things to think about and it's boggling my brain."

Posy held the door to the study open wider and Miss Sissy scampered in. More hair had escaped from the bun and now there was more hair outside it than inside it. The floral dress she wore was even more the worse for wear, since she'd eaten several meals in it—it almost appeared as though she'd eaten several meals *on* it—and had slept in it, to boot. She was clasping something in her arthritic hands and had a gleeful, childish grin on her face.

Posy sat down in a leather armchair and smiled gently at Miss Sissy. "Miss Sissy told me she had something she wanted to share with you," she told Beatrice.

Beatrice tried to be encouraging, although she wasn't quite sure she was going to like Miss Sissy's surprise. Depending on whether she was having a good day or a bad one, Miss Sissy's surprises could be various levels of extraordinary. Posy gave Beatrice a comforting wink, so it couldn't be too bad.

Miss Sissy sprang over to Beatrice's side and put

her hands over Beatrice's outstretched palm, laying a chocolate bar there. Miss Sissy's beady eyes greedily watched the chocolate.

"Miss Sissy!" said Beatrice. "You're giving me your chocolate? How sweet of you." She smiled at the old woman, then reached to deposit the somewhat mangled chocolate bar on the end table next to her chair.

"Eat it!" commanded Miss Sissy.

Beatrice demurred. "I'm not really hungry right now, Miss—"

"Eat chocolate!"

Not wanting to turn Miss Sissy's good day into a bad day, Beatrice speedily unwrapped the chocolate and put it in her mouth. She had to admit that the sweet taste of the chocolate had a relaxing effect on her.

Miss Sissy bobbed her head in satisfaction. "That will help."

Surprisingly, Beatrice thought that it might.

At that moment Meadow walked right into the study without knocking. "Are y'all having a party in here? Without inviting me?" She glimpsed the wrapper in Beatrice's hand. "And with chocolate?"

"It's all gone," said Miss Sissy fiercely. "Only had the one piece in my pocketbook."

"If you say so," said Meadow in a suspicious voice. "Although I'm not altogether convinced that's the case. Anyway, Beatrice, I wanted to hear how it's going. What have you found out so far?"

"I think I've ended up raising more questions

than I'm answering," Beatrice replied glumly. "Alexandra offered up a little information—vague information. Really, just inferences and innuendos. I think they're both holding back something, too. Alexandra hinted at a romantic relationship of some kind between Colton and Muriel. Colton denied any current involvement."

"Lies!" offered Miss Sissy, predictably.

"I can't really picture Colton Bradshaw and Muriel Starnes together," Posy said thoughtfully.

"What else did you find out?" Meadow asked.

"Alexandra mentioned that Winnie Tyson and her mother had been friends but had some sort of falling out. She didn't say what. Alexandra said she heard her mother and Winnie arguing last night."

"The plot thickens!" said Meadow in a dramatic voice.

"And Alexandra said that she and her mother weren't close," Beatrice continued.

"Clearly," agreed Meadow.

"Colton said that one of the reasons he was here was because Muriel had planned on changing her will after we had our meeting. She still wanted to go through with the changes after supper last night, but he discouraged her from doing so. He felt uncomfortable doing it with all of us in the house."

"Mmm." Meadow gazed thoughtfully at the ceiling. "It sounds like perhaps someone was getting cut from the will or maybe receiving less money."

"Well, if the quilting foundation had gone through,

the amount of the inheritance would have been reduced anyway," Beatrice explained.

Meadow gasped. "Are you saying—are you saying that the quilting foundation hadn't yet been added to Muriel's will? That it's kaput?"

Beatrice sighed. "That's my understanding, yes." Now Meadow was going to be completely fixated on the foundation—the murder investigation would be a thing of the past.

"Well, that stinks!" exclaimed Meadow, hands on her hips.

"But it sounded like she'd made provisions in her old will for quilting groups," Beatrice said hurriedly. It would be good to distract Meadow now before she got completely obsessed with the contents of Muriel's will. "This might be a good time to talk about what we all did last night and if we saw or heard anything."

Meadow stared at her with wide eyes. "You think one of us might have had something to do with Muriel's murder?"

"No, no. Why on earth would we have killed Muriel? None of us even knew her."

Posy said sadly, "I don't think I'll be any help at all. All I did after supper was help Miss Sissy hunt down additional quilts for our beds. We found a few really lovely ones, too—there were a couple in the most beautiful shades of red. It made me wonder if Muriel especially liked that color. After we gathered the quilts, though, Miss Sissy and I went to sleep."

Beatrice frowned at Miss Sissy, who was staring

with great determination at the fire. Miss Sissy had once stayed with her at her house, so Beatrice knew that the old woman was afflicted with chronic insomnia. "Is that right, Miss Sissy?" she asked. "Did you sleep soundly all night?"

Miss Sissy kept staring at the fire.

Beatrice sighed. "How about you, Meadow?"

"Well, you should know, Beatrice, considering that we are roommates. I didn't stir all night."

She'd snored most of the night, too. So Meadow would be no help.

"Did you hear anything last night, Beatrice?" Posy asked.

"I heard a couple of things," Beatrice said slowly, "but I'm not sure what they mean or if they are significant in some way. Before I went to sleep, I heard Holly Weaver talking to Muriel. She was very upset—actually, she was crying. Muriel was concerned about her, but Holly said she was tired and needed to get a little sleep."

Meadow frowned. "What on earth could have been upsetting Holly? She acts so determinedly cheerful and happy. Dimples flashing merrily at us all the time. And she has all those freckles."

"I don't know, but I think Muriel must have said something to upset her. I remember that Muriel said that there was somebody she wanted to talk to after supper. I guess it was Holly. I'll try to find out what Muriel told her," said Beatrice.

"Was there anything else?" Meadow asked. "Or were you as dead asleep as I was?"

"I slept pretty well last night, but I did hear a door creaking open at one point in the middle of the night sometime."

Posy gasped. "Beatrice, do you think that was when Muriel was murdered in her bed?"

"As far as I know, it could have been somebody up getting a cup of water. But it *could* have been Muriel's murderer. Wouldn't you think that the murderer would have wanted to sneak to Muriel's room very late to avoid being seen? After all, if the killer had gone out too early, someone might still have been getting ready for bed or just turning in."

"It all seems really risky to me." Meadow sighed. "What kind of crazy person would kill somebody with a whole houseful of potential witnesses right there?"

"Think about it, though," Beatrice said. "When else would the murderer have had an opportunity like this one? Maybe Alexandra would, but she might have been in a hurry to murder her before the will was changed. No one else had regular access to this house—certainly not to stay overnight, anyway."

Loud voices were raised somewhere behind them. Beatrice said, "Looks like people are already getting testy." They left the study and headed in the direction of the voices.

Winnie and Dot were facing each other angrily in the kitchen. Winnie's hands were on her hips and her expression was furious. She spun to face them. "Dot has taken it upon herself to eat all the peanut butter. All of it!"

Dot gave them a placid smile as she carefully wiped the gooey remnants of the peanut butter off her fingers with a napkin. "Somebody had to eat it. Might as well have been me. I was hungry. It was there. Case closed."

"You didn't give the rest of us a thought! You thought you were *entitled* to it," Winnie spat out.

"There couldn't have been all that much peanut butter," Beatrice said. "What's done is done, anyway."

Miss Sissy wasn't about to let it go, either, though. "Wickedness!" she hissed at Dot.

Dot gave them all a good-natured grin. "It was only wickedness if it was premeditated. It was pure instinct that drove me to that peanut butter, y'all. Hunger. I like to think y'all would have done the same thing." She winked at Miss Sissy, who scowled back at her.

Peacemaking Posy had already moved over to the pantry and peered in. "There are plenty of other things for us to eat in here. If we got particularly creative, we might be able to warm things up over one of the fires we've made. I do see canned soups in here."

"That sounds like a lot of trouble," grouched Winnie. "It sure would have been a lot easier to put peanut butter on bread or crackers."

"We would've had to break into the soup and other foods after lunch anyway." Meadow shrugged. "That peanut butter wouldn't have lasted more than one meal. Besides, this will give Posy and me a challenge. We'll find a pot to put the soup in and stick it over the library fire since Beatrice is busy in the study. It's not a big deal, Winnie."

Winnie didn't seem convinced.

Beatrice said, "Dot, since you've already had lunch, would you like to come talk with me next?"

Relief passed across Dot's broad features. "That sounds like a good plan," she said quickly.

Once in the study Dot sat down in the chair next to the fire and pulled it away from the fireplace a little. "Kind of warm in here, isn't it?" She mopped her face with a tissue she pulled out of her jeans pocket.

It wasn't really, not with that miniature fire. But Dot was in the hot seat, after all. "I guess the room is small enough to get stuffy," Beatrice said noncommittally.

Dot shifted uneasily in the chair, drumming her fingers on the arm. "So what do you need to ask me?" she said, looking Beatrice steadily in the eyes.

"How well did you know Muriel Starnes?" asked Beatrice. "It seems like most of the quilters that Muriel had specifically invited here were people she'd known for years."

Dot held her gaze. "I did know Muriel. Have done for years. She and I were in the same quilting guild for ages."

"Did you get along?"

Dot snorted. "Did anybody get along with Muriel? Not really. Only if Muriel was in the mood to get along."

"Muriel said she had a couple of different reasons for bringing this group here. We all knew about the quilting foundation and scholarship program. But there was another reason she'd gathered everyone—to make amends."

Dot grinned. "That's right. Muriel also said that she knew that the people she wanted to make amends with wouldn't come simply because she asked them here—that she'd had to *lure* them with quilting."

"Were you one of the ones she was trying to lure?" Beatrice asked.

"Absolutely," said Dot, stoutly.

"What was it that Muriel was trying to make amends with you for?"

"Oh, just general nastiness," said Dot in her cheery voice. "Nothing specific."

Beatrice somehow thought that wasn't the case. "You can't think of a particular instance that she might have been trying to apologize for?" she pressed.

Dot shrugged and stared down at her American flag T-shirt, which now had a small peanut butter smear on it. "Not particularly," she said. "Although I still think it's hilarious how Muriel thought that an impersonal, general apology was going to make everything better. It doesn't usually work that way in life, does it? People hold grudges. More than just *hold* the grudges, they cherish and nourish them! They don't want to give them up . . . They're almost like pets. Muriel, though, was the last person to understand human nature."

Beatrice thought about pushing Dot more on the reasons that she and Muriel had fallen out, but decided not to . . . yet. She had a feeling that Dot could, very abruptly, decide to stop being cooperative.

"What were your movements last night after supper?" asked Beatrice. "And did you see or hear anything after you turned in?"

Dot picked at the peanut butter stain. "I was tired of the whole situation by the time supper was over and ready to get away from Muriel. I went upstairs and helped Holly find quilts for our beds—the closets were stuffed with them, you know. And a few of them were absolutely gorgeous." Her eyes glowed as she said this.

So Dot was definitely a quilt lover. "I saw some beautiful ones myself," said Beatrice with a smile.

Dot grinned at her. "If we start getting bored with investigating Muriel's death and trying to survive without heat and good food, we could always put on our own quilt show in the library. I'd love to see all these quilts laid out." She smiled to herself at the prospect and appeared to be planning a quilt show in her head. "One of the quilts I dug out last night was a lovely botanical print. You've gotta see it, Beatrice. The plants are almost animated and the colors are amazing . . . all forest greens and light greens and cranberry reds."

"I'll be sure to look for it. I think Muriel was particularly fond of botanicals; there was a beautiful one in the closet in Meadow's and my room, too. So after you and Holly got the quilts, what happened then?"

Dot sighed, reluctant to continue. "We got ready to turn in—as well as we could, anyway. After all, there was nothing to do. I didn't bring anything to read, obviously, and the books in Muriel's library are only there for show, I think. Anyway, the books are all about a hundred years old and not a single thriller in the bunch. No, thanks. Holly managed to find a copy of *Little Women*, so she was happy. I wouldn't have had any light to read by even if I'd wanted to read. Holly and I didn't have a candle."

Beatrice frowned. "I thought we handed out candles to the rooms that had two people in them. It seemed only fair. Meadow and I had a candle."

Dot made a face. "Well, we *did* have a candle, before Holly gave it away. She's too sweet, that one. She started worrying about the old lawyer stumbling around and thoughtfully handed him *our* candle. I think he must have burned it out when he used it—there wasn't that much of it left. Hey—one of us should go back into Muriel's room and swipe her candle. That way we could all have one for tonight."

It was a good idea, but Beatrice couldn't help but shiver at the mere thought of spending another chilly night in the dark house. With a murderer afoot. "We'll have to think about it. I guess if one of us puts gloves on and is careful not to disturb anything. So, after you went to sleep, did you wake up at all? Did you see or hear anything?"

Dot bobbed her head. "I sure did. I was thirsty in the night and got up to get water. Then I got cold and got up to find another quilt to throw on the bed.

Most of the time I'm hot-natured, but not last night. Holly was sound asleep, by the way, whenever I woke up. I'm not saying she *couldn't* have done it, but it sure would have been tricky. But one of the times when I left our room, I saw that old lawyer walking around. Didn't even have the candle that Holly had given him!"

"He was just walking around, or could you tell where he'd been?"

"It sure looked to me like he was coming back from Muriel's room. Unless he somehow accidentally lost his way en route from the toilet."

Chapter Six

Winnie Tyson came into the study next. Her mouth was already pursed in disapproval before she even set foot across the threshold. Somehow her white blouse was just as crisp as it had been the day before. It must have really been starched to death, Beatrice mulled. Still, it hung loosely on her thin shoulders, as if several sizes too big. She was shivering from the drafty chill of the house and had wrapped one of Muriel's quilts around her.

Winnie sat as far away from Beatrice as she could possibly get, sitting very straight in her chair with the quilt pulled firmly around her. "I suppose we should get on with it." Her voice indicated she could barely tolerate the situation.

Beatrice glanced down at her notebook. The only person who had mentioned Winnie in the interviews so far was Alexandra. Winnie had a room to herself, so she definitely had the opportunity to sneak out of it. "What was your relationship with Muriel Starnes like?" Beatrice asked her.

Winnie sat even straighter, if that was possible. "I wouldn't say that we had a relationship at all," she said almost haughtily.

Beatrice suppressed a sigh. "Clearly, though, at one point in the past you did have a friendship of some kind with Muriel. Can you tell me a little about that?"

"We had quilting in common and met at a guild meeting long ago. She was quite a fine quilter." Winnie acted as if it physically pained her to say the words.

"I'm guessing that you saw each other apart from quilting, too?"

Winnie reluctantly said, "We did. Lunches and suppers and movies, and those kinds of things. We were friends."

"So this friendship changed . . . It ended?" said Beatrice. Winnie's mouth pursed up again and Beatrice added, "Well, clearly it did, since it seemed like you could barely stand being in the same room as Muriel."

"Muriel simply displayed her true colors," said Winnie in a disapproving voice. "She'd been giving me signs all along that she didn't really know how to be a friend, but I'd foolishly ignored them. Finally, she went too far and the friendship was over. It's as simple as that."

But things were rarely as simple as that. That Alexandra knew about this rift between the two women just went to show how big it must have been. Alexandra was hardly the kind of daughter someone confided in; she must have observed the end of the friendship. "Alexandra mentioned that the two of you had been friends until the friendship abruptly ended."

Winnie's lips tightened more. She hesitated a moment, as if revising her words. "Alexandra never liked me. Not even when she was a child. Anything that Alexandra might say about me is colored by that fact and can't be treated objectively."

"Was there a reason that Alexandra didn't like you?"

"Alexandra," said Winnie with a cold laugh. "She doesn't like anyone. Never has."

"Since you knew Muriel since Alexandra was a child, could you give me a little insight on the relationship between the two of them? What was it like when Alexandra was little?"

"It was the same." Winnie shrugged a bony shoulder.

Beatrice frowned. "Even when Alexandra was a child? It wasn't any warmer?"

"Alexandra wasn't a bubbly, loving child," said Winnie. "Not all children are. They had a distant relationship from the start and it certainly didn't get any closer as Alexandra grew older."

"So there was no big falling out between them?" asked Beatrice.

"No. It was a rift from the get-go." Winnie had a nonchalant air as she said this.

Beatrice glanced down at her notes again. "Did

you see or hear anything after everyone turned in last night?"

Winnie said quickly, "I certainly did! I saw that crazy old woman wandering around."

"Crazy old woman? You mean Muriel?"

Winnie made a croaking laugh. "No, Muriel wasn't crazy. Crazy like a fox, maybe. I meant that woman that your crowd brought in."

Her crowd? "You mean Miss Sissy?"

"That's the one," said Winnie.

"She was probably getting up for a drink of water," said Beatrice.

"She certainly wasn't. As I said, she was *wandering around*. She wasn't doing anything productive. She was walking the halls, going up and down the stairs, eating food in the pantry . . ."

Beatrice raised her eyebrows. "So you were wandering around, too?"

"Certainly not!"

"How else would you know that Miss Sissy was in the pantry?"

"Because she's always in the pantry," snapped Winnie. "She's going to wipe us out of food if we don't keep an eye on her." A flush crept over her sharp features.

"I can't think what motive Miss Sissy would have for murdering Muriel Starnes," Beatrice said.

"It's simple. She's crazy. Perhaps she's a homicidal maniac," Winnie said primly, tightening her fingers on her black patent leather purse, as if Miss Sissy had designs on her pocketbook.

"Pooh," said Beatrice. "She might be an insomniac, and she might be a little odd, but she's no killer."

Winnie glared at her.

"Who else did you see last night?" asked Beatrice.

"Dot was out of her room a lot. I saw your friend Meadow, too."

That was news to Beatrice. She'd have sworn Meadow hadn't stirred all night. "How do you know all these people were walking around?" Beatrice asked. "Weren't you sleeping?"

"I sleep with the door open," Winnie said with a shrug.

After Winnie left, Meadow came back into the study. "So you only have Holly Weaver left," she said. "Unless you think the others are going to demand that everyone is interviewed and you have to interview Posy, Miss Sissy, and me."

"I've already talked with y'all about last night," Beatrice said. "Although Winnie is sure that Miss Sissy had something to do with the murder."

Meadow burst out laughing. "Yeah. Sure. Miss Sissy . . . Ha!"

"Since none of us were really even *invited*," said Beatrice pointedly, still irritated that Meadow had dragged her here, "and didn't know Muriel personally, I can't imagine anyone would seriously consider us as suspects. Although Winnie indicated that you were wandering around last night, too, Meadow."

Meadow continued chuckling. "Miss Sissy! Ha!" She didn't even blink an eye at the suggestion that she might be a murder suspect.

"Care to share what you were doing up last night?" Beatrice asked, feeling very tired.

"I got up to lock the door," Meadow said immediately.

"Our bedroom door? I didn't think it had a lock."

"It doesn't. No, I meant the front door. It was unlocked."

How Meadow thought that a bandit would scale an icy mountain to get to the dilapidated Victorian mansion was a mystery to Beatrice.

"I think I need a break before I talk with Holly," Beatrice said, rubbing her eyes wearily. "I must not have slept as soundly as I thought I did."

"Why don't you go upstairs and put your feet up for a while?" suggested Meadow. "You deserve it. These interviews are hard work."

"I might just do that," said Beatrice, her voice sounding very meek to her own ears. "What are you and Posy doing? Will you rest, too?"

"I don't think so. She and I were saying maybe we'd give this house a good scrubbing. You know? It would look a whole lot better if it were rid of all the cobwebs and dust. I sneeze just looking at the piled-up dust. Posy said she felt the same way, so we're going to attack the dust bunnies in a little while. I found cleaning supplies in a closet off the kitchen." Beatrice recognized the fervent look in Meadow's eyes.

The thought of cleaning made Beatrice even more tired. "Well, good luck. That's nice of you to do. It seems like a massive job, actually."

"We won't be doing it all at once. We'd fall over! No, we're going to start with the kitchen and library and then we'll work on other rooms other days," Meadow explained. "Now head along upstairs and rest before *you* fall over."

Beatrice trudged up the dimly lit stairs into the dark upstairs hallway. As she turned toward her room, she stopped and frowned. The door to Muriel's room was cracked.

She strode to the hall bathroom and grabbed a towel to prevent making fingerprints, then pushed the door to Muriel's room open wider. Everything looked much the same at first glance—Muriel's body was still in her bed, the room was just as tidy. But on further inspection, it appeared as if someone had been in the room in a hurry. Drawers were still slightly open; a few ruffled papers were visible. And Muriel's candle remained at the side of her bed. So whoever had been in the room hadn't been on the errand to retrieve Muriel's candle. Something seemed different, though. Yet Beatrice wasn't familiar enough with the room to know what it was.

Beatrice turned to head out. She'd have to see if someone else—maybe Alexandra or Colton—could offer more information about what was ordinarily in Muriel's room. She spun to see Colton there, and gasped.

"I thought we were leaving this room locked," he

said, frowning. "And I thought you were downstairs
still doing the interviews." He had his hands on his
hips and was still wearing the immaculate dark suit,
a carefully pressed handkerchief barely visible from
the front pocket. He looked as if he might be headed
for a corporate board meeting instead of waiting for
rescue in a decaying mansion.

"You startled me! I needed a break before I talked
to Holly . . . that's all. I came upstairs to put my feet
up until it was time for supper and I saw that Muriel's door was cracked. You hadn't noticed that?"

Colton stiffened. "You mean someone broke in
here?"

"Could they? Or are there keys to these doors lying around somewhere?"

"Maybe Alexandra knows of some keys, but I
don't." Colton backed up a little to study the bedroom lock. "As I thought, these locks would be very
easy to pick. Someone would only have to stick in
almost any object and turn it, and the door would
open. We all have keys—someone could easily put
in one of their keys and fumble around until the lock
turned."

"Very comforting," Beatrice said grimly. How
were they going to stay safe? How were they going
to protect the crime scene?

"So someone—obviously in a hurry before anyone wondered where they were—hurried up here,
picked the lock, and entered Muriel's bedroom,"
said Colton, mulling it over. He glanced around the
bedroom.

"Do you see anything out of place?" asked Beatrice. "Or anything missing? I can tell that the papers in the desk have been riffled through."

Colton nodded slowly. "Muriel's bedside table has been tampered with. Her bottle of sleeping pills is gone."

"The sleeping pills?" Beatrice said quickly. "That prescription bottle that was beside the bed?" Her heart sank as she turned to look at the nearly empty bedside table.

"Yes. Don't you remember it there? You'd wondered if maybe she'd deliberately taken an overdose."

"Is there anything else missing?" Beatrice asked.

Colton glanced around the room, then said cautiously, "Offhand, I can't tell if anything else is missing. But then, I'm trying to go off my memory from this morning—and I was in such shock that I wasn't as observant as I usually am."

"What could someone have been searching for in Muriel's desk?"

Colton frowned, studying the open drawers and the messy papers. "Maybe Muriel's will? Notes she made regarding her will? I can't think what other documents someone would have been interested in."

"While we're here, we should at least get the candle," said Beatrice. She walked over to retrieve it.

Colton and Beatrice left the room. Beatrice handed Colton the candle and used the small towel to lock the door and shut it behind them. "Not that the lock will keep anyone out, clearly, but at least it will slow them down and give us a chance to spot someone trying to break in."

Colton said quietly, "What do you think we should do now?"

"Should we organize a search for the sleeping pills?" asked Beatrice.

"Those pills will be almost impossible to find," said Colton. "Think about it. They could shake them out of the pill bottle and put them in their pockets or shoes or purse . . . Unless we're prepared to search people, it's going to be futile. Besides, the thief could have put them anywhere in the house—in the curtain seams, behind the cleaning supplies in the kitchen closet . . . It would take us a week to search the house and we still probably wouldn't find them."

Beatrice put a hand up to rub her forehead.

"You were on your way to lie down, weren't you?" asked Colton gently. "If you're getting a headache, this might be a good time to have that nap."

"Sure," said Beatrice glumly. "But what if I don't wake up again?"

"Just be sure not to have anything to drink."

Beatrice didn't end up lying down after all. After putting her feet up, she found that she couldn't shut her brain off enough to take a nap. Her mind kept whirling, thinking over her interviews, thinking about Muriel. Finally she gave up and wandered back into the library, where she watched with interest as Holly and Dot quilted on the bay window seat in the dying gray light of the day. Posy joined them soon after, holding a bag with an unfinished project of her own.

"That's a really fun pattern, Holly," said Beatrice, looking over at Holly's twelve-inch quilt blocks.

"My guild is quilting for a children's hospital, so we were trying to work with blocks we thought the kids would enjoy," Holly said, smiling at her as she made her quick and confident stitches.

"It's a tic-tac-toe pattern, right?" asked Beatrice, studying two of the blocks that Holly had completed nearby. The blocks were in a cheerful red and white.

"That's right. With sort of square-looking O's and a funny X," said Holly with a laugh. Beatrice noticed that the X's and O's were in different red fabrics— checkerboard, paisley, and gingham.

"Who's going to win the tic-tac-toe match?" Beatrice asked.

"Oh, I think the X's will win—in the diagonals," Holly replied.

Beatrice glanced over at Dot, perched next to Holly on the bay window seat.

"I have a feeling I'm going to get plenty of inspiration for my quilt here," Dot said with a deep chuckle, gesturing with a needle out the window.

"What is it that you're working on?"

"A winter medley!" Dot grinned at her.

"Yes, I think you'll have plenty of inspiration. More than you might have wanted," said Beatrice with an answering smile. "So, what? A snowflake for one block, a snowman in another?"

"Definitely those. And mittens in one, ice skates in another. A sled, a cup of cocoa, a snowy evergreen—you get the idea. I'm going to have a border of snowflakes just like the one in this block." Dot held up a block with a glowing, silvery snowflake.

Beatrice smiled again. "I love those rich, warm colors you're using. Deep reds and golden browns and dark greens. It's going to be lovely."

"I . . . uh . . . well, I didn't come with any blocks or a quilt or anything," said Dot ruefully. "But Posy had half a quilt store in the back of her car and very generously allowed me to use her fabrics, template, and notions." She hastily added, "Which I'll be paying her back for, of course."

Posy said kindly, "Oh, no worries, Dot. It did seem kind of odd to come here armed with quilts, didn't it? We were only supposed to be here for a little while. All the vendors give me fabrics and things because they want me to buy more for the store. I end up with all this extra stuff. I'm happy to share it."

Posy had likely noticed that Dot's clothes were fairly worn and that she might not have much extra income for quilting, so she had decided to help out.

Supper that night was a quiet affair. Meadow heated up canned vegetables in pots over the fireplace. Beatrice finished her corn and peas and cleared her throat. "Colton and I made a discovery earlier this afternoon. I'm afraid it was an unpleasant one."

Meadow gaped and her hand flew dramatically to her chest. "Not another dead body!" She swiftly glanced around the table, counting everyone.

"No. But when I went upstairs to put my feet up, I noticed that Muriel's door was cracked." Beatrice told them what she and Colton had seen.

The meal went from quiet to completely silent as they all stared at Beatrice.

"Wickedness! Evil!" hissed Miss Sissy, finally breaking the silence.

Posy said in a small voice, "This means that someone plans to use the sleeping pills as a weapon? To murder someone else?"

They all stared suspiciously at their food.

"Or does it simply mean that someone has trouble sleeping and wants a sounder night's sleep?" Alexandra asked tartly.

Winnie let out a short laugh. "Why would anyone want to sleep soundly in this house? With a murderer afoot—according to Beatrice." She twisted her napkin anxiously, though, as if she, too, took the accusation seriously.

Holly's eyes were large. "Beatrice, did you make any progress with your interviews? I know you haven't spoken to me yet."

"If you don't mind, I'll talk with you after supper. Then, yes, that's it for the interviews," Beatrice said.

"Get any clues?" Dot asked. "Think you can track this person down?"

Beatrice said carefully, "It's really too early to say."

Winnie pushed her plate away with a thin hand. "I've lost my appetite."

Miss Sissy launched herself at the remains of her meal.

Chapter Seven

Holly, Beatrice decided, was a very likable sort of person. She had an open face with wide eyes that made you think she was hanging on your every word.

"I can't believe someone would do something like this," Holly said to Beatrice. "Muriel seemed like such a nice person. I wish I could have gotten to know her better." Her face was wistful.

"So you're someone who *didn't* know Muriel well," Beatrice said thoughtfully. "Like Meadow, Posy, Miss Sissy, and me. But, unlike you, we weren't invited. Muriel actually *invited* you here. And she appears to have had a personal connection with everyone else."

Holly knitted her brows. "Not Dot Giles, though, right?"

"They knew each other from their quilting guild," Beatrice said. "They'd known each other for years and apparently there was bad blood between them."

Holly gazed steadily at Beatrice.

"What I'm trying to figure out," said Beatrice, "is whether you had a personal connection with Muriel Starnes."

Holly twirled a strand of red hair around her finger. "I think she invited me because I'm a quilter and she was interested in possibly having my guild administer the scholarship for her foundation."

Beatrice paused, then said carefully, "I'm afraid this house is a difficult place to find any privacy in. Last night I did hear you in tears after a conversation with Muriel."

Holly looked back up at Beatrice. "I did have an emotional conversation with Muriel. But I'm not ready to talk about it yet. It didn't have anything to do with her murder, if that's what you're wondering. And as I mentioned before, the first time I'd met Muriel was yesterday."

Beatrice decided it would be better not to press her too hard. "After you turned in last night, did you see or hear anything?"

Holly was thoughtful for a minute. Then she regretfully shook her head. "Sorry. No. Since I was rooming with Dot, I plugged my ears up with my headphones and listened to music while I slept. So I'm afraid I'm no help at all. I did get up once to go use the restroom, but I didn't see or hear anything while I was up." She sighed. "I'm not sure what I'm going to do tonight. I have a feeling that my music player has a dead battery now."

"You could still sleep with the headphones on,

couldn't you?" asked Beatrice. "That would help muffle any sounds at least."

Holly brightened. "That's a great idea, Beatrice." Then she hesitated. "Unless you think that might be dangerous. Under the circumstances, I mean."

"You'll have Dot in the room with you, listening out for any unusual noises," said Beatrice.

Neither of them mentioned that Dot could be the murderer. Beatrice guessed that, when you were rooming with someone you didn't know, that was the kind of thing you didn't need to dwell on.

Meadow stuck her head in the study door after Holly left. "Coast clear?" she asked. She glanced around, saw no one, and happily came in. She bore a plate of black olives and a glass of water. "Just a little snack to enjoy next to the fire," she said, plopping into the empty armchair across from Beatrice. Then her eyes opened wide in consternation. "Shoot! I should have brought you a snack, too."

Beatrice quickly shook her head. "I appreciate it, but no. I don't think I'm quite at the point yet where I want to eat a plateful of black olives."

Meadow said, "You might want to lose that attitude real quick, missy. There's not a whole lot of food in that pantry to be picky over. And you don't have the generous quantity of fat reserves that I have."

Meadow wasn't at all chubby, actually. She simply had big bones. She wasn't a small woman, but she wore her weight well.

"Anyway, you're looking kind of piqued," said Meadow, frowning at Beatrice as she munched her olives. "What's going on?"

"I think I might be getting a headache," Beatrice said shortly. She was starting to feel out of sorts, in fact. She always tried to shake bad moods before they completely took over, or else she'd have that bad-mood mind-set the rest of the day.

"Why is that?" Meadow squinted at her as if she couldn't fathom what Beatrice might possibly find headache inducing about the situation they were in.

"Oh, I don't know, Meadow. Stress perhaps? You know—from having no heat or decent food. Oh, and having a killer running around, of course." Beatrice bit her tongue, realizing how cranky she sounded. But honestly, Meadow's determinedly sunny attitude brought it out in her sometimes.

"It's not that bad. We're alive, aren't we?" Meadow asked stoutly.

"For the time being," Beatrice said in a gloomy tone. "I'm wondering if I can really get to the bottom of this murder. I've gotten the impression during these interviews that everyone is hiding something from me. Or even outright lying to me. I'm not sure if I can figure out who's behind this."

"You certainly can!" said Meadow, sounding almost offended. "You're the smartest person I know. You'll figure out the murderer and we'll all attack her at the same time and lock her in the broom closet."

She clearly had it all mapped out. "I wish I were as confident in my abilities as you are, Meadow."

"All you need is more clues," said Meadow placidly. "And you'll be sure to get them soon. We're all stuck in this house together and people are getting on each other's nerves."

Hardly something Beatrice hadn't noticed. And Meadow was one of the people who was getting on her nerves the most. That infernal humming she did all the time—usually to unrecognizable show tunes.

"When people get all tense and irritable, they lower their guard and start saying things they weren't planning on saying," Meadow said. "They act on their emotions, too. I know that no matter how cold and calculating the murderer is, she's going to end up breaking at some point."

"Just as long as that process of breaking doesn't involve more dead bodies," said Beatrice.

There was a light tap on the door and Posy peeked around the corner. "All right if I join you ladies?" They invited her in. "Sorry to interrupt. What were you saying before I came in?"

Meadow's face suddenly darkened. "We were saying how being stuck indoors makes others get on our nerves."

Posy looked alarmed.

"Not you, of course, Posy," amended Meadow. "Mostly that nasty Alexandra. Bleh."

Meadow appeared to have a real beef with the woman.

"I'm not so sure she's even a quilter," she said huffily.

Posy's eyes opened wide. "You think she was

only pretending to be a quilter to make her mother happy?"

"Exactly. To get in her mother's good graces," said Meadow. "To please Muriel so she could be on her good side when a will was drawn up." She was really warming to her subject now. "She *knew* how much Muriel loved quilting. It's all a sham!"

"Except that we've watched her working on that log cabin pattern," Beatrice reminded her.

"Clearly a ruse. Maybe she paid someone to put the blocks together and she's simply unstitching and restitching the same little piece over and over." Meadow thumped the arm of her chair triumphantly.

Posy hesitantly offered, "Although . . . well, I did notice that she has these callouses on her left hand."

"She's probably left-handed, then. Alexandra would have gotten them from gripping a pencil or garden shears or something," said Meadow.

"I think I also noticed she's right-handed," said Posy, looking apologetic.

"Nice detective work, Posy!" said Beatrice.

Posy beamed at her, flushing with pride.

"Don't you have something to work on, Beatrice?" Posy asked.

"Beatrice wasn't cooperating," Meadow clucked with a disapproving glare in Beatrice's direction.

"I was just along for the ride," Beatrice said sadly. "Meadow dragged me off with her at the last minute. She did say something about bringing my current project, but I didn't see the point for what was supposed to be a short business meeting. So I ended up carrying in Meadow's quilts for the show-and-tell without actually bringing any of my own."

Posy's face brightened. "I have a trunkful of fabric and blocks and templates and notions from the shop. I'd be delighted if you'd use them, Beatrice."

"It's the quilting mobile," said Meadow, grinning.

"Oh, I don't know," said Beatrice quickly. "You've already given away too much of your fabric and supplies already. I know Dot has gotten a bunch from you."

Posy made a dismissive gesture with her hand. "Pooh. We all need some stress relief. Besides, I've got oodles and oodles of fabrics and things. I get samples from vendors all the time, too."

Beatrice said cautiously, "I'm not sure I can handle too much hand-piecing. I've gotten kind of dependent on my sewing machine lately, although I'd love to do more sewing by hand."

"I've got exactly the project for you," said Posy. "I'll help you with it, too, although I don't think you'll really need any help. I think you'll love hand-piecing, Beatrice."

"It does always seem very relaxing. I've done a little appliquéing, but what I've done has been limited."

"Hand-piecing gives you a much more intimate experience with your quilt," Posy explained. "I think you'll love making cathedral windows."

"The pattern sounds lovely. How big are the squares? Twelve by twelve?"

"Nine by nine," Posy said. "Then you fold it in

half, and in half again. Then you fold the corners into the center and iron them— Oops! I keep forgetting that we don't have electricity."

"Yes, ironing might be a problem," Meadow said thoughtfully, then snapped her fingers. "I bet we could use the bottom of the saucepan after we warm up our canned soups and vegetables. It's flat and it would surely be hot enough."

"Might get sooty, though." Posy frowned.

"If I'm bored enough—which I think is very likely—I'll try anything!" said Beatrice.

Posy said, "You can iron all the squares at once and put them in a pile until you're ready for them. It probably won't be as bad when you're doing all your pressing at once."

"Striking while the iron is hot?" asked Meadow with a grin. "It makes sense to me to do the squares that way anyway. Even if we had electricity."

"You know," Posy said, "I think I saw some flat-irons used as doorstoppers somewhere."

"That's right!" Meadow exclaimed. "Maybe over by the back door?" She dashed out and returned with one of the flatirons. "You could pretend you're a pioneer woman, Beatrice!"

Beatrice realized, not for the first time, that she was in for an adventure.

Meadow, Beatrice, and Posy joined the rest of the group in the library, where they were chatting in a desultory fashion.

"I never thought I'd miss my smartphone so

much," said Alexandra, gazing listlessly at the ceiling.

"Did you forget to bring it?" Posy asked, her brow wrinkled.

"No. But it runs through batteries really quickly. It was practically dead on arrival," drawled Alexandra.

Just like we all were, thought Beatrice. Then she chastised herself for not squashing this rotten mood of hers. "Well, I guess we could find things to do to keep us occupied. Posy was nice enough to give me some fabric to quilt. Of course, I saw that you came with your own quilt."

Alexandra nodded. "Sure, I did. But there's only so many hours in a day that I want to quilt."

"You could always join in the cleaning project that Posy and I have undertaken," Meadow said heartily. "I felt like I'd really accomplished something with the cleaning we did. Didn't you, Posy?"

Posy smiled at her. "I did. But then, I've always loved cleaning."

"We started out with the kitchen, and we're going to move on to the library and study next," said Meadow.

"No, thanks," said Alexandra. "I get enough cleaning at my own house."

"Why didn't your mother have someone to help clean the house?" Beatrice asked curiously. "There's quite a bit of dust and cobwebs here."

"She did have someone helping her," said Alexandra, a smile twisting her lips. "The woman just didn't come all that often."

"Why not? Your mother could afford the help," said Meadow, squinting at Alexandra as if trying to understand.

"Mother was just too cheap. Those cleaners would have slapped on a travel fee to come way up the mountain to a decaying mansion. And she didn't mind the dust and spiderwebs—obviously."

"The way she was living didn't bother you? You didn't check on her?" asked Meadow, putting her hands on her hips.

"*She* never checked on *me!*" Alexandra said fiercely. "Maybe I needed help myself."

The room got quiet. Obviously, Meadow's question had hit a sore spot.

Meadow cleared her throat. "Colton, you're kind of skittish. Everything okay?"

"Besides the fact I'm trapped in an ice storm with a murderer? Absolutely."

"You seem like you have something on your mind," said Meadow. She eyed him suspiciously. "You're not struggling with a guilty conscience, are you?"

"Hardly," said Colton with a long-suffering sigh. "Although I've got the feeling I know someone who *is*."

"I don't have a thing to do with it!" Meadow replied indignantly.

"Not you," Colton said.

Meadow's eyes were wide open. "You know who the murderer is?"

Colton shook his head impatiently. "I'm not saying another thing about it." He pressed his lips into a thin line.

Meadow shrugged. Beatrice decided she would talk to Colton alone as soon as they could arrange it.

Dot said, "Has anybody even *tried* to walk down the driveway?"

Winnie said sourly, "You can *see* the ice on the driveway. It's a sheet of ice that must be at least an inch thick. We can't walk on it. Unless you have skates in your car." She let out a snort.

Dot continued on in a chipper voice, "Well, I'm going to give it a go. Nothing ventured, nothing gained, right? Besides, I've got some fat to cushion a fall . . . unlike you skinny minnies." She was almost as sunny as Meadow, thought Beatrice.

"If you're determined to break something, go ahead," Alexandra said with a languid shrug.

Posy said quickly, "Oh, Dot, I wish you wouldn't. There's no reason to get hurt. My husband must have a group out searching for us now. I think it's better if we just sit tight and wait to be rescued. It's freezing out there—I know there hasn't been any melting."

"There might not even be bandages here!" said Meadow. Her eyes were agog.

Dot was already getting to her feet. "Pooh. Let me try it. I don't have anything else to do. And who knows? Maybe I can get down to the bottom of the driveway." She reached for her navy blue puffy coat. "Are y'all coming out to cheer me on?"

"I've no desire to watch you break your neck," Winnie said.

"I'm planning on giving myself a manicure with polish I found in the upstairs bathroom," Alexandra said without looking at them.

Colton said, "I highly recommend that you not attempt walking down that icy driveway, Dot." But he was already carefully putting his long wool overcoat on. Meadow, Posy, and Beatrice followed Dot outside. Miss Sissy brought up the rear, muttering, "Foolishness!"

The small group stood on the covered porch, shivering as Dot carefully made her way down the wooden stairs, slipping several times and tightening her grip on the underside of the railing, since the banister was also covered with a sheet of ice.

"One foot in front of the other," Dot said slowly. Her tongue was stuck out in concentration.

They watched as she scooted past the parked cars. With both arms held straight out from her body for balance, Dot slowly put a foot down where the driveway's steep slope started. And it flew out from under her.

Dot slammed to the icy surface, to the gasps of the group behind her.

"Dot! Are you okay? Dot!" called Meadow.

Dot slowly and experimentally moved her arms and legs until she winced. "I've messed up my right ankle," she said in exasperation.

Beatrice carefully stepped out onto the ice and promptly fell to one knee.

"Beatrice!" Posy gasped.

"I'm all right," said Beatrice, trying to sound positive instead of positively grouchy. She surveyed the situation. "I think I'll scoot over to you on my rump, Dot. If I stand up, I'll just fall over again. Even if I *did* manage to walk over to you, I might make us both fall down when I tried to give you a hand."

"Won't you end up sopping wet from the ice?" asked Meadow.

"Maybe a little damp. I don't know. But it's better than falling on the hard ice. Besides, I'm getting heartily sick of these clothes. I'm on the point of rooting through Muriel's clothes for something to borrow. Dot, how's that ankle? Is it swelling up?" Beatrice scooted toward her.

Dot peered at her ankle. "I don't think so. But it sure does hurt."

"Maybe it's so cold that it's keeping her ankle from swelling up," Meadow said breathlessly.

Beatrice finally made it over to Dot and studied her ankle. "Maybe it's just sprained," she said. "It would be blowing up really quickly if it was broken. Do you think you can move toward the house? Would it help if I tried to pull you?"

Dot sighed. "You know, I think I can scoot like you were doing. I'll try to use my arms. I'm not sure you're strong enough to pull me anyway."

That was good. Beatrice wasn't sure she was strong enough, either.

After a few minutes of muffled exclamations, imprecations, grunts, and groans, Dot made it to the side of the house. Meadow and Colton helped support Dot from both sides as she hopped on one foot up the stairs to the porch. Beatrice followed slowly behind.

They helped Dot back to the library and pulled up a chair close to the fire so she could get warmed up.

"I think we need to keep her foot elevated." Beatrice frowned as she tried to remember rudimentary first aid. "Does anybody have ibuprofen or anything?"

Posy had ibuprofen in her purse and Meadow ran for a glass of water.

"What else are we supposed to do for a sprained or broken ankle?" asked Beatrice, tapping her finger against her chin.

"Aren't you supposed to wrap it? Something like that?" asked Dot, staring down at the offending ankle.

"There should be plenty of cloth around," said Alexandra, who was still applying polish to her fingernails. "I'm sure you could find something to make a bandage out of."

"You can probably roll those blue jeans up a little on that leg and put the bandage underneath the pant leg," said Posy.

"You're supposed to put ice on it," Winnie said in a snarky voice.

"It was ice that put me in this mess to begin with!" Dot howled.

"After you warm up, why don't you go upstairs and lie down for a while?" Posy said soothingly. "I know it always does me a world of good to have a nap."

"Maybe I'll do that," muttered Dot. "As long as somebody can help me up the stairs."

"I'll even bring you supper in bed!" Meadow said with a clap of her hands.

Supper was hardly worthy of the flourish that Meadow later served Dot's meal with—it consisted of buttery lasagna noodles with no sauce. But Dot seemed pleased at everyone fussing over her. Beatrice got the impression that Dot wasn't ordinarily the center of attention.

Posy had brought Dot's current quilt in progress upstairs so she could work on it whenever she got bored. "How is your ankle doing?" she asked, brow wrinkled in concern.

"Oh, I expect I'll live," Dot said, then covered her mouth with her hand. "Oops. Not the best joke in this house."

Meadow said, "It hits too close to home, doesn't it? And apparently we can't even lock our doors, is that right?"

"Some of the doors have locks," said Beatrice. "Not ours. But even the doors with locks are easy to pick."

"Which makes it pointless!" Meadow was huffily indignant again.

Posy said, "I can't really see why anyone would want to murder anyone else here." She blushed. "Not that I can really see why anyone would have wanted to kill Muriel, of course. She seemed very nice."

But she really hadn't. At least—well, she was nice enough yesterday afternoon. But it was easy to see how she might have gotten on someone's bad side. And apparently she'd been much worse as a younger woman.

"Meadow, I can't think anyone would be brave enough to try to break into our room to kill one or both of us," Beatrice said reasonably. "In fact, we're all sharing a room with someone else. Posy is with Miss Sissy, who doesn't appear to sleep. Dot, you're still sharing a room with Holly, right?"

"That's right," Dot said gloomily. "Except that Holly sleeps like the dead." She covered her mouth again. "Oops."

Chapter Eight

Everyone was jumpy that night. When the women walked downstairs to eat their own buttery lasagna noodles, the dining room was full of awkward mentions of murder. They all appeared nervous about the night ahead.

Finally Beatrice was ready to escape. She cleaned her plate as best she could, then said, "I'm ready to call it a day."

Meadow raised her eyebrows. "It's so early, though, isn't it?" She tried to look at her watch in the low beam of the candle. "It's not even eight o'clock."

"You could help me explore Muriel's wine and liquor cabinet," Colton said with a small smile. "I'm planning on having another glass or two to help me fall asleep." He motioned to the large wineglass near him.

"There's nothing else to really do, is there?" asked Meadow.

"Quilting. We could quilt," Posy said quickly.

"I think that's an excellent idea for y'all," said Beatrice. "But I'm not nearly at your skill level and I need a lot more light for quilting than the rest of you."

"I found a deck of cards," said Dot, pulling the cards out of her slacks pocket and holding them out in a chubby hand. "You could play solitaire. That's what I've been doing."

"Thanks, Dot. I might take you up on that another time, but I don't feel like playing cards right now," said Beatrice.

"There are gobs of books here," said Alexandra. She was lying listlessly back in a chair and didn't seem inclined to check out any of the books herself.

"But they're all dusty and ancient and dull," said Winnie. She made a face.

The books didn't look particularly appealing to Beatrice. "I don't think I'll read tonight. I think I might try to heat up that flatiron and press those squares."

A couple of hours later, Beatrice reflected that heating up the flatiron in the fire and using it to press the folds in the squares had given her new respect for her ancestors. It had worked just fine, and now she had a number of crisply pressed squares. She had an inkling of what she needed to do with them next, but wanted to confirm it with Posy first.

"Am I sewing the pieces together by matching up two triangles from separate squares?" she asked.

"That's right. You're matching up the corners and

stitching together the triangles. Oh, it's going to look lovely. Cathedral windows are a favorite of mine and you always do such a nice job, Beatrice."

Posy was always wonderful at making Beatrice feel better about her quilting abilities. "Then I guess I'll sew fabric into the diamond that the two triangles in the middle form."

"You sure will. But you'll want to pin down those other triangles first—the ones that aren't in the center. That will keep them out of your way as you work. We'll need to measure the diamond to see how much fabric we'll need, too."

"Thanks, Posy," Beatrice said in a heartfelt tone. "I think I'd go batty if I didn't have anything to work on here."

"You have the case, though," reminded Posy. "You do such a good job investigating."

"Yes, but I can't do that *all* day or else I'd be next in line to be murdered," she answered dryly. She couldn't hold back a yawn. "I'm actually feeling a lot more worn out than I should be at this hour. I'm going ahead and turning in."

"Won't I wake you up when I come in to get ready for bed?" Meadow asked with a worried frown.

"I don't think even an apocalyptic event could wake me up tonight," said Beatrice. "I'm exhausted." But she did still want to find out what it was that Colton was so suspicious about. "Uh . . . Colton. Could I see you in the study for a minute before I go upstairs? I wanted to follow up on something from our interview earlier."

He gave her a sharp look. "Okay. Sure."

Colton followed Beatrice to the study. She closed the door behind him. "I didn't actually want to ask you about anything from our interview."

"I gathered that," he said, smiling. The faint scent of his cologne reminded Beatrice of her father.

"When you were talking to Meadow earlier, you said something about having an idea who might be behind Muriel's death," Beatrice said.

Colton continued staring steadily at her.

"Aren't you going to tell me who you suspect?" Honestly, this was the most secretive group of people ever, Beatrice thought.

"No, I don't think so," Colton replied, appraising her coolly. "For one thing, it's only a suspicion, as I mentioned. I believe we'll do much more harm than good if we throw out wild accusations against people without any facts to back them up."

"How are you proposing to get those facts? It's not as if the house is full of hidden cameras or anything. You can't check the security tape. We can't run a forensics-style investigation."

"I think," said Colton quietly, "at some point I'll simply ask her to explain herself. I think the reaction will be most telling."

"At some point. So not tonight?"

"Like you, I'm pretty tired. I'm going to finish my wine and turn in for the night. I'll sleep on how to proceed and will have a plan tomorrow morning."

"Understandable," Beatrice said grudgingly. "But— one thing. When you do decide how you want to proceed, could you let me know? I want to make sure you're approaching it in a safe way."

"Of course," said Colton, a little stiffly.

Beatrice was truly exhausted. Under the circumstances, she decided as she stared toward the ceiling after waking when Meadow had come into the room, it was amazing that any of them could sleep. When Meadow had gone to bed, she'd whispered that she was sure she wouldn't be able to sleep a wink. Yet there she was, snoring away in the other twin bed.

Beatrice found that she woke up at every small noise. There were larger noises, too—squeaking doors as various people visited the restroom. She heard Miss Sissy muttering and cackling to herself at one point, along with Posy's hushed voice saying, "Come along, Miss Sissy. Don't you want to lie down and rest for a while?" She thought that maybe the next night, if they were all still here, she should offer to switch off with Posy so that maybe Posy could get a little sleep instead of dealing with her resident insomniac roommate.

And so, at breakfast the next morning Beatrice wasn't feeling as chipper as she ordinarily would. There wasn't much food left in the pantry that could even be considered in the realm of breakfast food. Beatrice was currently staring with disinterest at the smattering of grits on her plate.

"Eat up!" Meadow commanded. "It's hot food, Beatrice. And there isn't much to go around, so you should be grateful for what you have."

"I know." Beatrice let out a small sigh. "It's not that I mind grits—and I'm glad for something warm to eat, too. I just usually have other things in my grits."

"What? Like shrimp, you fancy thing?" asked Meadow.

"Well, like bacon. Or grated cheese. Or maybe a pat of butter."

"We've totally run out of those things," Meadow said, gulping down a big spoonful of grits.

Posy said, "Beatrice, I opened the canned salmon and put salmon in my grits. Would you like some? A few of us have been sharing it."

"Is it good?" asked Beatrice doubtfully.

"We think so. If you like shrimp and grits, you might like this."

She forked out a little bit of the salmon, mixed it into the grits, and tried a bite. "Mmm. Not bad, actually. And salmon is good for us, of course. I feel like I need a shot in the arm, and this might help provide that."

"Didn't you sleep well last night?" asked Meadow, surprised. "I thought you were so tired."

"I was. But it was harder to sleep than I thought it would be," Beatrice said.

Winnie took the last bite of her grits and salmon and sighed at the sight of her empty plate. "I don't think I slept one bit last night. Not one little bit."

"You at least closed your door last night, though, didn't you?" asked Beatrice. Surely the woman wasn't going to just leave her bedroom door wide open with a murderer running around.

"No," Winnie said scornfully. "I left it wide open and put a welcome mat for the murderer right outside the bedroom door."

Beatrice ignored her. "Holly, how did Dot sleep last night?"

Holly winced guiltily. "I'm not really sure. I'm afraid I put my headphones on again. I feel pretty safe with Dot in there, so I don't worry about it. But one time I did hear Dot. It sounded like she was having a nightmare or something . . . lots of moaning and groaning and thrashing around. I woke her up and then went right back to sleep again."

"Sounds like that ankle was bothering her in her sleep," Meadow said with a knowing nod. "Probably causing her the bad dreams."

"Unless, of course, she was having nightmares about being murdered in her bed," Alexandra said in a dry voice. "Which, according to Beatrice, is a total possibility."

"I think I'll run breakfast up to her," said Meadow. "Was she awake when you came down, Holly?"

"No, she sure wasn't. She didn't stir at all, not even when I left."

Beatrice's breath caught in her throat.

Meadow didn't seem at all concerned. "Well, it's been a while now. Surely she's up by now. I'll bring her up a plate . . . She'll be wanting hearty food on a cold morning like this."

Unless she was dead, thought Beatrice grimly. "I'll go with you, Meadow."

Meadow raised her eyebrows in surprise. "Don't

bother. I've got it, Beatrice. You haven't even finished your salmon and grits."

"Well, I've . . . I've got to go upstairs anyway."

"There's a restroom downstairs, you know," Meadow said helpfully.

"Yes. Thank you. I do know that. Look, I'm going to come upstairs."

"Suit yourself." Meadow glared at her.

As they headed up the stairs, Meadow said, "What was that all about?"

"It just occurred to me that Dot Giles might not have a pulse, Meadow. That's all," Beatrice said with asperity. She tried to keep her voice low since voices definitely carried in the drafty old house.

Meadow tripped up a step. "Ohh. Really? Do you think so?"

"No, I don't *think* so, but I wanted to make sure for myself that it wasn't the case."

When they reached the top of the stairs, Meadow paused and said, "Well, she's not the only one who didn't come downstairs, you know. There were others. It's not like there's anything else to do around here—I guess people decided they may as well sleep in."

"Who else? Who else didn't come down for breakfast?"

"Let's see. I'm sure Miss Sissy didn't. She'd have eaten those grits before you'd had a chance to complain about them."

That was true. "Anybody else?"

"Colton," said Meadow. "But then, I guess he did

say he was really tired before he turned in last night. He went to bed really early, Beatrice."

"So shouldn't he already be up?" asked Beatrice.

Meadow nodded slowly. "So we should check on Miss Sissy and Colton, then?"

"After we've checked on Dot Giles."

Beatrice gently tapped on Dot's door. She felt tremendous relief when Dot called out in a sleepy voice, "Come in."

"We've brought you breakfast, Dot," Meadow said cheerily. "Hot grits! But you have to eat them now or they'll be cold grits, which is somewhat less appealing."

Dot grinned at her and struggled to push herself up in the bed. "Cold or hot, I'm a grits fan. Can't go wrong with grits."

Meadow said, "If only these were my favorite grits. Garlic cheese grits! But I couldn't find any garlic and the cheese Muriel had in the fridge was a bit moldy. So I gave up on the idea."

Beatrice cleared her throat. "Sorry we woke you up, Dot. We were also checking in to make sure you're okay."

"Oh, I'm not at all upset that you woke me up," Dot said. "It's so bright outside that I must have really slept in. I guess I was even more worn out than I thought I was."

"Having an accident can take it out of you," said Meadow.

"How do you feel now?" asked Beatrice.

Dot considered the question, gingerly moving her

leg around. "I think it's a little less sensitive than it was last night."

"But you're not putting any pressure on it," said Meadow. "The real test will be when you try walking on it."

Beatrice shifted restlessly, thinking about Miss Sissy and Colton. "Meadow, why don't we go ahead and leave Dot to her breakfast?"

Meadow glanced quickly over at her. "Good idea. Enjoy, Dot!"

They gently closed the door behind them. Beatrice said quietly, "Thank goodness she's okay. I was really worried about her when Holly said she didn't stir this morning."

"I know. But like I said, when you hurt yourself, just dealing with the pain really *can* make you exhausted. I broke my arm once and I napped all day long." Meadow paused. "Who are we checking on next?"

"Let's see how Miss Sissy is doing. Although she's probably simply worn out from wandering around the house all night. Poor Posy had to chase her down and plead with her to go back to bed."

"Eventually she gave up trying, though," said Meadow. "At least that's what Posy said over breakfast. She decided to let Miss Sissy wander around since she wasn't making a lot of noise and waking everyone up."

They tapped on the door to the room Miss Sissy and Posy shared. There was no welcoming "Come in," but the door suddenly flew open and a suspicious, wizened face appeared, surrounded by the iron gray hair standing around her head like a halo.

"It's just us, Miss Sissy," Meadow said in her jolly voice. "Good morning!"

Miss Sissy gave a distinct growl.

"You certainly appear to be alive and kicking this morning," Meadow said playfully.

Miss Sissy glowered at her.

"You've slept in kind of late, didn't you?" Beatrice asked. "I thought you'd be downstairs helping to knock out all the breakfast food."

"Didn't sleep well," Miss Sissy offered in a grouchy voice. She moved past them and hurried down the stairs, presumably to make sure there was enough breakfast left for her.

"That leaves Colton," said Beatrice, watching the cadaverous old woman sprint down the stairs like a youngster. "I guess our track record for living guests here is pretty good. Let's knock real quick at Colton's door."

They knocked and heard nothing.

Meadow frowned. "Try it again. These doors are heavy—we might not have heard him."

Beatrice rapped again at the door, harder this time. They strained their ears listening, yet couldn't hear anything from inside the room.

Beatrice and Meadow stared at each other.

"Maybe he's in the bathroom?" Meadow wondered.

They peered down the hall and saw that the bathroom door was open.

"Should we just go in there?" asked Meadow.

Beatrice was already slowly opening the door and calling through the crack, "Colton? It's Beatrice. Can we come in?"

There was no answer, so she continued to push the door open. Then she stopped short. Colton Bradshaw was lying very, very still in the tall four-poster bed. Beatrice saw his empty wineglass on the bedside table.

Meadow whispered, "Oh, no."

Chapter Nine

Beatrice strode to the side of the bed and gently felt for a pulse on the side of Colton's neck. She felt nothing. She turned to shake her head at Meadow.

"What do you think happened?" Meadow asked quietly. "Did he have a heart attack or something? Maybe all the stress here caused him to have a heart attack. That can happen, you know."

Beatrice gestured to Colton's empty wineglass. "No, I don't think *that's* what happened."

Meadow gasped. "You think—the sleeping pills?"

"Yes."

"You think he killed himself?" Meadow asked, reaching a hand to her throat. "That maybe he killed Muriel and decided to do away with himself?"

"No, I can't see it. Colton told me he had an idea who Muriel's murderer was. He was thinking about approaching her to get some kind of an explanation for what he'd seen or heard. It appears he was intercepted before he could do that. Somebody took those sleeping pills from Muriel's bedroom and put them in Colton's drink."

Meadow's brows knit together. "When would someone have been able to do that? We were all sitting together at supper last night. Colton had his glass with him—obviously, since he even took the glass upstairs with him. How could someone possibly have—? Oh!" Her eyes widened as a thought occurred to her. "Beatrice. When he left the room to talk with you?"

Beatrice nodded sadly. "It would have given his murderer the perfect opportunity to swipe his glass while everyone was clearing the table. She could have put the powder in the wine, stirred it up, and then put it right back on the table for Colton to find it. He might not even have realized what was happening when he fell asleep . . . He'd said he was very tired."

Both women stared silently at the still figure on the bed.

Beatrice sighed. "I guess we need to do the same thing we did before. Secure the crime scene. Although I suppose it's not really necessary, since it's probable that the murderer never even entered this room. We'll lock it behind us, though, and let the police deal with it when they come in."

"Are you going to talk to everyone again, then?" Meadow asked.

"I'll have to, I suppose. I think we also need to check again and make sure the phone lines haven't been repaired. And see again if any of us can get a signal . . . even for a few seconds. All we need is to connect just long enough for us to send out a text message."

"So you're going to ask everyone if they did it?" Meadow said. "Well, I guess that's not very subtle. You'll ask everyone to retrace their movements? Something like that?"

"I'm going to ask them if they saw anyone take Colton's drink or put Colton's drink back. Or, I guess, if they saw someone put something in Colton's drink . . . although I'd like to think that anybody here would have immediately said something if they'd actually seen someone tampering with his drink. I think it's more that they might have seen someone take Colton's glass 'by mistake' while they were all cleaning up and then put it back down later."

They left, carefully locking the door and pulling it shut behind them. Beatrice stood there for a moment in the hall before heading downstairs. "You know, I really liked Colton."

"I did, too," Meadow said. "He was pedantic and boring sometimes—remember when he was telling us all about the endowment? I thought I might nod off in the middle of it, and I was *excited* about the endowment! But you could tell he was a very decent guy."

"Which makes me wonder why he was so close to Muriel," said Beatrice. "Who, from all accounts, *wasn't* the most decent person." She heard the sounds of the dishes being cleaned and sighed. "Let's go on down and tell the others."

There was a lot more shock registered on the faces of the quilters than there had been after Muriel's death. Even Holly Weaver was swallowing hard, as if trying to hold back tears. But Beatrice knew that one of the women was faking her shock.

"Do you think he had a heart attack or a stroke or something?" Winnie asked, exhibiting more curiosity than she ordinarily did. She usually just sat around looking sour.

"No, I sure don't. He seemed in excellent health to me. It's very coincidental for him to die right after Muriel's death," Beatrice explained.

Alexandra shrugged and pushed a lock of black hair from her face. "He might have been in excellent shape, but he wasn't a young man. And guess what? This is a stressful situation. Every single thing about it is stressful, Beatrice—from lack of food, lack of heat, lack of clean clothes, to the fact that there *may* be a murderer in our midst. I think Colton's ticker gave out from the stress."

Meadow frowned at Alexandra. "Why do you say there *may* be a murderer?"

"Because I haven't heard a compelling case made for murder. I think my mother was an old, sick woman who passed away by natural means. Beatrice says she was smothered and that there's evidence of that. I'm thinking for myself, that's all. I'm not blindly accepting Beatrice's point of view." Alexandra gave a small smile.

"You can think what you like," said Beatrice. "But it's important that we treat both rooms as crime scenes to let the police decide how to handle it."

"Agreed," Alexandra said with a nod.

Meadow was still fired up, though. "So you think that two people just happened to die in this house while we've been here? While your mother was in the process of changing her will? And you don't think that's coincidental at all?"

Alexandra yawned. "Life is full of coincidences, Meadow. I'm saying it's not out of the realm of possibility, that's all. I'm not going to freak out over this," she said, nodding pointedly at Holly, who still was on the verge of tears.

Holly turned beseechingly to Beatrice. "Are you going to check into Colton's death, too? Because I don't agree with Alexandra. I think that there's something really dangerous going on here."

Alexandra snorted derisively.

"Yes, I'm going to ask more questions," Beatrice said quietly. "For one thing, I think I'll go absolutely crazy trapped in this house if I can't feel as if I'm doing something. For another, our actions are all fresh in our minds now and we can give the police a statement that's hopefully more accurate than it would be later. And I'm convinced that neither of these deaths is natural."

"What do you think happened to Colton?" asked Holly.

"I think that whoever took that bottle of sleeping pills ground them up and put them in Colton's wine while he was speaking with me in the study last night," said Beatrice. "He was probably already a little tipsy when he finished off his wine and didn't notice if the wine tasted off to him. He was already tired, too, and turned directly into bed. He never woke up."

They were quiet for a moment.

Holly said, "But why would someone kill Colton?"

Winnie's mouth twisted downward with displeasure at Holly's naïveté. "Clearly, if someone did kill Colton, it must have been because he knew who the murderer was and they were trying to prevent him from sharing that information."

Meadow frowned. "Or maybe he really did change the will. Maybe he and Muriel made the changes and he was scared to say anything while we were all trapped here. Maybe he had an amended will in his possession and someone knew about it and killed him, not wanting the new will to be made public. Then they stashed away the new will so they could destroy it later."

Beatrice hated to admit it, but it was an idea she hadn't considered. It did make sense, although she wasn't completely convinced. "Either way," she said, "I'm sure his death wasn't natural. And I'm going to ask for everyone's patience again while I talk to each person here to learn more about what happened last night."

Posy said tentatively, "What are we going to do now? Besides your interviewing suspects, I mean."

Winnie shivered. "I'm not looking forward to going to sleep tonight. In this house, people don't ever wake up again."

"Is it worth searching for the sleeping pills?" asked Holly.

Beatrice took a deep breath. "I don't think it will do much good to search for the sleeping pills. They're probably all used up . . . To kill a grown man like Colton, the murderer likely used all of that full bottle. It would be easy to hide the bottle somewhere—I doubt anyone would keep it in their room. But if it would make everyone feel better to search for the pill bottle or any remaining pills, we could do that."

Beatrice glanced around, but no one appeared eager to instigate a search.

Alexandra said, "Sounds like an exercise in futility to me."

"Did anybody check on Dot?" Holly asked in a panic.

"Beatrice and I did," said Meadow quickly. "We brought her breakfast, remember? She was doing all right. Her ankle is still bothering her, but it sounds like she was able to get a good night's sleep."

"Can somebody come with me to help Dot down the stairs?" asked Holly. "I'm sure she's probably ready for a change of scenery."

"I'll help you," said Posy, and the two women headed for the stairs.

Alexandra languidly walked across the room and picked up the phone on a desk in the corner. "No dial tone," she said, dropping it back in its cradle. "We're well and truly stuck in this dump." She plopped irritably into a chair. "Why don't we get this travesty of a police interview over with so I can go back to bed? There's nothing else to do here."

Beatrice glanced at Winnie. "Do you want to join Miss Sissy in the kitchen, maybe?"

"Not particularly," said Winnie, making a face.

"Somebody probably should," said Meadow, giving an easygoing laugh. "Just to keep an eye on Miss Sissy."

"Because she might be behind all this?" Winnie asked.

"No, because she might eat all our food up," said Meadow. "Even the condiments." Since Winnie wasn't in any hurry to check on the situation with Miss Sissy, Meadow left to do it herself.

"Winnie doesn't have to leave," said Alexandra with a roll of her eyes. "I don't have anything to say that can't be said in front of her. Here, I'll do both the questions and the answers. Did I kill Colton? No. Did I kill my mother? No. Did I see anyone tampering with Colton's drink last night? No. Have I seen any sleeping pill bottles lying around? No." She smirked at Beatrice.

This monologue appeared to irritate Winnie, whose face grew even more pinched. "You're not taking it seriously, Alexandra. You're not even thinking about your answers!"

"What does it matter?" asked Alexandra. She shrugged.

"It matters because I want to get out of here alive! If we can figure out who's behind these murders, then we can lock them up in a room and keep ourselves safe until we're rescued," said Winnie.

"So she's got you believing these deaths were murders, too," said Alexandra with a sneer. "I thought you could think for yourself, Winnie."

"I don't know why you're being so stubborn. Why won't you consider the possibility that your mother and Colton were murdered? Is it because you're responsible? And you're trying to persuade us not to investigate?" Winnie's neck was splotchy red with emotion.

Alexandra gave her a chilling glare.

"Think back to supper last night," implored Winnie. "Remember how everyone was bustling around after the meal ended? We all pitched in to clear the table."

"I only remember that crazy old woman trying to eat the leftovers," said Alexandra.

"Do you remember anything else? Anybody taking Colton's drink and putting it back down again?" asked Winnie.

Beatrice stayed silent. Winnie was pushing Alexandra for answers harder than she would have herself.

"As I said before, I didn't see anything." Alexandra snapped her mouth shut to indicate that she was done talking.

"Did you hear anything last night?" continued Winnie.

"Last night? Last night doesn't even matter because he was poisoned at dinner, right? If he was poisoned at all," said Alexandra in that scornful tone.

"I guess this interview is over, then," Beatrice quickly said before Alexandra and Winnie descended into a full-blown argument. "Winnie, could I speak with you next?"

"Fine. But I *would* like to have a private conversation with Beatrice," she said defiantly.

Alexandra gave a put-upon sigh and stomped out of the library.

Winnie started speaking as soon as the heavy library door swung shut. "I saw something," she said in her clipped voice. "I saw Alexandra loitering around the table last night when Colton was talking with you in the study."

"Loitering?" asked Beatrice.

"Yes. See, the rest of us were trying to clear the table of all the glasses, plates, and silverware. Alexandra was hanging behind. She wasn't clearing anything or washing any dishes in the kitchen. She hung back for a few minutes, then left very abruptly."

"But you didn't see her actually tampering with Colton's wine?" Beatrice asked.

"No," Winnie admitted reluctantly, then quickly added, "But Alexandra was standing right beside his glass. Why would she have been doing that?"

Beatrice had the feeling that Alexandra had something of a lazy streak. She could have simply been trying to get out of work.

"You've known Alexandra for a while, haven't you?" Beatrice asked.

"Since she was a little girl," Winnie replied.

"What's your general take on her? As a person, I mean."

"You mean, she *is* a person?" Winnie's voice was snarky. "I hadn't noticed. I thought that perhaps she was a rodent of some kind."

Beatrice paused. "So you're not very fond of her."

"You could say that." Winnie sniffed.

"Why do you have that opinion of her? Was there a specific incident?"

"No, she's always been very unpleasant. Even as a child. She's a very rude person. I told you that she and her mother had never gotten along, and Alexandra is much of the reason why."

"I got the impression that Muriel wasn't particularly easy to get along with, either."

Winnie grew still. After hesitating a moment, she said, "Muriel wasn't always that way."

Might they finally be getting somewhere?

"I figured she must have at least been tolerable to be around, or else the two of you wouldn't have been friends," said Beatrice.

"She was tolerable," allowed Winnie. "Muriel could fake friendliness for short periods of time. We quilted together, went to church together, and even went out for dinner and to the movies together. When I first knew her, Alexandra was only a toddler."

"How old was Alexandra when you and Muriel ended your friendship?"

Winnie considered this. "She was a teenager."

"Can't you tell me what came between you and Muriel?"

"It simply doesn't have anything to do with Muriel's death," Winnie said in a harsh voice. "You're just wanting to satisfy your own curiosity."

"It helps me to understand the kind of person that Muriel Starnes was," Beatrice said quietly. "And that's one of the things I'm trying to figure out—her character. I only knew her for a few hours and she was pleasant enough during that time."

Winnie snorted. "As I said—she could fake friendliness for short periods of time."

"So it's hard for me to fathom why someone would dislike her enough to kill her," finished Beatrice. "It would be very helpful if you could explain what happened between the two of you."

Winnie looked down at her hands, carefully folded in her lap. Finally she said, "Muriel was, at one time, a very charismatic and handsome woman. It's probably hard to imagine that, since you saw her at the end of her life while her health was failing."

"No, I can see it," said Beatrice. "She certainly had a very powerful and magnetic personality."

"That's exactly it," said Winnie, nodding approvingly. "It was really the force of her personality that was so attractive. She wasn't a raving beauty—nothing like that. But she had a great strength of character."

"So she was charismatic. Muriel had lots of friends, then? And admirers?"

"She did." Winnie pinched her lips shut before finally responding. "And she didn't think twice about horning in on friendships. I'd have people I'd become friendly with at a guild meeting or at church. I'd eventually introduce these friends to Muriel at a quilt show or after a church service, and the next thing I'd know Muriel would have charmed them into becoming her best friends. I'd call them up and they'd tell me that they'd *love* to go to the movies with me but already had plans with Muriel."

This sounded practically like elementary school to Beatrice, but she nodded at Winnie to encourage her to keep going. "So she kept stealing your friends."

"Yes. But I let her." Winnie's hands tightened into bony fists. "I'll admit it. I let her steal them. I kept thinking that they were naturally drawn to Muriel, the way I was. Instead of realizing how manipulative Muriel had been and ending my friendship with her then, I kept right on with her. I was stupid. And one day I was even stupider than I usually was."

"You introduced her to the man you were dating?" Beatrice said.

It was apparently a good guess.

"That's right." Winnie blinked with surprise at Beatrice's astuteness. "I'd never been one to date much—I never had the opportunity. I was always this scrawny quiet girl. I'd have a date here and there, but the dates never ended up sparking a real relationship." She paused. "Until I met John."

"And you and John embarked on a serious relationship?" Beatrice had to wonder whether Winnie could have overreacted, considering her lack of relationship experience.

"We did." Winnie's head bobbed slightly. "We were both very much in love," she added almost defiantly.

"And you introduced John to Muriel. Why would you have done that?" It popped out involuntarily and Beatrice snapped her mouth shut. She tried again. "Sorry. I mean, what—?"

"What was I thinking?" finished Winnie. "I know exactly what I was thinking. I was thinking that I wanted to show John off. I wanted to show Muriel that she wasn't the only one who could develop a relationship with a man. Besides, John was so handsome. I guess I was feeling smug."

"What happened?"

"It was Christmas Eve," said Winnie, her words now coming out in a sob. "Muriel had a party. She always had a party on Christmas Eve . . . a big one. There were gobs of people there. I'd bought a new dress." She smiled at the memory. "I felt really beautiful—I *wasn't* beautiful, but I felt that way. John had a dark suit and a red tie for Christmas. He looked like a million dollars."

"Did Muriel also think he looked like a million dollars?"

"Apparently. She was positively glowing." Winnie's voice was flat now. "And she completely monopolized John the entire night. I was miserable. Not only was she flirting with the man I loved, but I was totally alone at the party . . . I didn't know another soul there. It was a relief when the party ended and John and I left."

"That's when you realized the kind of person Muriel was?"

"Not quite. I blamed myself for not being witty or fascinating enough to command John's attention."

"So did John end your relationship, then?" Beatrice frowned.

"No. I did. You see, I returned to Muriel's house the next morning to give her a Christmas present. I'd forgotten to bring it to the party. I discovered John there." Her eyes filled with tears of pain. "He'd dropped me off at my house, then gone right back to Muriel's."

Beatrice winced.

"I saw red. I thought for a crazy moment that I'd kill them both," said Winnie, still in that flat voice. "I never saw John again. I stopped taking Muriel's calls. I avoided her in public. And I didn't return to this house until two days ago. I wish I didn't come back then, either."

Beatrice said carefully, "You don't think that this is a long time to carry a grudge? What happened between you and Muriel was, what—thirty years ago or so?"

Winnie stared at Beatrice. "You don't understand at all. Why would you? You're such a pretty woman that you probably had all kinds of suitors. You've got pretty hair and a nice figure. But that was the last time that I ever had any kind of relationship with a man. No one else was remotely interested in me, as much as I tried to find dates. I've never had any close bonds with my family and Muriel destroyed my capacity for trust in a friendship, so none of my friendships have had any depth to them. My quilting guild is my only social outlet. I'm completely alone, Beatrice. And I've had to work hard, teaching, to support myself my entire life. Teaching is the hardest job in the world, let me tell you."

And Winnie hadn't forgotten whom she held responsible for this life she was leading. Muriel.

Beatrice had never heard anyone sound so bitter.

"So now you understand my opinion of Muriel," said Winnie with satisfaction. "And you know more about the kind of person she was."

"I do," said Beatrice, nodding. But she also understood more completely what Winnie's motive would be for murdering Muriel: revenge. What was it that people always said? Revenge was a dish better served cold.

"Since you knew Muriel so well—at one time—" Beatrice amended when she saw Winnie open her mouth to protest. "Why don't you tell me who you think could be responsible for her death?"

"I told you. It was that crazy old woman. I don't think it had anything at all to do with Muriel's personality. I think it was that witch of an old woman, who lost her mind, got confused, and did Muriel in."

Right at that moment the library door popped wide open and a particularly wild-looking Miss Sissy glared at them. "*Murder!*" she hissed.

Winnie shrieked, frightening Miss Sissy into shrieking back.

Beatrice sighed. "Miss Sissy, Winnie thinks you might have had something to do with Muriel Starnes's death. Did you?"

"Did *not*!" she hissed again. "Wickedness!"

It seemed to be a charge leveled at Winnie Tyson, who promptly burst into ugly sobbing.

Chapter Ten

Winnie returned upstairs to lie down for a while and recover from her emotional outburst and her embarrassment over it. Alexandra apparently went upstairs, too. Holly and Posy were just finishing wrestling Dot into the library when Beatrice found them. Beatrice shivered again as she entered the library—a reaction that had little to do with the cold. The dark wood of the heavy furniture, the unread appearance of the dusty books, and the dim light from the dirty windows contributed to the bleak effect.

Beatrice hesitated. "Do y'all mind if I talk with Dot for a minute in the library? It might be easier for her than moving her to the study and then back."

"Of course," Holly said quickly. Meadow, Posy, and Holly stepped out, closing the library door behind them.

Dot said, "Holly told me what happened. I really

liked that Colton, too. It's a plum shame that he's dead. So you think the same person who killed Muriel also took Colton out?"

"We're still trying to figure out what happened. But that does appear the most likely scenario, doesn't it?" Beatrice said.

"So old Colton was onto somebody," Dot said thoughtfully. "Then he let on that he knew something and the killer had to come after him before he could say anything."

Beatrice nodded.

"And in this case, instead of some diabolical murderer from outside, we're talking about middle-aged or old-lady quilters," said Dot with her guffawing laugh. "Quilters are a tough bunch, aren't they? People think we're all milk and cookies and grandkids and quilt shows. They don't know the real story."

Dot shifted in her seat to ease the pressure from her ankle. Beatrice said, "I know with your ankle injury you probably don't have a lot of information about anything that might have happened last night. Especially since you weren't even at supper with us."

"Which I'm feeling bad about. It would have been good for y'all to have had another set of eyes for that meal. So that's when you think it happened? Holly said it sounded like it was those missing sleeping pills. In his wineglass?"

This interview was unfortunately all one way. It was more like Beatrice was supplying the information and Dot was the one asking all the questions. But she did need to be filled in, after all. "That's right," Beatrice said. "And it most likely happened during supper because Colton said he was tired and turned in right after dinner. There probably wouldn't have been time for anyone to doctor his drink upstairs."

"Was his door locked this morning?" Dot tilted her head to the side, thinking.

"It wasn't," Beatrice said. "And I didn't think about it, but that could indicate that the reason he went straight to bed was because the sleeping pills had already taken effect at dinner. Maybe he felt so sleepy that he wanted to close his eyes for a few minutes."

None of this had occurred to Beatrice with the shock of finding Colton dead. But now that she thought about it, Colton hadn't really appeared to be about to turn in for the night. Wouldn't he have at least unbuttoned his collar or removed his shirt? Certainly he'd have gotten under the covers with a night as cold as last night had been. And yet there he'd been, lying on top of the carefully made-up bed, fully dressed, looking like he was just resting for a moment before addressing a board meeting. He must have suddenly been overcome by sleepiness when he got into his room, she thought.

"Let me tell you about what I noticed last night," Dot said eagerly. "It might be really helpful for your investigation."

Beatrice decided that Dot probably wouldn't be able to shed much light on the situation, but she wasn't going to burst her bubble. "Sure," she said.

"Well, as you know, I stayed upstairs after taking my tumble. Thanks again for coming to help me, by the way."

"It was really no problem," said Beatrice.

"You ladies brought me my dinner up here. This house has a lot of open areas, so I could hear y'all talking downstairs, but I couldn't make out the words or anything. I know I didn't hear your voice after a while."

"I actually was talking to Colton in the study." Beatrice again felt that small stab of guilt that she might have accidentally contributed to his death.

"That was all I knew about what was going on downstairs. I didn't even know that Colton had come upstairs," said Dot. But I did notice something else."

Beatrice suppressed a sigh. As she'd expected, Dot didn't know anything useful, although it wasn't for lack of trying. "What was it that you did notice last night?"

"Holly. She couldn't sleep, I guess. She was gone last night for a long time." Dot's eyes were lit up with excitement at the idea that she'd been able to provide a little information.

"Holly left your room?"

"For a *long* time," stressed Dot. "I don't have a clock, but I'm guessing it must have been one o'clock when she left. And I think she didn't come back to the room for a couple of hours or so. I wasn't sleeping all that great myself, with my ankle throbbing and all. I needed to go to the restroom, too, and that

QUILT TRIP   131

was a real pain, trying to lug myself over there. It sure would have been handy for Holly to have been in the room to help me."

"Where do you think Holly was?"

"Well, she wasn't in the bathroom, because I managed to lug myself over there and it was free. Maybe she was off murdering Colton." Dot's eyebrows shot up in alarm.

"But we've already decided that Colton's drink was tampered with at supper. He was probably already dead when Holly left the bedroom. Besides, I'm not really even sure what Holly's motive would be for killing either one of them."

Dot said slowly, "Well, Colton because he knew something. That's what we're thinking, right? And Muriel . . ." Her broad face twisted as she tried working it out in her head. "Let's see. With Muriel . . ."

"There must have been a connection between Muriel and Holly," said Beatrice, almost to herself. "Everyone here had a connection with Muriel. At least, everyone that she personally invited to come here." Beatrice still hadn't forgiven Meadow for dragging the Village Quilters into the mess.

Beatrice realized she was giving herself an opening to push Dot into explaining more about her own relationship with Muriel. "Speaking of personal connections, could you talk a little more about your relationship with Muriel?"

Dot's eyebrows lifted in surprise. "You think Muriel and I were friends?" She snorted and gestured at herself—her chubby physique, the too tight American flag T-shirt, the faded blue jeans. "Is that because I somehow look like a person who hangs out with rich folks?"

For the first time, Beatrice heard a bitter note underneath the good-natured veneer that Dot presented to the world. Feeling as if she'd struck a chord there, she pressed further. "It's not too far out of the realm of possibility, is it? After all, you were both quilters. Muriel seemed like she enjoyed spending time with other quilters. Winnie, for instance."

"Winnie was in our guild, yes. Of course, I never hung out with Winnie." Dot rolled her eyes at Beatrice. "You might have noticed that she's the type of person who thinks she's better than everyone else. Why she thinks that, I can't say. She's a teacher who doesn't have two cents to rub together."

Beatrice hadn't noticed that Winnie acted superior. In fact, she thought that Winnie was probably one of the most insecure people she'd met. It might be that Winnie covered up that insecurity by acting condescending.

"So you saw Winnie hanging out with Muriel, then?" Beatrice asked.

"Oh, they were real buddy-buddy, those two. For a long time. Winnie would rub it in everyone's face. You know—she'd drop these fake-casual mentions of going over to Muriel's house and having an amazing meal . . . that kind of thing. Used to make all of us in the guild talk about her behind her back."

"So you saw when Winnie and Muriel stopped being friends?"

"I sure did. None of us knew what had happened, but we saw an immediate change one day. Winnie stopped talking about Muriel, stopped making those little comments about dropping by her house. And then she got real uncomfortable when Muriel came to guild meetings. It was obvious that either Winnie was going to have to drop out of the guild, or Muriel was because Winnie was too upset whenever Muriel was there. Of course, it ended up being Winnie who dropped out. Muriel never batted an eye over whatever it was that had upset Winnie. And Muriel wasn't going to budge—she was naturally going to keep doing whatever she wanted to, no matter what."

"So Muriel is still in your quilt guild? I mean, she was still in your guild?"

Dot snorted. "Nope. Muriel quit the guild years ago. I don't think she stopped quilting, but she stopped coming to our guild. Before you ask, no, I don't think she joined another one. Winnie did, though. She joined another guild that met in Lenoir. That's kind of a drive for her, I think. I always wondered if she'd have come back to our guild if she'd known that Muriel was no longer in it."

"Why do you think Muriel stopped going to your guild?"

"Why did Muriel do anything?" Dot asked with a chuckle. "Because she *wanted* to stop, that's why. Could've been her health, could've been that the guild members were all getting on her nerves. Could've been that she simply didn't want to hang out with people anymore and wanted to be alone. That's probably what happened—she got sick of people. Why else would somebody with lots of money stay all by herself in a rotting mansion?"

Beatrice realized she still didn't totally understand Dot's connection with Muriel. "And you're sure you didn't have any other relationship with Muriel? It appeared to me that all of Muriel's invited guests did."

"Well, Holly obviously didn't," Dot said stoutly. "And Miss High and Mighty Muriel sure didn't with me, either."

Beatrice saw she wasn't going to get anywhere else with Dot. Besides, she realized that she hadn't asked Winnie about Dot. Surely Winnie could give more insight into Dot or Dot's possible connection with Muriel. Could she also shed some light on Holly?

Beatrice was about to ask Holly to talk to her about where she'd been roaming the night before, when an angry, piercing shriek came from upstairs.

Everyone rushed to the bottom of the staircase, anxiously peering up toward the source of the shouting.

It was Alexandra. "Who took my gun?" she said fiercely, eyes like flint, arms crossed. "Who took it?"

They all gaped at Alexandra. "Gun?" asked Beatrice. "You had a gun here?"

She snapped back at Beatrice, "Yes, I had a gun here. There's no law against it, you know. I frequently lock one in my car's glove compartment so that I feel safer on the road. With everything going on here, I thought it would be a good idea to have it in my room, so I took it out and concealed it in there. Now it's gone."

Meadow crowed, "So you *do* think that your mother and Colton were murdered!"

Alexandra glared at her. "I like covering my back, that's all. I'd put it in the house that very first night— *before* Mother died. Besides, I didn't like the thought of it being out in the car. Now I'm going to ask again . . . who took it?"

No one said anything. They all continued staring at Alexandra.

"Well, I certainly don't have it," said Winnie with an exaggerated shudder. "I hate the things. I wouldn't have slept a wink if I'd known there was one around here."

"And now there's one missing," said Meadow. "Guess that's not going to help you sleep much, either." She straightened up. "Well, I haven't seen a gun. I don't have a gun."

"I wouldn't even know how to *use* a gun," Winnie said, half sobbing.

Leaning against the downstairs wall, Dot said, "I sure know how to use one, y'all. And if I'd seen it, I'd have nabbed it. But I didn't."

"When did you last see it, Alexandra?" Beatrice asked. "Did you regularly check to make sure it was there, or did you bring it inside and hide it, and assume that it stayed put?"

Alexandra didn't meet Beatrice's gaze. "Well, naturally I assumed it was going to remain where I put it. No one knew I had a gun here, so why would I think that anyone would know to go into my room and take it? I hadn't checked to see if it was there since putting it in my room our first day here."

Holly's face was so pale that her freckles stood out in sharp relief. "What does this mean? Do you think that somebody plans to kill us all?"

Beatrice discovered that she was very, very angry. This in itself was fairly remarkable. She was frequently irritated or annoyed. But angry? And yet here she was, furious at the situation they were in, furious that they hadn't been discovered, furious that Alexandra had been shortsighted enough to introduce a gun into the vicinity of a killer, and furious that no one was giving her any straight answers.

"What this means is that Alexandra made a very foolish decision and was remarkably careless afterward," said Beatrice. Alexandra spluttered furiously at her, but Beatrice continued. "It also means that whoever is murdering people in this house is now armed. Frankly, I think that gives the killer way too much of an advantage. She hasn't needed firearms before now to murder two victims. We can't fix what's already happened, so the only thing we can do now is to try to find the weapon and disarm it or lock it away somehow."

"A search!" Meadow said ebulliently. "We'll go through the house methodically. Room by room."

Alexandra rolled her eyes. "It's pointless. Whoever has the gun won't be stupid enough to leave it in a place where it could be easily found."

"I think I'd feel a lot better if we searched for it," Posy said in a worried voice, pulling the fluffy cardigan up around her neck as if she'd felt a chill.

"Can somebody help me up the stairs?" Dot asked rather plaintively as the others were heading up the stairs to begin searching for the gun. "I want to be part of the search, too."

Meadow helped Dot up the stairs, pausing halfway because Dot was already winded and red in the face. Beatrice hoped that Dot wasn't going to end up with a major medical problem while they were stuck here. What if she had a heart attack? What would they do? A feeling of helplessness washed over her and she said, "Dot, you've already been pretty active today, especially considering your injury. Why don't you put your feet up for a while?"

Dot pouted. "I'm not an invalid, you know. It's not like I have to take to my sickbed. I'm a little out of shape and have a sprained ankle, that's all."

Beatrice said quickly, "I know you're not an invalid, Dot. It's just that it's been a stressful situation for all of us and you need more rest to heal properly—not stress."

"I'll be fine," Dot said stoutly.

"Why don't we find some of Muriel's home medical equipment?" asked Posy. "She had a walker when we first met her and probably had canes to help her move around the house. Couldn't they help Dot out since Muriel won't need them anymore?"

"Good idea!" said Meadow. She asked Dot, "Would you rather use a walker or a cane?"

"I think to take the weight totally off the hurt ankle, she would have to use the walker," said Beatrice.

"No, really, she needs crutches to take the weight completely off her ankle," said Alexandra briskly.

"I guess we could search for crutches, then. Otherwise, the walker will provide more support than a cane," said Beatrice.

Dot sighed. "This stupid ankle. I'm sick of it."

"Okay, we'll look around for crutches while we search for the gun, although most people don't have crutches lying around," said Beatrice with a sigh. "In the meantime, let's carefully remove the walker from Muriel's room."

"I feel sort of funny taking her walker," said Dot, shifting uncomfortably.

"As Posy said, she doesn't need it, Dot. I'm sure if we could ask her, she'd want you to use it," said Beatrice. Without waiting for a reply, she took a tissue from her pocket and opened Muriel's bedroom door. The walker wasn't far from the door, and Beatrice removed it and carried it over to Dot.

"Where should we search first?" asked Meadow. "To be fair, how about Beatrice's and my room?"

"Seems pointless to me," grouched Winnie. "Does anyone really think that y'all had anything to do with Muriel's or Colton's deaths? You didn't even know these people."

"That's exactly the kind of thinking that's going to get us killed," said Dot. "Who knows? Maybe Beatrice and Meadow had a connection with Muriel that we don't even know about."

"I agree," said Beatrice. "Let's check everyone's rooms."

Alexandra's room was right next to Muriel's and they automatically started in that direction.

"Wait a minute!" said Alexandra, stepping right in front of Beatrice to block her. "Why are we checking *my* room? I'm the one who *lost* the gun, remember?"

Beatrice said coolly, "Well, let's glance around anyway. Maybe there are crutches in the closet . . . or an empty bottle of sleeping pills. Maybe your gun got covered up by other things in the room and you simply didn't see it. We won't know unless we go in and check it out."

They pressed into the room. Beatrice peered under the bed and rummaged in Alexandra's closet. Beatrice frowned at the unmade bed. "I think we should pat down the bed, just to be sure."

This was enough to set Alexandra's temper to the boiling point. She grabbed a vase that was next to the bed and smashed it on the hardwood floor.

Meadow gasped. "That beautiful vase!"

"What do I care?" Alexandra sneered. "It's mine, anyway. As a matter of fact, *everything* here is mine. So, really, when I tell you to get out of my room and leave my stuff alone, I'm speaking as owner of the house and everything inside it."

Beatrice raised her eyebrows and said in a reasonable tone, "The will hasn't even been executed, Alexandra. In fact, we don't even know where the will is.

I assume Colton had a copy at his office. You can't be sure you're inheriting the house or its contents."

All Alexandra's show of anger had done was to demonstrate that she had a dangerous temper. Could she have gotten angry enough to kill?

They did a quick search of Alexandra's bedsheets and found nothing.

They moved onto Beatrice and Meadow's room, where Meadow made a big production out of carefully searching every square inch of the bedroom and closet. "Let's leave no stone unturned!" she cried, lifting up the curtains and examining the undersides with exacting scrutiny. It all took forever and, naturally, they uncovered nothing.

Next they visited Holly and Dot's room. This bedroom wasn't as heavily furnished as some of the others and it took very little time to search. Dot, already winded, sat down on a chair once they'd searched under the cushions. Holly, like Meadow, had taken an overzealous approach to searching her own room. Again, they turned up nothing.

"Can't we finish this exercise in futility another time?" asked Winnie. "I'm thinking there's no way we're going to find this gun. We're just doomed to our fate here."

"Cheerful," said Alexandra, crisply. "But you haven't considered the fact that, if we stop, then whoever has the gun could decide to conceal it in a location we've already searched. Besides, it would be awfully convenient for us to stop searching before we got to *your* room."

Winnie made a strangled cry. "You're certainly not going to find anything in *my* room! I'm scared to death of firearms. I have no idea how to operate them."

"Well, let's go in there and get it over with, then," said Alexandra icily. "It's not like we have anything else of any importance to do here, Winnie. And I'd really like my gun back."

Alexandra strode to Winnie's door and pushed it open with a flourish, smirking back at Winnie as she did so. Then she stared disbelievingly into the room before giving Winnie a scornful glare. "Scared to death of firearms, huh? What do you call *that*?" She pointed inside the room and everyone crowded over to see.

There was a gun sitting on Winnie's bedside table, right next to the door.

Chapter Eleven

Winnie gave a long, sustained shriek.

"Sure looks like my gun to me," said Alexandra, picking up the compact Ruger pistol and calmly sticking it into her pocket.

Winnie's eyes were wide with terror. "Someone came into my room." She gasped. "Someone came in and planted the gun here."

"Baloney," said Alexandra.

Winnie seemed to be on the verge of total hysteria. "You did it!" she screamed at Alexandra. "You put your gun in my room to throw suspicion onto me."

Alexandra raised her eyebrows. "And why would I do something like that?" she haughtily asked.

"Because you've always hated me," said Winnie with a sob.

Alexandra blinked twice with surprise, and then her mouth twisted in a cruel smile. "I've never thought about you much one way or the other," she said. "In fact, I felt sorry for you more than anything else."

"Mean, through and through," muttered Meadow, glaring at Alexandra.

Winnie cried, "You were always jealous of the friendship I had with your mother! You wanted to spend more time with her."

Alexandra gave a laconic laugh. "You've got that completely wrong. The last thing I ever wanted at any stage of my life—even, I suspect, at infancy—was to spend more time with Muriel Starnes." She turned to Beatrice. "Okay, so you've taken on police duties here, right? What are you going to do now? You've found a stolen weapon in a suspect's room. What will you do about that? I think we've found ourselves a killer."

They all stared at Winnie, who seemed in danger of melting into a puddle on the floor.

Beatrice said, "We found a stolen gun, and she denies taking it. I also have a hard time imagining that she would just leave it sitting right by the door of her bedroom in plain sight. We have no evidence that she had anything to do with the two deaths."

"So you're going to do absolutely nothing," said Alexandra.

"No. I'm going to make two suggestions. One, that you give me the gun and we lock it in a safe place."

"A safe place?" said Alexandra with a dry laugh. "There's no such place here, Beatrice. If there was, don't you think we'd all be trying to get into it? I think 'safe place' is code for 'Beatrice's room.' You want the gun for yourself."

Beatrice forced herself not to respond to the barb. "I was thinking of perhaps locking it in a glove compartment of one of the cars, if I could slide my way over to it."

"And who would have the key?" asked Alexandra. "You? You see my point. And I'll save you some time from thinking of another place to put the gun . . . I'm not going to give it up. So save your breath."

One idea shot down. "My other thought was that we should all try sleeping in the same room. For safety. That way we can effectively keep an eye on everyone at night."

Surprisingly, it was Winnie who wasn't impressed with this plan. "I don't think that's going to work out well."

"Of course you don't," said Alexandra. "That's because your plan of hunting us down one by one and murdering us would be foiled."

Winnie had regained her composure by now, however, and managed to ignore Alexandra. "The problem is that everyone here has very unusual sleep habits," she said. "Erratic, actually. I know, since I had my door open that first night. Lots of sleeplessness, lots of wandering around. I like the idea of feeling safe, but the only way I can deal with my stress is to sleep. I don't think I'd get a wink of sleep if I had to be around this group all night."

Her second idea, shot down. "Then I suggest that everyone locks their doors again tonight," Beatrice said. "At least that will slow down someone from entering a bedroom. Whoever is behind this is gaining confidence every time she gets away with murder. I'm worried that she's going to strike again."

After the search was over, Beatrice felt like crawling back into bed. Meadow saw that her energy was flagging, and she said chirpily, "Time for us to have lunch, Beatrice. I stashed away some of the remaining good stuff for you. Although it's nothing like I would be cooking if I were at home in my own kitchen. I'd give anything for a hearty chicken casserole or a meat loaf or a bowl of steaming hot chili right about now."

The remaining good stuff was composed of canned soup, which did hit the spot on a day when the temperatures were cold enough to keep the ice outside intact. Posy had made a small fire in the study and the three women gathered in there with their lunches. They ate quietly. Meadow kept glancing over at Beatrice. Finally Meadow said, "You seem really tired out, Beatrice."

"It's these people we're stuck here with," said Beatrice. "They're getting tired and scared and it's starting to make everyone seriously obnoxious. A couple of them were obnoxious even before all this happened. The way that no one is telling me the whole truth is also making everything a lot harder."

"What are you thinking so far?" asked Posy in a hushed voice.

"Wait a minute!" commanded Meadow. She leaped

up out of her armchair and checked outside the study door before closing it again behind her. "Okay, the coast is clear. Let's keep our voices down low, though," she suggested in her stage whisper that could likely be heard all the way upstairs.

"It's hard to know," said Beatrice with a shrug. "There's so much that's being hidden from me."

"True, but what's your *gut* telling you?" asked Meadow.

"Everyone is so un-murderer-like," said Posy, sighing. "Well, except maybe Alexandra. I hate to say it, though. The poor thing just lost her mother, after all. That might be behind the way she's acting."

"I doubt that very much, Posy," Beatrice replied. "You're sweet to look for the good side of Alexandra Starnes. But I don't think there's much there that's good. I don't think she cares a hill of beans about her mother's death. She's glancing at her watch all the time, waiting for the moment when we're all discovered and she can take over this property and Muriel's bank account."

"Alexandra is the one who's responsible for all this," Meadow said stoutly, still in the noisy whisper. "She had the most motive. It's always about money— isn't that what we've learned from watching cop shows on TV? And did you see that temper of hers this afternoon, Beatrice? I half thought she was going to sling that vase at you instead of at the floor. She's nasty."

"Grief affects people in very unusual ways,"

mulled Posy, still determined to think the best of Alexandra.

"Yes, she has a temper and, yes, she has a motive. Yes, she had opportunity," Beatrice said. "But I think we're really limiting ourselves if we decide she's definitely the murderer. We also have to admit, Meadow, that we're not very fond of the woman and that's probably coloring our judgment."

"That's because she's a total harpy," said Meadow in a completely even voice.

"True. But let's consider everyone else, too," said Beatrice.

"Holly is very sweet," offered Posy in a hesitant voice.

"Holly *is* very sweet," said Beatrice. "No one has had anything negative to say about Holly or seems to have even known Holly before we got here. She's been completely lovely to everyone, pitches in to clean, is polite, and spends her day working on a quilt for a children's charity or reading *Little Women*. The only problem is that I can't understand what she's doing here. Muriel appears only to have invited people who she had a personal connection to and had wronged in the past. How does Holly figure in? And where was she last night? Dot says she was out of her room for hours."

"Maybe she simply couldn't sleep?" Posy offered. "After all, Miss Sissy roams the halls all night with insomnia. Under the circumstances, maybe Holly hasn't been able to sleep and is going down to the library to read at night. She's a librarian and we know she loves reading."

"You should ask Miss Sissy," said Meadow, snapping her fingers. "She'll probably know."

"Depending on whether she's having a good day or a bad day," said Beatrice glumly. "But that's a good idea. I'll ask her. Which reminds me. Posy, do you want to switch rooms with me? It might give you the chance to get more sleep instead of chasing Miss Sissy down all night."

Posy beamed at her. "I really do appreciate that, Beatrice. That's so kind of you. But I think I'll be fine. I've decided that Miss Sissy is so much happier when she can just wander around. She's not hurting anyone, and I suppose she'll sleep when she's ready. But it makes sense to ask Miss Sissy what Holly was up to last night."

"And I'll ask Holly herself. She's the only one I haven't interviewed about Colton's death. What do y'all think about the others?"

"Like Dot?" asked Meadow. "I guess she knew Muriel back from when Muriel was involved with her quilt guild, right? So Muriel was ugly to Dot—is that what we're supposed to gather?"

"Something like that," said Beatrice. "Except that Dot refuses to say what happened, or even if there was a specific incident. So that drives me a little crazy. But yes, I think we can assume that Dot has a motive. She's a pretty hefty woman, too—I don't think she would have had any problems smothering Muriel Starnes. But I still want to find out more about her past and how it intersected with Muriel's. I'm thinking I'll talk to Winnie about it, since she's the one who knew Muriel the longest."

"Except for Alexandra," Meadow pointed out.

"The problem is that Alexandra doesn't know anything about her mother or her mother's life. She did know about Winnie, but that's only because Winnie was at her house a lot growing up. But casual acquaintances of Muriel's? I'm thinking that Alexandra didn't know and didn't care. Once Alexandra grew up, I think she left home and didn't return often."

"So you're going to talk to Winnie to see if you can find out more about Dot," said Meadow. "And I guess you're going to ask Winnie more about how the gun showed up in her room?"

Beatrice nodded. "Sure. I'll ask her about it. But I don't think Winnie even knows how it got there. Unless she's a really good actress, she was surprised and upset to learn that there was a gun somewhere on the premises. She appeared even more shocked that it was in her bedroom."

"Of course, Winnie *is* set up pretty well to have carried out these murders," said Meadow, still in her loud whisper. Beatrice shushed her and she continued in a slightly quieter voice. "After all, she doesn't have anyone sharing a room with her. It would have been easy for her to slip out and murder Muriel."

Posy said, "But Muriel had been a good friend for a long time. Could she have done something so awful to someone she'd been so close to?"

"Muriel had also done something unforgivable in Winnie's eyes," said Beatrice. "She'd betrayed their friendship by stealing away Winnie's one true love. Winnie is still teaching school and is bitter that the life she thinks she *should* have had was stolen from her. Winnie's friendship quickly switched over to hate."

"That was such a long time ago, though," said Meadow. "Do you really think that Winnie would carry a grudge for so long?"

"It's as someone said after Muriel's death: people hold grudges. Muriel didn't completely grasp human nature and thought that she could clear her conscience by giving a blanket apology to everyone she'd hurt. It doesn't work that way, though. Blanket apologies don't wipe away years of anger or hurt or resentment. Muriel didn't understand that," Beatrice explained.

"I can see why several of the quilters would be upset with Muriel," said Posy slowly, "but why would anyone kill Colton?"

"Maybe he guessed who the murderer was or witnessed someone leaving Muriel's room. I think he knew too much," Beatrice replied.

"Poor guy," said Posy. "I really did like him."

The three women were silent for a few minutes.

"And you're still thinking that it was an overdose of sleeping pills in his wineglass?" Meadow asked.

"It would have been easy enough for the murderer," said Beatrice. "He usually had a glass of wine in the evenings, and he left it unattended for a while last night. Everyone was bustling around, clearing the table. The murderer would simply have poured the powdered pills right into his glass and swished it around real quick. He'd never have known. And there was plenty of opportunity for everyone to have access to that glass."

Meadow gave Beatrice an evaluating look. "You seem a little more upbeat and less tired than you were before. See—Posy and I make good sidekicks!"

Posy beamed.

"You certainly do," said Beatrice. "And you've inspired me to hop back into my investigating. I'm going to talk with Holly next and then Winnie."

"Before we know it it will be night again," said Posy with a shiver. "I still like the idea of sleeping in the library. Particularly since my roommate wanders the halls at night and doesn't offer much protection from murderers."

"We can still camp out in the library tonight, Posy," said Meadow. "I don't think we'll be the only ones, either. I bet Holly will join us. Dot might, too."

"Alexandra is probably feeling pretty secure up in her room, considering she has a gun." Beatrice sighed. "And we already heard Winnie's feelings on it. I think Dot would be game for camping out in the library, but she might not be very comfortable. She's probably barely comfortable even in a bed. But we can plan on sleeping downstairs and leave it so that anyone can join us."

"What are you going to do now, Beatrice? When will you talk to the others?" asked Posy, her blue eyes looking worried.

"I'll try to talk with Holly and Winnie as soon as I can. Hopefully before suppertime," Beatrice said.

Holly, as usual, was completely amiable when Beatrice asked to speak with her in the study. She even managed a smile, although her eyes were hollow. If what Dot had said was true, then Holly probably didn't get much sleep last night.

"Here we are again," Holly said brightly. "You're awfully good to try to figure this mess out, Beatrice."

Beatrice smiled. "I think I'm desperate for something to do. I'm used to keeping busy, and when I don't have anything to do, I get very restless. So investigating is a way to try to keep us safe as well as to simply keep from going crazy with boredom."

Holly smiled back and then gazed reflectively into the fire. "And I want to help you out, Beatrice. I really do. I wish I had more information to give you, but I don't think I know anything that's going to help."

"It might be that there's a bit of information that doesn't even seem important that ends up being a clue," said Beatrice. "Why don't you start out by telling me what you noticed after supper last night? When Colton and I left the table, what did you see?"

Holly continued thoughtfully staring into the fire. "We all started clearing the table."

"Everyone did?" asked Beatrice.

Holly turned to grin at her. "Someone must already have tattled to you about Alexandra. She wasn't particularly interested in washing dishes."

"Did Alexandra have access to Colton's wine-glass?"

Holly considered the question. "Beatrice, I think everyone probably had access to Colton's wineglass. We were coming and going from the kitchen, leaning over the table to pick dishes up. Anyone could have put something in his glass. To answer your question, though, it did seem that it would have been very easy for Alexandra to slip something into Colton's glass. She could have timed it while more people were in the kitchen."

Beatrice was silent in response, hoping Holly would go on.

"She acted like she was deliberately ignoring us," Holly continued. "There we were, rattling silver-ware and dishes and glasses and talking to each other over the running water, and she never even glanced our way." She shrugged. "Alexandra might not be able to help it. With her background, she probably always had someone here cleaning up after supper. They probably had a housekeeper." An expression passed across Holly's face that Beatrice found difficult to read.

Beatrice said quietly, "Dot mentioned that you had a bad case of insomnia last night."

Holly's eyes were startled. "Poor Dot. I didn't realize I'd kept her up."

"It didn't sound like you'd really kept her up," said Beatrice. "I think that her ankle was making her uncomfortable and every time she woke up from the pain, she noticed you weren't there."

Holly nodded, gazing at the fire again. "I guess it's from all the stress. I found it really hard to fall asleep. Then I woke up and lay there for a while but couldn't go back to sleep again. I thought I might go downstairs and work on my quilt or read a little more of *Little Women*. I'd gotten to the point where Jo had moved to New York and met Professor Bhaer."

Beatrice studied her. "Ah. You know, I was always sorry that Jo didn't end up with Laurie. So that's what you did downstairs? Read your book?"

Holly continued staring at the fire. "That's right."

"For several hours? Dot said you were gone for hours. And that part of *Little Women* isn't far from the end, as I recall."

"Was it that long?" asked Holly. "It didn't seem like it."

She wasn't really answering the question. Beatrice would be interested in peeking at Holly's quilt later and seeing if it had progressed a few hours' worth.

"Maybe," Holly said quickly, coming up with an explanation, "I dozed off while I was reading. I do that sometimes at home. I wouldn't even have noticed that I'd nodded off in the middle of it." She smiled eagerly at Beatrice, as if to gauge whether she'd believed her story.

Beatrice decided not to push her any further on that point . . . yet. "While you were up last night, did you see or hear anything? See anybody?"

Holly's eyes grew wide again. "Why do you ask? I thought y'all had decided that Colton's drink had been tampered with after supper. Do you think he might have been murdered after he turned in?"

"Not really. But I'm trying to put together a complete picture of last night from supper through to this morning at breakfast."

"I didn't see or hear a soul." Holly gave a small sigh. "And here I am not being helpful again."

But Holly had been more helpful than she realized, Beatrice thought. Because Holly hadn't seen Miss Sissy, who'd been wandering around downstairs for much of the night. So where had Holly been?

Chapter Twelve

After Holly left, Beatrice tried connecting with Winnie to ask her more about Dot and the gun's appearance in her room. But Winnie wasn't downstairs in the library or in the kitchen. She checked upstairs and Winnie wasn't in her room, either.

Beatrice frowned. Could she possibly be outside? In this weather? Last time she'd glanced out the window, it had started snowing. The temperature must have been in the twenties. If she was going to check outside for Winnie, she might as well try again to see if she could get a cell phone signal out there. She grabbed her phone from her bedroom, put on her coat, and headed downstairs and outside.

Beatrice spotted Winnie as soon as she was out on the porch. Winnie was sitting in her car with the engine running. Surely she wasn't going to try to leave? She'd smash that car immediately against a tree. Beatrice stood there, not sure what to do.

Winnie glanced her way and rolled down a window. "Beatrice, don't try to step on the driveway. You'll fall down and break your neck like Dot almost did."

"Then why did you step out on the driveway?" asked Beatrice, exasperated.

"I needed to get away from that house. Just for a few minutes. It's oppressive. Don't you feel it? I feel like the atmosphere in there pushes down on my chest until I find it hard to breathe."

That was rather excessive, but she didn't have the patience to argue. "How did you manage the ice?"

"It was okay. I slipped a few times, but I managed to catch myself. I feel much better now that I've spent some time out here. I'm warmer, for one thing. You know, I had one of the most miserable days of my life here in this house. Being here doesn't exactly bring back happy memories for me." Winnie paused. "You came out here to find me, I'm guessing?"

"Well, that, and I wanted to check my cell phone signal again. Sometimes you can find a small pocket where you can get a signal. But if I'm going to break something by stepping out on a sheet of ice, I guess I'll put that part off." There was no point in even turning the phone on if she wasn't going to be able to walk around the property to locate a signal. "At least you're all right. I was wondering since I couldn't find you anywhere inside."

"You needed to speak with me again?" Winnie's sharp features were strained.

"I did. I wanted to ask you a few more questions.

But we don't have to do that now—I can tell you're trying to de-stress."

"Can we wait until tomorrow morning?" asked Winnie. "I think I need to block everything out for a while. If we talk shortly before it's time for me to turn in, it's going to stick in my mind and I'll have nightmares about guns, sleeping pills, and depressing houses. I'll go in soon and quilt for a while. That will relax my nerves a bit."

"That's fine, of course," said Beatrice. Although an unwelcome thought popped into her head, reminding her that tomorrows sometimes didn't happen in Muriel Starnes's house.

As she quilted in the library along with Meadow, Alexandra, and Winnie, Beatrice was still itching to talk to Winnie. Winnie might have suspected Beatrice wanted to talk, which was why she was staring with great focus at her Grandmother's Flower Garden pattern.

"That's the perfect thing to have brought along," said Meadow. "No background needed—just cut your hexagons, sew your strips, and bingo!"

Winnie continued staring fixedly at her quilt pattern. "True. Although I'm planning on appliquéing these flowers to a background when I get back."

Beatrice said, "I love the mosaic of all the hexagonal flowers, Winnie. And I'm with Meadow—you couldn't have brought a better project with you. You can easily hand-piece it—no need for a sewing machine. The effect is really lovely. The pastels you're using are perfect—the robin's egg blue, that faint mint color. It's a very soft, comfortable look."

Winnie gave a small, pleased smile before clamping her thin lips tightly together again, as if reminded that she was supposed to be miserable.

Beatrice glanced curiously at Alexandra's quilting. "What are you working on?"

Alexandra drew the fabric closer to her instinctively, as if hiding it. After a moment, she relaxed enough to briefly hold up the fabric.

It was a log-cabin print of darker colors. The stitching was excellent, if primly perfect. Somehow, though, the quilt lacked soul. Beatrice was instantly irritated with herself for thinking that. Wasn't she just transferring her feelings about Alexandra onto her quilt? How could a quilt be full of soul anyway?

But her experience with quilts in the art world from her days as museum curator had taught her that inanimate objects can, paradoxically, be full of life and joy and have souls of their own. Not Alexandra's quilt, however.

Beatrice was careful not to let any of her thoughts show on her face. She gave Alexandra a quick, perfunctory smile. "It's very well made," she said.

Alexandra appreciated the compliment. Beatrice noticed that she looked pleased as she resumed her quilting.

The mood was a little lighter in the room, but the chatting that Beatrice hoped might follow—full of insights into the murders—was sadly not to be.

*   *   *

Supper wasn't the organized meal it had been the night before. Perhaps the ordeal of the previous night was enough to quell everyone's interest in sharing a meal together. This night everyone rooted around in the pantry on their own, heating up cans of vegetables or broth for themselves and sitting by the fire in the library. Alexandra took her food upstairs. Winnie claimed not to be hungry and had gone to bed early. No one—not even Meadow—was in a chatty mood.

After they'd eaten and washed up, Beatrice, Posy, and Meadow set out pillows and quilts in the library. Holly joined them, but worried about the fire. "We're not going to use up all the wood, are we? Just for the four of us? I know there wasn't a whole lot of wood to begin with."

"Five with Miss Sissy," Meadow reminded them.

"If Miss Sissy actually goes to bed," said Beatrice with a sigh. She turned to Holly. "We're going to burn only a small amount of the wood. There should still be plenty left for our stay. I'm hoping that this cold snap is almost over and that soon the ice will melt and we'll be able to drive home."

Posy said sadly, "Cork has got to be crazy with worry. And for me to say that simply goes to show how long we've been missing. You know how laid-back Cork can be."

Beatrice thought Cork was actually more crotchety than laid-back. But she was sure he must really be worried about Posy's whereabouts. "Do you think he's not quite as worried as he might be? Because he must realize you're with us?"

"Maybe he suspects we're together, which might have been comforting at first. But by now he's got to be wondering if we were all in a car together and the car slipped off the side of the mountain in the bad weather." Posy gasped. "I hope we're not putting rescue teams in danger. Do you think there are rescue teams out in these conditions, searching for our cars off ravines?"

"Maybe not," Beatrice said. "The thing is that we arrived here in two separate cars. So the likelihood that both of them would careen off a mountaintop isn't big."

Meadow said glumly, "Well, there's no way Ramsay can even *be* concerned about this situation. He doesn't even have cell phone service where he is. He's in the middle of nowhere."

"He's in good company." Beatrice sighed. "What I wouldn't give for one signal bar on my phone right now. I wonder if Cork has gotten in touch with Piper."

"I kind of doubt it," said Meadow. "After all, Piper is in California visiting Ash—does Cork have Ash's phone number? Or Piper's?"

"He wouldn't," said Posy. "So Piper and Ash are in blissful ignorance. And poor Miss Sissy doesn't have anyone to be called."

"She has us!" said Meadow. "But we're all here with her." She thought for a moment, then grinned coyly at Beatrice. "I bet Cork called Wyatt."

One of Meadow's goals in life appeared to be matchmaking Beatrice with the handsome older minister. This was a problem because Beatrice hoped to embark on a relationship with Wyatt and the last thing she wanted was Meadow mucking things up. "I'm sure that calling the local minister would be natural in these circumstances," Beatrice said in a rather prim voice. Meadow laughed.

"How about you, Holly?" asked Beatrice. "Do you think there are people actively searching for you?"

Holly shrugged and tilted her head down, her red hair forming a curtain that made it hard to see her face. "I don't know. I sort of doubt it, though. I grew up in foster care, as Muriel made reference to, so no family is out searching for me. I was married once, but not for very long. We didn't have any children, so I'm on my own, for the most part."

"How about coworkers?" asked Beatrice.

Holly nodded. "I'm in an office, so they'd definitely see that I was missing. I'm always very punctual about coming to work, so this absence would be something really out of the ordinary for me. They'd probably report it to the police."

Meadow said, "And the police would go by your house to check on you. Would they find any clues to lead them here? Maybe you jotted down directions? Or maybe you wrote it on a calendar?"

Holly frowned, then apologetically shook her head. "I don't think so. But I can't really remember."

"The police would put two and two together pretty quickly," said Beatrice. "After all, we're all quilters. How often do a bunch of quilters go miss-

ing? How did Muriel get in contact with you to begin with?"

"She sent me an invitation," said Holly. "My name
and address are listed on our Web site as the contact
information for my guild."

"But Muriel didn't use the Internet," Beatrice said
slowly. "There's not even a computer here."

"Maybe she got Colton to take care of it for her,"
suggested Meadow. "That could be a kind of law-
yerly chore, couldn't it? Muriel would simply have
told him that she was interested in setting up a foundation and wanted to get in contact with several
guilds that could help her decide how to manage
different aspects of the charity. Colton would have
found that information in a snap."

"I guess," said Beatrice. "But something about
that still doesn't make sense to me. How genuine
was Muriel about creating a foundation? It seemed
like it was a ruse to get everyone over here so that
she could apologize to them and clear her conscience."

"It sounded like she wanted to make a foundation
to me," said Meadow. "That's the whole reason we
came over here!"

Holly was looking away again. Beatrice was sure
there was more to her connection with Muriel than
just quilting.

Beatrice was surprised how quickly she fell asleep,
considering she was in a room with several other
women and lying on the floor. But the fire put out a

pleasant warmth and the emotional day had exhausted her. She drifted into sleep nearly as soon as she closed her eyes.

Sometime in the middle of the night, they were all awakened by a piercing scream from upstairs. The fire had burned out and the library was completely dark.

"What on earth?" muttered Meadow.

Beatrice stumbled toward the door, feeling around her to keep from running into any furniture on her way out. The other women were close behind her.

Winnie was standing in the middle of the hall with Alexandra and Dot gaping at her. Miss Sissy joined the others at the bottom of the staircase, then snorted derisively when she saw the distraught Winnie. She disappeared back into the kitchen.

"A ghost!" Winnie gasped. "I saw a ghost!"

Alexandra rolled her eyes. "I'm going back to bed now." And she stomped off to her bedroom.

Beatrice hurried up the stairs. Winnie didn't really seem like a fanciful person. She might have seen something . . . but Beatrice didn't believe it was a ghost. Perhaps the stress she was experiencing was playing out in weird ways. "Winnie, can you tell me exactly what it was that you saw?"

Winnie took a deep breath. Once Beatrice got close enough, she could see that the woman was shaking.

Winnie finally made out, "I heard a noise of some kind outside my bedroom. I didn't hear it again, but it was enough to fully wake me up. I decided I'd visit the restroom. I stepped out into the hall and there was this billowing thing that jumped out at me with a hissing, groaning noise. I've never been more terrified." The last words came out in a sob. "This horrible house!"

"Are you sure you weren't half asleep?" Dot asked skeptically. She leaned heavily on her walker and seemed half asleep herself. Her short gray hair stood up on her head.

"I know what I saw and what I heard," Winnie said stubbornly, her voice still wavering.

"It's so dark up here," said Beatrice. "Are you sure about what you saw? Where was this billowing thing coming from?"

"It was dark, but I could feel and see this moving mass. It was out of the corner of my eye, but I did see it!"

"Did anyone else see or hear anything?" asked Beatrice.

No one said a word.

"Okay, I'm going to say that we all need to go back to sleep," Beatrice said.

"What about the ghost?" Winnie asked in a shrill voice.

Beatrice sighed. "I'm not sure what you saw, Winnie. If it was something supernatural, as you're claiming, there's nothing we can really do, is there? It's not like we can hunt down a ghost by going room to room and then banish it outside in the ice. Besides, we all need a good night's sleep. We can't stay up all night worrying about this."

Winnie said, "I can't sleep in there! There's no way I can fall asleep now!"

Posy gently suggested, "Why don't you join us all in the library, Winnie? We can light the small fire again. Grab your pillow and a couple of quilts and settle down in front of the fire. There's safety in numbers, anyway."

"I guess I might as well," said Winnie. "I don't think I'll sleep a wink, though."

While Winnie got her quilts and pillow, Beatrice lit another small fire in the library. Winnie set up her bedding with much ado, complaining about the situation they were in, the hardness of the floor, and the fact that they were trapped in a haunted house. Beatrice had the feeling they were going to be subjected to hours of sleeplessness with Winnie's tossing and turning and muttering, but was amazed that Winnie fell instantly asleep as soon as she closed her eyes.

"Well, that's a gift," murmured Meadow, staring in amazement in the dim firelight at Winnie, who was now snoring gently.

"As long as it's not because she's been given sleeping pills," said Beatrice with a sigh. She lay down and soon fell blessedly back to sleep herself.

The next morning, Beatrice was awakened by Miss Sissy, who stuck her head in the library, hissed, "Wickedness!," and then abruptly disappeared again.

Beatrice sighed. She had a feeling that Miss Sissy was getting lonely with her self-imposed solitude and was reaching out in her odd way. Everyone else was still sleeping, so she decided to join the old woman in the kitchen for a snack—that, almost certainly, was where Miss Sissy would be heading.

Miss Sissy was already opening up a can of white potatoes when Beatrice entered the kitchen. The old woman glared at Beatrice and held the can closer to her. "I'm not that hungry, Miss Sissy. You're welcome to the potatoes." Beatrice surveyed the pantry, by now quite picked over, and wondered whether she could stomach a breakfast of olives.

She discovered a small can of beets in the back of the pantry and pulled it out instead. "I hope the weather changes fast," she said to Miss Sissy. "Otherwise, our diet is only going to get even weirder."

Miss Sissy greedily ate a potato and nodded. "Blue sky out there," she said, pointing vaguely to the window.

Beatrice glanced out. "Well, that's a good sign. Maybe the sun will help to melt some of the ice."

Miss Sissy said, very reasonably, "Driveway is in the shade, though."

Yes, that wooded driveway was going to be an issue. Beatrice was starting to wonder if they were ever going to get out of there.

She remembered that she was planning on asking Miss Sissy questions and now appeared to be a very good time, since the old woman seemed to be fairly lucid. Beatrice munched delicately on a canned beet, then began her questioning. "Miss Sissy, I know you have a hard time sleeping. What kinds of things have you seen and heard at night lately? Have you seen people walking around? Heard any strange noises? Seen any ghosts?" She smiled at her.

"Ghosts!" snorted Miss Sissy. "No such thing." She cackled to herself.

Beatrice figured if anyone was likely to see a ghost, it would be Miss Sissy while wandering though the huge house all night. "Okay, so no ghost. What about people? Who have you seen while you've been up?"

Miss Sissy grunted and stared imploringly at Beatrice's beets. Beatrice carefully fished one out with a knife and put it on Miss Sissy's plate, where it was quickly gobbled up.

Miss Sissy sighed contentedly and glanced up at Beatrice. "Saw that younger gal."

Everyone was a gal to Miss Sissy, who many days appeared to be staring one hundred in the eye. Beatrice's mind whirled as she tried to imagine who Miss Sissy would consider young. "Holly?"

Miss Sissy nodded. "She wanders around at night."

"Wanders around? Does she sleepwalk or something?"

Miss Sissy said scornfully, "Not her. She's awake. Being snoopy."

"What makes you think she's being snoopy?"

"Goes through desks and anyplace there are papers. Goes into closets and every room. Poking around."

Beatrice sat back in her chair in surprise. It didn't gel with her impression of Holly at all. "Have you gotten any idea what she's searching for or doing?

Has she seen you or talked to you while she's up at night?"

Miss Sissy shook her head and more wiry hairs tumbled out of her poorly constructed bun. "I've seen her, but she hasn't seen me." The old woman looked pleased at this.

"What do *you* think she's hunting for?"

"Secrets!" hissed Miss Sissy, staring scornfully at Beatrice.

Beatrice was happy it all made such good sense to Miss Sissy, but she really didn't have a clue why Holly would be looking around for secrets or anything else. Miss Sissy was starting to look irritated, so Beatrice needed to back off before she shut up for good.

"So you've seen Holly at night. Who else have you seen while you've been up?"

"That mean gal. She's up at night. Yelled at me, too." Miss Sissy's expression was vicious.

"Who is that?" Beatrice asked with a frown.

"The *mean* one!" Miss Sissy bellowed, as if Beatrice were hard of hearing.

"You mean Alexandra?"

"If she's the one who's so mean. She's snoopy, too. Checks the same spots that the young gal does. She hollers at me when she sees me watching her." Miss Sissy's catlike eyes glowered.

It could be that Alexandra was hunting around for a will. Beatrice had a feeling that, if she found one that wasn't in her favor, she'd have no problem destroying it.

"She's all the time talking about a key, too," said Miss Sissy.

"A key? Key to what?"

"Don't know. Won't tell. Wickedness!"

Having grown up in the house, Alexandra likely knew where all her mother's hiding spots would be. "I'm thinking I should take a tour of this house," mused Beatrice.

"You've seen it," said Miss Sissy with a shrug of a cadaverous shoulder.

"Not really. Nothing except the main downstairs rooms. I did check out the bedrooms really well, but that was only because we were searching for that gun. Now I think I should investigate the attic. There's a turret room up there, too."

Miss Sissy glared at her apparent ignorance.

"I've been hearing all this stuff about people searching for things and wills and missing sleeping pills and ghosts," said Beatrice. "It would be good to have a better understanding of the entire layout of the house."

Miss Sissy continued glaring at her.

"Who knows," said Beatrice lightly. "There might even be food up there. Some people stockpile food for emergencies, you know."

Suddenly Miss Sissy was a lot more interested. Beatrice wondered whether she might leap up and start for the attic herself. She quickly added, "So you saw Holly and Alexandra about. Was there anyone else, Miss Sissy? Any of the others?"

"Not Posy!" said Miss Sissy, viciously. She apparently thought that Beatrice might be suspicious of her dearest friend.

"Of course not. Nor Meadow or me. But none of us are really going to be suspects with the police, since we didn't know these folks. You didn't see Dot or Winnie walking around at all?" Beatrice was starting to think that everyone had a secret life in the middle of the night here.

"Seen both of them!" muttered Miss Sissy. "Evil! Wicked! Liars!"

Beatrice raised her eyebrows. Miss Sissy was going downhill fast. "Nothing specific you want to tell me about them? Were they doing anything?"

Miss Sissy stared blankly at her.

"Okay, well, I've kept you long enough, Miss Sissy. I should be cleaning up my breakfast things. Want me to clean yours, too, while I'm at it?"

"I've seen my friend, too," Miss Sissy whispered, looking vague.

Beatrice stared at her. "Your friend? Who is your friend?"

"It's *my* friend, isn't it? Not yours! Won't tell," Miss Sissy said stubbornly, banging an arthritic fist on the wooden kitchen table.

Chapter Thirteen

Meadow joined Beatrice in the kitchen after Miss Sissy had stomped out. "Well, you got up awfully early this morning for someone who was up in the middle of the night with a ghost."

"Miss Sissy and I were having a visit, that's all," said Beatrice, rinsing off the plates.

"How did *that* go?" asked Meadow. "You never know what you're going to get with Miss Sissy."

"It started off well, and then deteriorated after that." Beatrice placed the plates in the dish drainer.

"This is going to be interesting," mused Meadow. "Stuck in the house with a completely crazy Miss Sissy."

"Winnie is another one in danger of cracking up," said Beatrice quietly. "She was better when she was quilting yesterday, but the stress still must be too much for her. What did you think of her ghost story last night?"

"I thought she must have been having a real lulu of a nightmare," said Meadow. "Or that maybe she'd gotten into the wine."

"But she was up walking around," said Beatrice. "So a nightmare doesn't fit."

"She could have been sleepwalking. People do. Especially when they're really stressed out."

Beatrice shook her head slowly. "She struck me as being completely awake and alert when I saw her last night. She was hysterical—but not sleeping."

"She might not have been sleeping then, but for the last few hours she'd been sleeping pretty hard," said Meadow. "Maybe now would be a good time for you to talk to her. Before she has a chance to get all hysterical on us again."

"Is Winnie awake now?"

"She was just stirring when I left the library. You could bring her breakfast," said Meadow. She opened the pantry door and peered inside. "Maybe a nice meal of . . . canned salmon. It's the fanciest thing we have left and I think it would make a nice gesture for you to offer it to Winnie. She'd probably really appreciate it."

"I can't believe Miss Sissy didn't devour it already. I strongly believe the whole reason Miss Sissy is up so much in the middle of the night is because she's plundering the pantry."

Meadow said smugly, "Ah. But I hid the canned salmon behind the tin of sardines. Miss Sissy hates sardines."

Winnie was indeed very grateful to have the last

decent can of food in the house. In fact, she was so grateful that she was moved to tears. This distressed Beatrice more than any amount of ravings over ghosts. She was relieved to set upon a mission to find Winnie some tissues.

When she'd returned with tissues for Winnie, she was glad to see that the quilter had composed herself for the most part. It was a fragile recovery, though, and she seemed she could fall apart at any moment. Beatrice vowed to tread carefully. It would probably be better to start out with something safe—like Dot and Holly.

"Winnie, I was wondering if you could maybe give me a few insights into Dot and Holly," Beatrice began. "I don't really have the full picture for how they figure in."

Winnie finished chewing a mouthful of fish and said, "I really don't know Holly at all, Beatrice. I have no idea what her connection with Muriel was. She says she didn't know Muriel, so I guess we'll have to take her at her word. I had heard of her through the quilting world, though. I knew that she was a very accomplished quilter in a good guild."

Beatrice sighed. "I guess we'll just have to accept that, then."

Winnie raised her carefully drawn-on eyebrows. "Muriel *was* trying to actually set up a foundation, you know. Why else would she have had her lawyer here? I think—yes, she was trying to kill two birds with one stone with others of us. But Holly was probably only here because of her quilting."

"Can you tell me more about why Dot is here? I understand she did have a connection with Muriel. A quilting one, I'm guessing, since Dot doesn't appear to run in the same circles as Muriel would have."

Winnie giggled. "Dot is pretty blue collar and Muriel wouldn't have been friends with her, no. But she would have been acquainted with Dot through her quilting guild. I don't have money, but at least I'm educated. Dot was likely a high school dropout."

Beatrice knit her brows. "So, if Dot wasn't really in the position to have been friends with Muriel, then why did Muriel feel she owed her an apology? It seems she wouldn't have known her well enough to have hurt her."

Winnie said in surprise, "Didn't you know? Dot worked for Muriel. She was one of her mill employees."

Beatrice stared at Winnie. "She was an employee?"

"She sure was. A pretty important one, too. She was a manager over there. But when Muriel shut down the mill, Dot got laid off. And she's never found anything as well paying since. Of course, she's not qualified to get another job that's going to pay as much, considering she doesn't really have an education. I understand that she had a good standard of living before the mill closed and that her life was really impacted by it. She had to sell a lot of stuff. She even had to move." Winnie said this a bit gleefully, appearing to rejoice in Dot's misfortune.

"So this all happened while you and Muriel were still friends?"

"Mercy, no! Muriel and I haven't been friends for decades. No, this was something I heard about through the quilting grapevine. Quilters were trying to help Dot out by cooking her casseroles and that kind of thing. That's how I knew about it. It's the kind of thing that would make one very vengeful, wouldn't it?" Winnie's eyes glinted maliciously.

"Oh, I don't know," Beatrice said mildly. "Getting laid off is a nasty part of life these days. I can't imagine that Dot would hold the loss of a job against an employer."

"It wasn't only that. Dot felt a sense of entitlement. Apparently, she'd argued for a higher salary while she worked at the mill, but was told that she'd get more money along with the promotion she'd get when she became manager. Then she finally *became* manager—and Muriel sold the mill. So Dot apparently felt that she'd been cheated. She'd been working hard all those years at a dirt-cheap salary because she'd been promised this prize—a prize the company, and Muriel, knew would be denied her. Yes, she became manager—but only for a month."

"I know I keep playing devil's advocate, but I can't see how that was Muriel's fault."

Winnie blinked at her. "Well, of course it was! The mill was her business."

"But as owner she probably had no idea of the inner workings of the place, her employees, or anything else. She wouldn't have been responsible for telling Dot that she wasn't getting a raise until her promotion. She likely wouldn't have been aware of any of it except for the sale of the mill."

"She certainly *was* aware of it! Muriel Starnes knew everything that went on in that place. Everything. There wasn't a whispered rumor she hadn't heard. If someone so much as sneezed, she was aware of it. I'm sure that she was the one person responsible for keeping Dot at a low salary and lying to her about her prospects at the company."

"Why would she have done such a thing, though? It doesn't make any sense to me why Muriel would have been so determined not to give Dot a raise or to give her a heads-up that she might want to start hunting for a new job. Especially since they were in the same guild and knew each other socially."

"They were only acquaintances in the guild," Winnie explained, seeming bored with the conversation. "There was no feeling of real friendship there. And besides, Muriel brought frugality to a new level. She pinched pennies like crazy. It wasn't because she needed the money—it's just the kind of person she was. It made her feel clever, I think. And it made her feel smug that she had piles of money in her bank account."

Now Winnie's thin face flushed and Beatrice figured she was probably thinking about how Muriel had cheated her, too, in a way—keeping her from marrying a prospective suitor with means.

Beatrice remembered that there was one other thread to this mystery that she didn't understand.

"Winnie, were you acquainted with Colton before you came here?"

"No. I knew who he was, but I'd never actually met him. Colton and Muriel got involved after Muriel and I had ended our friendship."

"You knew who he was?" Beatrice frowned. "So you saw him with Muriel in town?"

"Well, they were married. I was aware of that, of course, even though Muriel and I weren't talking to each other. The other quilters would gossip about Muriel."

"Married!" Beatrice stared at Winnie.

"Didn't you know?"

"No! I thought that perhaps they'd dated. Or maybe even that Colton had admired Muriel from a distance."

"No, they were married, all right. But not for very long. Don't take the fact that they were married too seriously, Beatrice. Muriel certainly didn't take marriage seriously. She was married five times."

Beatrice's mind boggled at this. She'd had only one husband and had been widowed for ages. *Five* husbands?

"But I will say this—Colton was her last husband. Muriel never married again after that," Winnie said.

"Do you think that Colton broke it off? Or Muriel?"

"Well, the gossip around the quilting guild was that Colton had actually broken it off. Oh, he was crazy about her—couldn't you still see it? He was very deferential to her. But the other quilters said that he realized that her feelings for him weren't the same as his for her. It broke his heart and he decided to end their marriage instead of living a lie." Winnie snorted. "Very tragic." Her voice was bitter again, as if she were thinking about her own failed relationship.

Beatrice hesitated, then said, "Winnie, tell me about the gun. And more about what you saw last night."

Winnie tensed. "I hate guns, Beatrice. I've never had one in my house, nor wanted one, even though I've lived alone almost my entire life. They terrify me. When I tell you that I have no idea how that vile thing got into my room, it's the truth."

Beatrice was inclined to believe her. If she was acting, it was an excellent performance. "And what about last night?"

Winnie shuddered. "I've already told you about that. I hate to even think about it. I got up to visit the restroom. I felt a chilling draft sweep over me." She stared at Beatrice. "Why would I feel a draft when there were no windows open?"

Beatrice shook her head.

"Then I had this sensation of movement out of the corner of my eye. I turned and there was this swooshing, billowing form leaping out at me from near the hall window. I screamed." She spread out her hands to indicate that Beatrice knew the rest of the story.

"And you were completely awake?" asked Beatrice, after clearing her throat.

Now Winnie's eyes grew hard. "Is that what you think? You think I was dreaming? You're one of those people who likes to deal in facts and numbers and data, aren't you? Let me tell you, Beatrice, there are some things in life that we can't understand. But they're as real as you and me."

"Oh, I know," Beatrice said quickly. "Yes, I believe you."

"Faith is real and we can't see it. Evil is real and we can't touch it. And this ghost was real, Beatrice. I can't explain it or even describe it very well—but it was real."

Beatrice thought again about the key that Miss Sissy had mentioned. Where hadn't they looked in the house? There were several closets downstairs—coat closets and storage mainly—as well as a few upstairs, for linens and other storage. And none of them appeared to be locked.

The turret room and the attic—those were the two main unexplored areas. And considering how dark the house was, daytime would be the only time to explore, although the attic was bound to be fairly dark even then, despite the dormer windows Beatrice had spotted from outside the house.

She hated to use one of the precious few candles, but there was really no other way.

Meadow saw her lighting it. "Where are you going?" she asked.

"Miss Sissy mentioned that Alexandra has been searching for a key at night. I figured I'd check to see if the attic or turret room was locked. If one of them is locked, I'll spend some time poking around for a key," Beatrice explained.

"You don't think I'm going to let you go roaming around in the attic by yourself, do you! With a crazed killer around? No way. I'm coming with you. In fact, let's get Posy to join us."

"Won't we draw a lot of attention to ourselves?" asked Beatrice. "I really don't want the whole household up there."

"Okay, so no Posy. You and me, Beatrice! A team." Meadow beamed at her and Beatrice successfully repressed a heavy sigh. Still, Meadow was very energetic. Beatrice could probably use a little extra energy to feed off of.

"Let's attract even less attention, though," said Beatrice. "Let's go up to the attic separately. I'll go first, and then you follow me a few minutes later."

"Okay!" Meadow agreed. She paused. "Do you know how to get to the attic? I mean, I know it's *up*, but I don't know how to go any farther up than the second floor."

"There's a very narrow wooden spiral staircase tucked into an alcove directly next to Muriel's bedroom. You might not have noticed because it's so dark upstairs. And every time we go near Muriel's room, there's so much excitement that it overshadows everything else."

Meadow blinked at her. "No, I've never noticed it. Okay, so I'll give you a few minutes to go upstairs, and then I'll follow. What if you find that the door at the top of the stairs is locked?"

"Then I'll be coming back down again quickly, of course, and we'll search for the key."

The upstairs was dark and quiet. Everyone had gone downstairs to warm up by the fire. Beatrice walked quickly down the long hall and over to the narrow staircase beside Muriel's room.

She hesitantly put her weight on the bottom stair. The staircase sure was rickety. Beatrice wasn't a big woman, but she wondered if the rather delicate staircase could hold her weight. The idea of the staircase collapsing and sending her plunging back down to the second floor was a scary thought.

The stairs appeared to be sturdier than they seemed, although they did squeak a fair amount. Beatrice quickly climbed them.

There was a door at the top of the stairs and Beatrice turned the glass knob. The door didn't budge. Beatrice sighed. There could be clues in the attic and she was going to have to figure out how to get in. Obviously Alexandra had been searching for a way in, too.

As Beatrice stood frowning at the door, she heard a distinctive squeak on the bottom step. She leaned over to peer down and saw Miss Sissy, who quickly put a finger to her mouth and held up a key.

Miss Sissy scampered lithely up the stairs and handed her the key. Beatrice inserted it in the lock, turned it, and then turned the door handle once again.

The attic door swung open and Beatrice smiled at Miss Sissy. She lit her candle and they walked into the dark space that was only slightly lit by attic vents. The musty smell was even more pungent up here and Beatrice jumped as a moth flew past her. The large space appeared to be used just for storage, judging from all the clothes racks full of hanging bags, steamer trunks, old furniture, and picture frames she saw up there.

"How did you find the key?" Beatrice asked Miss Sissy quietly.

"Remembered where my own mother hid keys," said Miss Sissy. "Wondered if the old gal had done the same thing."

It was funny to hear "old gal" coming from Miss Sissy, considering she was clearly much older than Muriel had been.

"Where was that?" asked Beatrice.

"Taped to the bottom of one of the linen closet shelves." Miss Sissy's bright eyes showed her to be much more alert than she had been earlier. It was amazing how fast her mental aptitude came and went.

They could hear more squeaking out on the staircase, and Miss Sissy tensed up. Beatrice quickly said, "That's only Meadow, Miss Sissy. I told her to join me up here separately so that we wouldn't draw a lot of attention to ourselves."

Meadow stuck her head through the attic door, then smiled as she spotted Beatrice and Miss Sissy. "Almost like a party up here!" she said delightedly. Meadow glanced around. "Although I don't think we're going to find anything but a bunch of old junk up here." She squinted across the attic. "What's that over there, though?"

Beatrice peered across the attic and saw a turret alcove. She frowned. "I thought the turret functioned as Muriel's private bath off her bedroom," she said to the others.

"It did," said Meadow. "But it was probably a two-story turret. So the bottom part was the private bath off Muriel's room and the top part was a small alcove off the attic. Don't you just love this house? Secret hiding places and creepy attics and cupolas and turrets . . ."

"Why would you even have an alcove off an attic?" asked Beatrice.

"For an element of mystery, Beatrice! These old houses are rife with the element of mystery, didn't you know? This place reeks of Southern gothic."

"Complete with the dead bodies," said Beatrice glumly.

"There are probably all kinds of secrets over in that alcove. It's fantastic!" Meadow said.

"Secrets!" chorused Miss Sissy, clapping her hands.

They trod across the attic toward the turret. "I'm not even going to pay any attention to this other stuff," said Meadow in her stage whisper. "It looks like the same stuff that I've got in *my* attic. But that desk over there looks a lot more interesting."

And it did. Because, for the life of her, Beatrice couldn't figure out why there would be a desk in the attic. Right up there in the turret, too.

Chapter Fourteen

"Do you think she fancied herself a writer?" Meadow asked in a doubtful voice. "Having a desk up here seems like something Jo in *Little Women* would do—write in the attic."

"You know," Beatrice said, "it might just be a spare desk—just like the extra chairs and chests of drawers and tables all piled up here. But perhaps then she realized it was a great place to keep papers away from prying eyes."

"It wouldn't exactly be comfortable to sit up here, though," said Meadow, making a face. "It's freezing up here now, and in summer it would be three hundred degrees."

"Maybe not so bad in the summer. These turret windows actually open. She could have sat up here with a window open and it might have been fairly pleasant at this elevation."

Miss Sissy scowled at the alcove. The massive

wooden desk was full of pigeonholes and cubbies. A swivel chair faced it. There was nothing else in the alcove.

"Okay, let's get at it," said Meadow, rubbing her hands together and plopping into the chair.

Beatrice reached for a stack of papers on the desk and Meadow reached for another. Miss Sissy wandered off to explore the other parts of the attic.

After a few minutes, Beatrice frowned. "I'm seeing a lot of baby pictures here," she said.

"Recent ones?" asked Meadow.

"No, some really old color pictures. A few black-and-white snapshots, too. They're mostly of a little girl."

"Is there a name on the back?" Meadow asked.

Beatrice flipped several of the pictures over. "No. And that's annoying. I always label the backs of my photos. After all, *I* might know who's in the pictures, but that doesn't help anyone else if I'm not around to identify the people."

"They're probably old pictures of Alexandra," Meadow said with a dismissive wave of her hand. "Muriel must have been like everyone else in the world and had a pile of pictures she kept meaning to put in an album. Finally you get to the point where you want to hide the pictures out of view and not even see them anymore to remind you how slack you've been."

"Probably," Beatrice muttered. "Although I wonder where all these pictures were taken."

Meadow started chuckling, which ended up in a

coughing fit. "Dust—" She gasped. Once she'd gotten control of herself, she handed a photo across to Beatrice. "Colton with hair!"

Sure enough, there was a picture of a younger Muriel staring triumphantly straight at the camera. Beside her was a younger version of Colton, with hair. He had his usual serious features, but in his eyes was an expression of pure joy. He was obviously thrilled to be marrying Muriel. They apparently married here at the house. The old Victorian home appeared much younger in the pictures, too.

"He looks to be devoted to Muriel," Beatrice said as she stared at the picture. "No wonder he was happy to come over and help her set up her foundation. He was also concerned about the way she'd brought heirs here while in the process of changing her will. He must still have deeply loved her."

Meadow peered back over at the photo. "You're getting all that from the picture? I was laughing at seeing him with hair."

They continued going through pictures and papers. "There are lots of letters in my stack," said Meadow. "And lots of them are correspondence with Colton. I guess I must have happened into the official Colton stack of stuff."

Beatrice was almost halfway through her pile. "My pile is chock-full of Alexandra pictures. From a distance, which is kind of odd. Long lens." She stopped and peered closer at one of the photographs. "Okay, this is a picture of an older child. A teen. But she sure doesn't resemble Alexandra. In fact, even the baby pictures don't resemble Alexandra. You know how Alexandra has that really distinctive, aquiline nose? I don't see it in these photos."

"Maybe she had her nose done," Meadow said, with a shrug.

"But wouldn't her nose appear *better* if she had it done, not worse?" Beatrice kept staring at the pictures in front of her. "I don't think these are of Alexandra at all. And the child isn't even smiling at the camera in any of these. It almost appears like the child doesn't know her picture is being taken."

Meadow leaned over to see. "You're right—this kid doesn't really look like Alexandra much. Do you think it's a niece or something? There's a resemblance to Alexandra, but it's definitely not her."

"Aren't these a lot of pictures to have of a niece?" Beatrice frowned.

Miss Sissy made a squawking sound and held up an expanding file folder. "Clues!" she barked.

Beatrice walked over to Miss Sissy and took the file folder. "Let's take this over to the window, Miss Sissy. It's too dark to read it over here."

They huddled around the folder. "Anything interesting?" asked Meadow, peeking over Beatrice's shoulder.

"They're receipts," Beatrice said as she slowly leafed through the papers. "Mostly from AAA Investigative Services."

Meadow snorted. "Was she trying to keep tabs on Colton? Maybe he wasn't as boring as we thought."

"I think," said a quiet voice behind them that

made them gasp and spin around, "that Muriel was trying to keep tabs on *me*."

It was Holly.

Beatrice tried reading Holly's expression, but she couldn't. "We're sorry to snoop around, Holly. We're trying to find clues to help us figure out what's going on."

Holly said sadly, "That's what I've been doing, too, so don't feel bad about snooping. You've just as much right to come up here as I do."

"Is this where you were the other night when Dot noticed you were out of bed?" asked Beatrice.

Holly nodded. "I came up here to look around. Practically burned the candle down to a nub—it was so dark up in the attic at night. I should have simply found a quiet time to sneak up here in the daytime so I could see what I was doing." She sighed. "And no matter what I found, it didn't *explain* anything to me."

"Explain?" Meadow asked.

"Those pictures," said Beatrice. "They are all of you, aren't they? You are Muriel's daughter, aren't you?"

Holly's eyes filled with tears. "I am. Not in any real sense of the word, though. I had no idea she was my mother until she told me that night before she died."

Beatrice remembered that Muriel had told Colton she'd been determined to speak to someone. She also remembered overhearing Holly's tears during their conversation. "What did Muriel tell you?"

Holly took a deep breath and resumed her frequent nervous habit of winding her red hair around a forefinger. "She said that she'd become pregnant with me and that it would have created a huge scandal because she wasn't married at the time. Muriel said it was hard enough to be taken seriously at the mill without an accidental pregnancy. She concealed her pregnancy as best she could with loose clothing, and then told everyone she was going abroad for a while. No one thought anything of it because she frequently traveled and because she'd had a rough time in the years before with a failed marriage and the death of her mother."

Meadow's eyes were wide. "So she left town to have you?"

"There was a home for unwed mothers somewhere up north. Muriel stayed there the last few weeks of her pregnancy. As soon as I was born, she gave me up for adoption."

"But you didn't get adopted," said Beatrice gently.

"No," said Holly. "I went into foster care."

Meadow said quickly, "But we can see that your mother kept up with you during your entire childhood! There are tons of pictures in that stack from the time you were little on up."

Holly thought this through, head down so that her hair formed a curtain around her face. "But it's not the same, is it? She hired an investigator to take pictures of me so that she could see how I was doing. I guess she could tell from the photos that I was healthy and well and what I looked like. She couldn't see what I was like on the inside, though. And that's where I was really hurting."

"How long did she keep up with you, Holly?" Beatrice asked. "Did you find any pictures from when you were an adult?"

"I did. Not as many, of course. I think by then she was content that I'd grown up. But there are scattered pictures in there. Muriel was particularly interested in the fact that I was a quilter." Holly was fighting tears again.

"How did you react when Muriel told you that she was your mother?" asked Beatrice. "That must have been a tremendous shock."

"I had no idea what Muriel wanted to talk to me about," Holly said. She sank down on the top of a nearby steamer trunk, reliving the memory. "We were down in her study with a candle and she was telling me she was my mother and I could only stare at her. It didn't seem real at all—just with the lighting and all. It was almost as if it had been staged. I guess she thought I didn't believe her, although why would she make up a story like that? She gave me a key to the attic and told me to see for myself—that she'd kept all kinds of pictures of me throughout my lifetime. She told me where to find them."

"Did you go up here that night?" Beatrice asked.

"No. After Muriel gave me the key to the attic, I suddenly fell apart." Holly sighed. "It made it more real somehow. I only wanted to go to bed and hopefully the weather would improve and I could get away the next day."

"Did Muriel say anything about why she was suddenly getting in touch with you after all these years?" asked Beatrice.

Holly stared at the file folder. "She was apparently trying to make amends for not being a part of my life. She told me she was sorry I'd had such a rough life, and she planned to make it up to me. Colton was here to help her change her will to favor me. She hoped that she and I could have some sort of a relationship before her terminal illness ended her life. Muriel said that . . ." Holly hesitated. "Well, it wasn't very nice of her to say, but she said that Alexandra had been a disappointment as a daughter to her."

"What did you say to that?" Meadow asked, drawing in a breath.

"What *can* you say to that?" said Holly. "I was so overwhelmed from what she'd told me that I wanted to go turn in for the day. I didn't know that would be the last time I'd talk to her. How could I know?" She stretched out her hands helplessly to Meadow and Beatrice.

Meadow said thoughtfully, "Muriel was really hopelessly naive in many ways, wasn't she?"

Beatrice frowned. "She seemed very complex to me. Why do you think she was naive?"

"To think that a simple apology could wipe away all the hurt and stress over the decades," said Meadow. "Why would she think it would be so easy?"

"Muriel was the kind of person who was used to

people doing what she said," Beatrice explained. "To her, this was probably no different. So if she apologized and asked someone to accept her apology, in her mind it wouldn't be any different from any other request she made—people would hop to it."

"It all makes me feel so sad," Holly said. "Mostly, I'm sad that I never got the opportunity to know her. And it makes me angry, too. There were so many wasted years." She glanced down at the key in her hand. "Here, Beatrice. You take this. I don't want it. Being up here only makes me more confused."

They all went quietly downstairs, glancing around them to make sure that no one was watching them exit. Miss Sissy hurried off to make herself a snack— being in the attic had apparently made her hungry— and Beatrice and Meadow adjourned to their room to discuss what they'd found out.

"What do you think?" Meadow asked in her stage whisper.

"It's all very sad, isn't it?" Beatrice said quietly. "Here you have Holly, who seems like a really good person. She had a very tough life, growing up in foster care. Her childhood may even have had implications for later in life—we know she had a failed marriage. Maybe this belated apology and Muriel's assumption that it would make everything okay was enough to push Holly over the edge."

"Maybe," Meadow said judiciously. "Although that would have been kind of a stupid thing for Holly to do, right? I mean, Colton was here at the house to alter Muriel's will in her favor. All she had to do was at least wait until that will was drawn up."

"And probably become a very wealthy woman," said Beatrice. "But who knows if her emotions got the better of her? From what I overheard the night Muriel was murdered, Holly was very distraught."

Meadow snorted. "I think if Holly murdered anybody she should have gone after Alexandra. It would have annoyed the hang out of me to see that smug face and know that selfish creature grew up totally catered to while I was struggling to survive. *That's* who would have driven me to murder."

"Alexandra had been obviously snooping around searching for that key," Beatrice said. "She wanted to check out the attic herself."

"Do you think she knew about Holly's true identity?" asked Meadow. "Or suspected it?"

"I don't think Alexandra knew anything about it," Beatrice said. "After all, she would have been one of the last ones that Muriel would have told about another daughter. Think what would have happened if Alexandra had realized that Holly was a potential heir. Holly might have ended up as a victim herself. No, I think Alexandra was searching for the key because she suspected there might be a copy of the will up there."

"Don't you think we should go back up to the attic and poke around for a will?" Meadow asked.

"Finding a will isn't going to help us solve these murders, though. It's only going to clear up who was an intended heir. And that doesn't even particularly matter since Colton was obviously here to draw up another will."

"What should we do with the keys to the attic?"

"I'll put one of them in my pocket so it'll be with me at all times. The other one . . ." Beatrice glanced around their bedroom. She spotted a small framed photograph on the bedside table picturing a very dour person from the early twentieth century. "How about we put the other key in the back of that picture frame?"

"Good idea." Meadow raised her eyebrows. "I'm impressed! Have you had much opportunity to hide things in your life?"

"Not a thing, except maybe Christmas presents." Beatrice laughed. "But that's a spot where we can still easily access the key but it's completely out of sight."

Beatrice felt restless again after the attic discoveries. She felt as if they were on the brink of discovering who was responsible for the murders and her brain didn't want to shut off. Ordinarily when she felt this way she'd take a walk with her corgi, Noo-noo. There was no way she could take a walk in these icy conditions without breaking her neck. And thinking about poor Noo-noo, who must surely wonder where her mistress was, put her into a brooding mood. She was peering out the library window to look for signs of melting ice when Meadow spotted her. Posy followed Meadow in a few moments later and settled down at a leather card table, where she immediately proceeded to cut circles out of colorful cloth.

"You're acting broody, Beatrice," Meadow said with arched eyebrows. Then she frowned. "Which I understand, since I'm not really in the best of moods myself."

Posy put down her fabric to stare at Meadow. Meadow was so rarely in a bad mood that it was fairly earth-shattering when she was.

In fact, it was almost a relief to have Meadow finally feeling the effects of living in a dilapidated mansion with no electricity and a murderer on the loose.

"Starting to feel the stress?" asked Beatrice, nodding.

Meadow gazed blankly at her. "Stress? No. But I've gotten myself all fired up about the fact that Muriel and Colton didn't have the time to come up with a will to set up that quilting foundation."

Beatrice sighed. "I thought we decided it was all just a ruse to get everyone here so that she could apologize to them."

"No, I really think she was going to also do something about the foundation. After all, she got Holly here and she didn't even *know* Holly. She wasn't exactly making the Village Quilters leave, either—Muriel could have simply had Colton send us away when we showed up."

"Well, I know you're disappointed . . ."

"I am! I really wanted to have some funds to start after-school clubs or something. We always try to get the young people involved in quilting, but they're always so busy. They never can commit to something that takes as long as a quilt." Meadow's eyes were sad behind her red glasses.

Posy said quickly, "The young people are so accomplished, though, Meadow. Soccer and lacrosse and tough classes and—"

"Yes, of course they are!" Meadow replied. "Take my Ash and Beatrice's Piper. Brilliant children! And so talented. But it would be nice to pass on a real *art form* to the next generation."

"Piper is a member of Village Quilters, Meadow," Beatrice reminded her dryly. "She's a much better quilter than I am."

"Well, of *course* she is!" said Meadow. She swung her arms around in a dismissive gesture. "Our children are much more gifted than the norm! But I'm talking about regular young people—high schoolers or college or regular folks in their twenties. They need to be indoctrinated, too."

Beatrice hit back a laugh at the word "indoctrinated," which made her picture Meadow brainwashing youngsters into quilting. Instead, she said, "I'm sure we can do a little fund-raising to establish a club of some kind in the schools, Meadow. Perhaps Posy could donate older fabrics or give us a deal on bulk."

Posy was nodding eagerly.

Meadow still appeared grumbly, but brightened a little at the thought.

"Now can we get back to the case at hand?" Beatrice suddenly felt grouchy again.

"Are you getting fidgety?" Meadow put her hands on her hips. "I know how antsy you get when you can't do what you want. I saw you staring out those windows."

"I think there's some melting happening," said Beatrice, gesturing outside. "See? It's even dripping off the roof. And right there on the driveway? Doesn't that look like a puddle?"

Meadow peered dubiously out the window. "Not much like a puddle, no. Maybe it's starting to melt, but it's still icy on the top. Like a lake that hasn't completely frozen over. You're not thinking about us hopping in the van and taking off, are you? Because I'm too fond of my life to end it by running slap into a tree while going down a mountain of a driveway."

Beatrice sighed. "No, I guess I'm not thinking about doing that. I wouldn't want you to wreck your van and I'd be too guilty if anything were to happen to us if we tried it. But, boy, I sure wouldn't mind some of the others trying to drive out." She kept her voice low in case anyone came in.

"I know!" said Meadow, rolling her eyes. She tried to keep her voice low, too, but was as loud as usual. "Especially that Alexandra. Although Winnie has been getting on my nerves, too. She's so shrill and whiney. I can't handle it."

"Maybe I'll try to find something in the bookshelves," Beatrice said. "I did spot a few Agatha Christies in the study, so I'm thinking the study might actually have the good books. The library has those wretched collections. I've already tried reading a few of the anthologies and they were pretty awful. Maybe I've just got more modern taste."

"Let's quilt for a while," said Meadow, as if proposing something new and different. Naturally, they'd all been quilting at least once a day since the ordeal started. After all, it was the way most of the women relaxed when they were under stress.

Beatrice reluctantly agreed. She still felt fairly limited in her quilting abilities, and being around expert quilters who'd been practicing the craft for a lifetime wasn't exactly the way to make her feel more confident. But after she'd started hand-piecing, Meadow helpfully jumped in with a few tips. After a half hour had passed, Posy joined them and Beatrice heard even more helpful tips. Soon she felt that she was getting a free master-level class. When Miss Sissy entered the library, she thought she'd really hit the jackpot. Miss Sissy was a fabulous quilter and a fairly able teacher, despite her frequent odd behavior. But Miss Sissy was apparently only in the library for a spot in front of the warm fire and a comfortable chair to nap in. She was soon snoring loudly.

While they were in the library, the other quilters came and went. Winnie listlessly joined them for a few minutes before putting her project aside and wandering off again. Dot came in with her squeaky walker and cheerfully chatted with them while playing a quick game of solitaire before heading to the kitchen in search of a snack. Alexandra came in, apparently searching for a book, glared at them, and left again. Holly spent nearly an hour with them and made quick progress on her own quilt, a homey-looking double ring quilt. Then she got sleepy and went upstairs for a nap.

When it was only Meadow and Posy and the sleeping Miss Sissy in the room again, Beatrice said quietly, "You know, Posy might be a good person to poke around in the attic a little."

Meadow nodded. "You could be right. If *I* go into the attic, there'll be someone looking for me about food or firewood. I seem to have gotten elected cook and fire maker. And if *you* go up to the attic, Beatrice, someone will be trying to talk to you about the case or about getting out of here . . . You're sort of the group leader. But no one wants to bother Posy, since she's in charge of keeping up with Miss Sissy and that's trouble enough."

And Posy was quiet, too, which was something that Meadow was decidedly not.

"Oh, I'd be delighted to help, Beatrice," Posy said. "I feel I really haven't been able to do very much to help you out."

"Are you going to give her your key?" asked Meadow. "Actually, why doesn't Posy just take the other key? The one you've hidden away."

"Honestly, it probably would be a good idea for Posy to have possession of that key," said Beatrice thoughtfully. "That way, if anything happened to you or me, she'd have it."

"God forbid!" said Meadow stoutly. "Nothing will happen to us, Beatrice. Not unless we try to get out of here with the van, and we've already decided against that."

Beatrice quietly told Posy the key's location on the back of the picture frame. Posy listened carefully, nodding. "So I'll get the key and wait for the coast to be clear before I go up to the attic. I'll search for official-looking documents, right?"

"Exactly," Beatrice told her.

Posy put down her quilting and headed upstairs.

"This is all so exciting sometimes!" said Meadow, still doing some hand-piecing. "I wonder what Posy might uncover upstairs."

A few minutes later, though, an apologetic Posy rejoined them. "I'm so sorry, y'all. I must not have heard you right. I checked in the back of the picture frame on one of the bedside tables but there wasn't any key in it. It had a picture of a real serious woman on the front. Was that the wrong one? But I didn't see another one. Did you hide it, maybe?"

Chapter Fifteen

Beatrice and Meadow stared at each other. "No, that was the right picture frame," Beatrice said slowly.

"Do you think maybe it somehow got into another part of the frame or something?" asked Meadow, squinting her eyes in thought. "Could it have slipped underneath the picture, maybe?"

"I don't know." Beatrice put her quilt aside and stood up. "But I'm going to go up right now and check it out."

"Me, too!" said Meadow.

"I'll wait down here so it won't be too obvious that we're trying to be secretive," said Posy.

Beatrice and Meadow headed upstairs and into their room, quietly closing the door behind them. Beatrice picked up the picture frame and carefully dismembered it, putting each piece separately on the bed. They stared at the bits: glass, a back, cardboard filler, the photograph. No key.

"Are we losing our minds?" Meadow asked in an excited whisper. "Did we hallucinate the whole thing?"

"No, we put the key right in the back here," Beatrice said. "Someone must have overheard us talking about it."

"They must have," Meadow agreed. "Because *I* didn't move the key."

"Of course you didn't," said Beatrice. "Nor did I. Someone heard us and took it."

"Let's go back downstairs and ask Posy and Miss Sissy if they noticed anyone lurking outside our door earlier," said Meadow. "I want to know who's been eavesdropping on us!"

But Posy hadn't seen anyone outside their bedroom door. "Don't you think that would have been pretty obvious?" she said doubtfully. "Our murderer seems to be more clever than that."

Miss Sissy, when they'd woken her up from her nap, was adamant. "Nobody snooping!" she said.

"This was earlier, Miss Sissy. Before Meadow and I started quilting," explained Beatrice.

"There was nobody!" repeated Miss Sissy vehemently.

"Miss Sissy would likely know," said Posy. "She played solitaire in our room and had the door open the whole time. I'd think she'd see anyone coming or going."

"Nobody!"

"Okay, so what are we going to do now?" asked Beatrice. "Clearly someone listened in on us. I'd love to know how they did it and what they were hoping to find out. I wonder if we can set a trap for them? And maybe keep half an eye on the stairs to the attic?"

Meadow clapped her hands with delight, causing Miss Sissy to startle and glare at her. "A trap! I'd love to set a trap. Makes you feel so smug, doesn't it? Being in the know while someone else falls into it."

Posy said in a hesitant voice, "So maybe give her another chance at taking something? A red herring?"

"Exactly. A red herring," said Beatrice. "Over supper tonight, I'll say something to Meadow about needing to talk to her. Then we'll make sure that someone has an opportunity to hear us. We'll make up a story about some important papers that are hidden in the study. Then, when our culprit goes to the study to find the papers, we'll have caught her red-handed!"

Posy said, "But can we be sure that the same person will hunt for them? What if someone else comes searching for the papers?"

Meadow said, "What are the odds? I'm thinking that out of a smallish group of quilters there could only be one person that sneaky."

Beatrice said quickly, "Did y'all hear something?"

It was Dot. She called downstairs to them again. "Can y'all find me that cane you were talking about? Somebody had it in their closet, right? I'm getting tired of this squeaky walker and want to try a cane instead."

"Oh, I think there was one in my bedroom closet," Posy said. "Hold on, Dot. I'll run and get it."

Posy scurried off and Beatrice muttered, "Hope Dot is really ready for a cane. All we need is for her to go tumbling down that oak staircase and get seriously injured. What would we do then?"

"She's probably fine." Meadow shrugged. "She's been off that ankle for a while now. I've seen her put ice from outside on it. It's got to be better."

Beatrice had her doubts, though, when Dot tried to navigate the stairs holding the cane with one hand and the banister with the other. Posy hovered anxiously at Dot's elbow. "Can I help you, Dot?"

Tiny Posy would likely fall down the stairs herself if Dot took a tumble. "No—here, I can help you, Dot," said Beatrice firmly. Dot scooted to the side and held on to Beatrice instead of the banister and they slowly made their way down the stairs. Dot stuck her tongue out in concentration.

When they reached the landing, Beatrice frowned as she heard an unusual sound. "Dot, did you hear that?"

Dot gazed blankly at her. "Hear what?"

"I don't know. There was a funny sound when your cane hit the landing."

Dot picked up her cane and rapped against the floor again. Again there was that hollow sound.

Beatrice stooped down and Dot moved out of the way. Beatrice rapped on the floor around the area and then sat back on her heels. "It sure seems to me like there's a hollowed-out spot here in the floor."

Miss Sissy appeared behind them. "Secrets!" she hissed.

Meadow put her hands on her hips. "Well, if this isn't divine providence, I don't know what is. Just when I'm thinking I'm going to go stir crazy and that this house is the most boring place in the world, we find a secret compartment. I love it!"

"That's only my guess," muttered Beatrice. "This house might just have a serious case of termites."

"Dot, I'll help you the rest of the way down," Meadow said. "Do you want to go put your feet up in the library?"

"I sure don't. I want to watch the action!" Dot's eyes danced. Meadow helped her to the bottom of the staircase and they watched as Beatrice stooped down to carefully examine the landing. Posy also studied the floor.

"I'm looking, too, Beatrice," said Posy. "But I'm not really sure what I'm searching for."

"Maybe the outline of a door?" Beatrice said slowly. Then her eyes fell on a slight depression in the wood. It was hard to see because the staircase wood had warped over the years. "Or something like that," she said, gesturing to a thumbhole.

No one seemed even to breathe as Beatrice put her thumb into the depression and tugged. She felt something give, but hadn't put enough force behind her pull. She tried again, this time bracing herself. A square section of the floor started coming up.

"A trapdoor," Posy breathed.

Meadow chortled with delight. Dot grinned.

"Wickedness!" said Miss Sissy decidedly.

Beatrice carefully opened the door all the way

back until she leaned it against the wall. The door was hinged on the inside. She could see a rickety wooden ladder leading down into a space that was about four feet deep. "Should I go down there?"

"Yes! You should!" Meadow said with delight, and complete disregard for Beatrice's safety.

"Don't you think you might get hurt?" Posy worried. "That wood is awfully old."

"You don't want to take a tumble like I did," said Dot.

"I'll be careful," said Beatrice. She eased herself onto the small ladder, testing her weight on it. "The ladder appears pretty sturdy, actually."

Beatrice slowly descended into the space, then paused. "Could someone hand me one of the flashlights, please? Or a candle. I won't be able to see a thing down here without a little light." And the thought of accidentally brushing against some sort of creature that made the hidey-hole a burrow made her shiver. She wasn't particularly fond of large spiders, either.

Meadow dashed off for a flashlight, returning in seconds. The flashlight wasn't very generous with its light, but it at least gave off enough so that Beatrice would be able to get an idea of what was in the space. This time she continued down the ladder until she got to the floor, crouching herself over as she descended.

"Are you going to be able to breathe down there?" called Meadow.

Beatrice carefully stood all the way up and her

head was over and through the trapdoor. "Well, as you can see, I'm a lot taller than the space is. But I can crouch in half and look around for a minute."

She felt a little like Alice in Wonderland after eating the cake marked *Eat Me*. Beatrice hunched over and pointed her flashlight into the musty air and saw the space was lined with wooden shelves. And something else. Beatrice grinned.

She stuck her head up through the door again. "There's a very old collection of whiskey and wine down here. This must have been someone's hiding spot during Prohibition."

"Pooh," said Meadow. "I was hoping for more secrets than that."

Posy leaned over the trapdoor as Beatrice hunched over again to reexamine the shelves. "I think it's pretty cool," Posy said. "I love the idea of a hidden space."

"Wait," said Meadow. "You don't see any old wills down there, do you?"

"That's what I was wondering," said Beatrice. "I'm sure Muriel must have known this space was here after living in this house so many years." She glanced around her, pointing the dim beam around the dusty shelves. "All I see is old bottles." Then her foot brushed against something and she quickly pointed her beam down to the floor. "Wait a minute." She stooped all the way down and gazed at an anachronism. Everything else in the space was 1920s era. But not this. "I've found the missing sleeping pill bottle."

She heard the women murmuring their surprise. "What? On the shelf?" Meadow asked.

"No. It's on the floor. I think someone must have just chucked it in the hole," Beatrice said slowly.

"Aren't you going to bring it up?" Dot asked.

"Evil!" said Miss Sissy.

"I think I should leave it here," Beatrice said. "In case there are fingerprints on it. Or if the police want to see it where I found it." She swept the flashlight once more all around the space, this time illuminating the floor and ceiling in her sweep. "I think that's all." Beatrice carefully climbed back up the ladder and through the trapdoor, brushing herself off after she climbed out.

Meadow gave Beatrice a meaningful wink that said she wanted to discuss what they'd found. Beatrice supposed she should count herself lucky that Meadow hadn't blurted out what was on her mind the way she usually did.

"How fascinating!" Posy said. "Aside from the pill bottle, I mean. But it's like seeing a little bit of history, isn't it? A hidden stash. Imagine!"

"I wonder if there are any other hidden areas in the house," said Beatrice. "Since we've found a hidden storage room, maybe there are other hidden places."

"Like a secret passage!" said Meadow, breathless with excitement. "Wouldn't that be wonderful? I've always wanted to see a hidden passageway. Just like in *Nancy Drew*."

They stared at the trapdoor as if hoping it would

spill its secrets about other hidden places. They jumped at a harsh voice from the top of the stairs. "So you found the secret hole in the floor, I see."

It was Alexandra, smirking at them from the top of the stairs. "It's not like there was hidden treasure in there or anything. The way y'all are acting, you'd think it held a magic lamp with a genie inside."

Beatrice raised her eyebrows and worked to keep her irritation from boiling to the surface. She was pleased with her cool tone when she said, "Maybe it didn't have treasure, but it did have the sleeping pill bottle. And I'm wondering who in the house would be most likely to know where that hiding spot was."

Alexandra's eyes narrowed. "What are you saying? You think that I'm the one who killed Colton and then threw the bottle of sleeping pills down there? I don't think the police will be pleased by the lack of evidence. The fact I may have known something about the hiding place doesn't mean I killed anybody. Besides, Mother told everyone about it— she was quite proud to be descended from people who were lawbreakers. Winnie almost certainly knew about it and Dot probably did, too."

Dot rolled her eyes. "This is the first I've heard about it. Your mother and I weren't exactly buddies, you know."

"I'm simply saying that I'm not the only person who knew about it, that's all," Alexandra said sulkily.

Meadow said in a reasonable voice, "Let's stop talking about it. Everyone's in a grouchy mood at being stuck here. Let's go our separate ways until supper. I know I'm always in a better mood when we have supper."

"Except that we're probably dining on a can of kidney beans," Alexandra grumbled.

Alexandra must have taken inventory of the pantry. They were indeed dining on a can of kidney beans. Well, several of them were. The others were eating French-style green beans. Beatrice unenthusiastically ate her meal. She was really going to enjoy going out for a steak when she got back home.

Meadow and Beatrice had made their plans for setting up their trap. At the end of the meal, Meadow cleared her throat and said, "Beatrice, is everything all right? You're acting like you're concerned about something."

Beatrice said absently, "Yes. Yes, I am concerned about something. But I'll talk to you about it later, Meadow. After supper."

For a moment, Beatrice felt sure that Meadow was going to wink at her. Thankfully, she didn't. Posy dissolved into a fit of coughing, which Beatrice thought covered up a giggle.

They cleaned up the dishes and the kitchen. Then Meadow said again, "Want to go upstairs for a chat, Beatrice?" Beatrice thought this was a bit of overkill, but they headed upstairs.

"Now what?" Meadow asked in a hushed voice. "Should we wait or go ahead?"

"Let's give whomever a chance to get into place.

So let's talk about other things and be natural for a minute."

Meadow's idea of natural was to immediately spring into a very animated discussion about her dog Boris's eating habits and stomach issues. Apparently, some digestive distress had necessitated changes in dog food brands. This was actually a surprise to Beatrice. On most of the occasions when she'd had contact with Meadow's huge beast, he'd eaten whatever struck his fancy. In fact, Boris was very goatlike in his eating.

After a couple of minutes of this, Beatrice felt the urge to finally interrupt. Surely whoever was trying to eavesdrop on them had gotten into position and was probably about to run away after hearing Meadow's Boris the Dog monologue. "Meadow, about that issue I wanted to talk to you about."

Meadow gave her an excited nod and said in an overly casual voice, "Oh, that's right. What's on your mind?"

"When I was in the attic earlier, I came across some papers. It was so dark up there and that flashlight is so pitiful that I took the papers down with me so that I could see them in a brighter light. After taking a closer look, I can tell they must be a will. And a few other legal papers and notes, too."

"Really?" said Meadow. "Imagine that."

"Yes. Well, we knew there should be papers like that here, so I guess it's not too much of a surprise. But considering the circumstances, I thought it would be prudent to put the papers in a safe place."

"Very clever of you," said Meadow. "Where did you put them?"

"Well, I wanted to let you know in case anything were to happen to me. You just never know in this house, do you? So I put them down in the study in an Agatha Christie book. In *And Then There Were None*."

"Even more clever!" said Meadow. Then she gave an exaggerated yawn. "You know, I think I'll go ahead and turn in. Are we sleeping downstairs or upstairs tonight? I'm so exhausted that I really don't even care."

"I think I'm going downstairs again," said Beatrice. "That little fire in the library was actually very comforting to fall asleep to."

A couple of minutes later Beatrice walked downstairs—not to the library, but to the study. She'd noticed earlier that there was a closet in the room filled with things like books, old chessboards, and even more quilts. She took several of the quilts down from the shelves and put them on the floor of the closet as a cushion while she waited for someone to come looking for the fictitious papers. She hoped that whoever had been listening would hurry up with their snooping.

Unfortunately, no one did hurry. And Beatrice was starting to get fairly uncomfortable in her hiding place. It was a shame how muscles cramped up when you got older.

After a couple of hours had passed, Beatrice was ready to give up completely. Perhaps no one had cared to listen in on her important conversation. Or perhaps the eavesdropper had gotten turned off by the talk of Boris's dog food. Or perhaps no one had even really registered that Beatrice and Meadow were going to have a discussion in the first place. Beatrice slowly started moving again as her muscles ached in protest.

She was standing up into a crouch when the door to the study opened and she dropped back down to the floor again. Beatrice couldn't see who the figure was in the darkness. Whoever it was walked right to the study's bookcase and searched through the titles. Beatrice waited until the figure pulled a book off the shelf and opened it. Then she jumped out of the closet, turning on her flashlight and saying, "Wait right there!"

Beatrice was faced with a very startled and irritated Alexandra.

"What are you doing here?" spluttered Alexandra.

Chapter Sixteen

"I think the question is more what are *you* doing here?" Beatrice said coldly. "You listened in on Meadow's and my conversation and stole down here to take the papers."

"Which aren't here," Alexandra said, eyes flashing. "Where did you put them?"

"There *aren't* any papers," said Beatrice. "They were our invention to trick you into revealing yourself."

Meadow and Posy came into the study, eyes wide. "We heard voices," said Posy, gazing at Alexandra solemnly.

"So Alexandra is the culprit," crowed Meadow, exceedingly pleased. She didn't bother trying to hide her dislike of the woman.

"I'm certainly not. Think again," said Alexandra icily. "All that I'm guilty of is trying to locate papers that have great significance to my personal life. And this is *my* house, I might add."

"A fact that's actually in some doubt," said Meadow with a sniff. "I'm not at all convinced that you're the heir to this mansion."

"Besides, you're not only guilty of searching for papers," said Beatrice. "You're also guilty of eavesdropping—and I would very much like to know how you're eavesdropping so frequently without getting caught."

Alexandra pressed her lips tightly closed.

"Are you standing with your ear outside our door?" asked Meadow.

"It seems like we would all have seen you in the hall if you were listening outside doors," said Posy, almost apologetically.

The three women stared at Alexandra, who appeared to be wrestling with herself over whether to divulge her secret.

Finally, Alexandra snapped. "Fine. May as well tell you since you're clearly all grabbing onto me like a pit bull over this. There's a secret passageway. It goes from a small door in the back of my closet to a couple of other bedrooms on my side of the hall. Including yours, Meadow and Beatrice."

Meadow appeared as though she might fall over from the thrill of it all. And Beatrice had to admit that her heart skipped a beat or two at the thought. Secret passageways!

Beatrice took control of her expressions again. "Alexandra, it occurs to me that your knowing about a secret passageway linking bedrooms would have made sneaking to your mother's bedroom or Colton's bedroom very easy for you."

"Maybe it would have. But I didn't kill anybody." Alexandra put her hands on her hips. "Just because I know about this house's secrets doesn't mean I'm a murderer. The police wouldn't even consider that evidence."

"This is sounding all very familiar," said Beatrice. "You knew about the hiding place under the stair landing and the secret passageway, yet you're innocent on all counts. You didn't put the sleeping pill bottle in the secret hiding spot and you didn't use the passageways to murder anyone."

"That's what I'm saying." Alexandra jutted out her chin.

"Well, I'll tell you this," Meadow said. "We could go on all night with this debate. Alexandra admits she knew about the secret places in the house—she grew up here, so of course she did. We don't have any other proof against her. Why argue back and forth all night long without getting anywhere, when we could be checking out a secret passageway at midnight in a house that might be haunted!" Her eyes glowed with excitement.

Posy breathed. "Do you think we might? Alexandra, could you show us where it is?"

Alexandra frowned at them with exasperation. "You do know you all sound like you're about five years old instead of the elderly ladies you are."

"Not so elderly!" said Meadow robustly. "You're only as old as you feel."

"All right, I'll show you where the passageway is," Alexandra said, sounding resolved. Beatrice thought she might actually be enjoying being the center of attention for the moment. Alexandra was more animated than usual and even had a small smile on her lips. Beatrice couldn't remember Alexandra ever giving more than a cynical smile.

They quietly went upstairs and Alexandra beckoned them to her bedroom. "How many flashlights or candles do we have?"

"Right now, only the one that I've got," said Beatrice, glancing down at her flashlight.

"Well, it's obviously pretty dark in there. I'll light the candle from my bedside table so at least we'll have two lights," said Alexandra.

She led them into her closet, where they could barely make out an outline of a door once she'd pointed it out to them in the very back of her closet behind a few old coats. In order to open the door they had to push on the nonhinged side of it, which appeared to activate a spring that opened it. Beatrice, who realized stooping wasn't her forte anymore after her stint in the closet, was glad that the passageway didn't require crouching.

They stepped into the darkness. "Narrow, isn't it?" muttered Meadow, whose sides were touching the walls.

"Shh," said Alexandra. "Unless you want the whole house up."

They walked through the passage in a line. They came across another door. "This is your room, Meadow and Beatrice," Alexandra said quietly.

"Can we open it?" asked Meadow.

"It hasn't been opened in years," said Alexandra. "But you can see if you can open it from this side."

"Wouldn't you have opened it when you were snooping on us?" asked Meadow.

"No. I listened through the door and could hear you perfectly," Alexandra said dryly. Meadow did have that loud whisper.

Meadow pushed at the door and it opened up right into their closet, just as in Alexandra's.

She closed it back and they continued down the narrow passage.

Suddenly Meadow bellowed, "Something on my foot! There are rats in here!"

Posy cried out and Beatrice held her breath as her heart pounded hard in her chest. Beatrice felt she could handle nearly everything in life with a certain amount of equanimity. But rats weren't one of them.

There was an accompanying shriek from the other side of the wall.

"That would probably be Winnie," said Alexandra coolly. "She of the ghost fixation."

"I'm guessing we need to come back out of the walls now," said Beatrice wryly.

"It might be best," said Alexandra.

"Poor Winnie," said Posy.

They turned around with difficulty and walked back to exit through Meadow and Beatrice's closet, since it was closer. By the time they'd finally made it back out, Winnie was hysterically babbling to Dot and Holly that the ghost or Miss Sissy or perhaps both had disposed of the rest of the group, since they were nowhere to be seen.

Dot patted Winnie kindly. "Look, Winnie. See everyone? They're all fine."

Winnie acted briefly relieved, then irritated. "Where were you all? Why didn't you come out? Where have you been?"

Posy said sadly, "We were trying not to wake y'all up. Alexandra told us about a secret passageway. It goes from bedroom to bedroom through the closets. We were exploring, that's all . . . We didn't want to disturb anybody."

Dot chuckled. "You did a poor job of being quiet, then! What was all that ruckus?"

Meadow said meekly, "I thought a rat had brushed up against me. But it was only one of Alexandra's old baby dolls rolling around."

They all stared at Alexandra, trying to picture her ever being childish enough to play with dolls.

"Well, gosh, that relieves my mind a ton," Winnie said in a sarcastic voice. "So there are secret passageways that connect other bedrooms to mine? Wonderful. That's just great. How am I supposed to block those off?"

"You could set up a homemade alarm system," Dot suggested. "You know—put the empty cans of food right outside the hidden door or something like that."

Winnie simply gave an annoyed sigh.

"Why don't you come downstairs and sleep?"

asked Beatrice. "It worked out well for you last night."

"I guess it did," grumbled Winnie. "Although I woke up very sore this morning from sleeping on the floor. I was kind of hoping I could sleep in a soft bed tonight without having any problems. How naive of me."

"Well, the invitation is open," said Meadow. "We keep a small fire burning in there, so it's nice and warm . . . which should keep you from getting too stiff. And there's safety in numbers, too." She glanced around at Holly, Alexandra, and Dot. "All of y'all are welcome to sleep in there."

"I'll pass," said Alexandra in her haughty way.

Dot said, "My bed was nice and warm when I left it, so I'm hoping to find that same warm spot when I get back to it."

They retreated to their separate spaces and Meadow, Posy, and Beatrice headed back downstairs to the library.

"I'm excited about having a decent night's sleep when I get back home," said Meadow. "This traipsing around in the middle of the night is about to kill me!"

Beatrice had finally managed to turn off her brain and drift off to sleep when they were awakened by yelling and thumping sounds from upstairs. "Not again," groaned Beatrice, half asleep.

"What is with that Winnie?" said Meadow.

They rushed upstairs again to see Alexandra and Holly gaping at Winnie, Dot, and Miss Sissy, who all seemed to be wrestling with one another.

"Stop!" Beatrice said in her loudest, firmest voice. "Stop it!"

They did finally stop, panting.

"What's going on here?" Beatrice asked, feeling a bit like a schoolteacher in a particularly unruly classroom.

"The ghost!" Winnie gasped triumphantly. "There!"

Beatrice stared in the direction Winnie was pointing, which was the curtained window at the end of the hall. She wondered whether Winnie was indeed losing it. Some of the curtain had been yanked off the rod and was lying on the floor in a heap. The heap did appear to be moving and Beatrice wasn't looking forward to seeing what type of creature was under it. One thing she was certain of, though—it was a living creature and not a dead one.

Dot was still holding her cane threateningly aloft. "Got to be a rat, Beatrice. Saw them all the time in the mill when I was working there. Nasty, awful things."

Miss Sissy hollered, "Murderer! Wicked! Wants to kill her."

Beatrice didn't want the situation to devolve back into chaos, so she gathered her courage and strode toward the moving curtained lump on the floor. "Winnie, I think we're going to find that this is a rat. You're acting almost as if you're about to faint—do you want to go back into your bedroom while I look around?"

Winnie shook her head wordlessly, but backed up against the wall for support.

Dot limped forward and proffered her cane to Beatrice. "Here. You might not want to get your hands too close to that thing. Use the cane to move the fabric out of the way."

"Don't hurt my friend!" bellowed Miss Sissy.

Beatrice frowned at the old woman. "So this is your friend?" She hadn't exactly figured out what she was going to do when she released the creature, but it certainly hadn't involved handing it over to Miss Sissy. She rethought the problem. "Maybe I should pull the curtain the rest of the way off the rod and gather it up and stick it outside as fast as I can." She gulped at the thought.

"No!" Miss Sissy was seriously up in arms now.

"Miss Sissy, you can't be hanging out with rats! They are not your friends. You'll end up with rabies or other nasty diseases," Beatrice said with a shudder.

"Isn't a rat," Miss Sissy said smugly. She marched over and gently bent to move the curtain to reveal a very indignant cat.

They gawped at the feline. "Where did *that* come from?" asked Beatrice.

Miss Sissy gave her a scornful stare. "From outside, of course. Wanted in."

"I bet it did," muttered Beatrice. It was freezing out there. "Does it seem domesticated?"

Miss Sissy stared blankly at her.

"I mean, do you think Muriel was in the habit of feeding the cat?"

"It likes tuna," Miss Sissy said with a shrug. "Knew it was in the pantry."

Alexandra roared at Miss Sissy, "You gave this animal our tuna? It was bad enough when I thought *you* were the one eating all the good food. You gave it to *that*?" She pointed at the cat, which was rubbing lovingly against Miss Sissy.

"Isn't a *that*. It's Clarisse," said Miss Sissy elegantly.

A wave of exhaustion rolled over Beatrice and she was reminded that this conversation was taking place in the middle of the night. And it appeared to be going downhill, at that. She quickly said, "I'm assuming that you've set up some kind of litter box for the cat, Miss Sissy." Miss Sissy was kind of vague on that point, but Beatrice really didn't want to think about this at what must be three o'clock in the morning. "All right, well, we'll revisit that later in the morning. Winnie, you should be able to sleep better knowing there's no ghost lurking around to attack you when you're up getting a cup of water. I feel confident that Clarisse is our ghost."

Winnie said sullenly, "Yup, only a murderer to fret about now." She was still staring at the cat and her expression softened. "Actually, Clarisse is sort of cute, isn't she?"

"And now I think we really all need to try to get a little sleep. We're going to seriously be at each other's throats if we can't get any rest."

Finally, blissfully, Beatrice got some uninterrupted sleep.

Beatrice quilted for a bit the next morning while she thought about her next step.

"Beatrice, you're doing a wonderful job with those cathedral windows!" said Posy, beaming at her.

"It's coming together nicely, isn't it?" Beatrice said, feeling surprised. "But that's because you had such beautiful fabrics for the 'windows.' I love all the different shades of blue. They coordinate beautifully, but are so different. Turquoise, robin's egg, indigo, midnight blue, periwinkle—I love how they all come together to make this beautiful whole."

Meadow squinted at the quilt over her red glasses. "I think that's because the patterns on the squares of fabric are all very simple and not busy. Faint flower prints and larger polka dots and paisleys. They meld together really well."

"It's all much easier than I thought it was going to be," said Beatrice. "It's the type of thing that *looks* complicated but is really not that difficult." She had a feeling she'd be making more cathedral window patterns in the future.

She glanced over curiously to see what Posy was working on. "Posy, you've been so good to get everyone set up with fabrics and notions and templates and tips that I haven't noticed you doing much quilting yourself. What are you hand-piecing? I saw you cutting circles out earlier. I was impressed by how perfect the circles you'd drawn were."

Posy give her a wink.

"Oh," Beatrice said. "Were the circles from a template you had in the quilting mobile?"

"No, but I can't claim them, just the same. I traced around a bowl I found in the kitchen."

"Are those going to be yo-yos?" asked Meadow, peering at Posy's fabric.

"They sure are. Aren't they fun?" Posy said in her gentle voice.

"Remind me what yo-yos are again?" said Beatrice, figuring they surely couldn't be talking about the bouncing stringed toy.

"They're circles of fabric," Meadow explained. "You turn down the edges and secure them with a running stitch so that the fabric gathers up when you pull the end of the thread. Then you can whipstitch the yo-yos together to make a quilt."

"Or to decorate another project. You know, to add texture to it," added Posy.

"I love those pink and white circles," said Beatrice.

"I thought they'd be sweet for a coverlet for a girl's bed," said Posy, beaming at her. "I've got a grandniece in mind."

They all worked quietly for a few minutes. Then Meadow said, "All right, I can't suppress my curiosity anymore. I know we're supposed to be de-stressing and all, but I'd like to know Beatrice's next move for the case. Who are you planning on talking to?"

"Dot was next on my list," said Beatrice. "I guess I'll talk with her after lunch."

Beatrice hadn't had a chance yet to ask Dot why she hadn't revealed that she'd been Muriel's employee for years.

After an uninspired lunch of canned pears and baby carrots, Beatrice asked Dot if she could speak to her in the study for a few minutes. "Okeydokey," said Dot cheerfully, thumping with her cane as she headed to the study.

As soon as she'd plopped into a chair and sighed in relief at being off her feet, she said, "What's up, Beatrice? Got a new lead you're working on?"

"Not so much a new lead, but more like a new line of questions," said Beatrice.

Dot nodded. "Well, get on with it, then. This has something to do with that harpy Winnie, I'd guess."

Beatrice bit back a laugh at her description. Really, she'd come to feel sorry for Winnie. She was emotionally fragile, and this wasn't the place for fragile people. "Yes, I guess it does. But don't blame Winnie. I asked her if she could give me some background on you, since you hadn't offered up much yourself."

Dot sighed. "I suppose she told you all about me working for Muriel for all those years. And here I was ready to let bygones be bygones."

"Dot, it sounded like you had every reason to be upset."

"Because Muriel and her minions promised me that if I waited I'd be rewarded for all my hard work by a promotion? A promise that they knew was just empty words because they already had plans to close the factory?" If Dot was bitter, it didn't show in her words.

"Most people would carry a real grudge against Muriel, Dot. After all, it practically amounts to theft. You asked for raises and bonuses and were told you'd get your payment later on . . . and Muriel knew you wouldn't."

"Oh, I was real steamed. *Real* steamed. Believe me, I gave Muriel a blowing out that I bet she never forgot. Nobody ever talked to Muriel that way because nobody dared to. I wasn't intimidated by her one whit, though. I let her have it. But then . . . why hold on to that kind of thing year after year? I don't believe in carrying grudges. My me-maw always told me that life was full of lemons. I could try to make lemonade with them. Or, if I couldn't, I could learn to swallow the lemons I was given—tart or not." She laughed. "It's not been easy. But me-maws are always right."

"And you've been all right since you left Muriel's factory?" asked Beatrice. "You've been able to find something else to do?"

Dot glanced away into the fire for a moment. "Sure, I have. I'm a survivor, right? I know how to take care of myself." She chuckled. "Now I won't say that I won't be jumping up and down with absolute joy if we find out that Muriel left money or trinkets to me in her will as a consolation prize."

Beatrice smiled at her. "I hope so, Dot. I think she owed you more than that blanket apology you got."

"I guess we haven't come any closer to finding any wills lying around, have we? Of course, if we do come across any wills, Miss Thing is likely to rip them out of our hands and throw them into the fire if they don't mention her as heir supreme," Dot said with a snort.

Beatrice felt like kicking herself. With all the talk of secret passageways and rats and ghosts—combined with genuine exhaustion—she'd completely forgotten that Alexandra had the key to the attic. She needed to get that back, not that it would be easy to pry it out of Alexandra's hands. And if she couldn't get it back . . . she was going to have to stay a lot closer to Alexandra than she would have wanted.

Chapter Seventeen

"Absolutely not," said Alexandra coolly. "I'm certainly not going to give you that key back. Why should I? This is my house. I should have a key to any room in the house if I so desire. Why should *you* have a key? You own nothing here and have nothing to do with the house. I should be asking you for *your* key."

"The reason I'm asking for the key," said Beatrice as patiently as she could muster, "is because I'm a neutral party here in this house. You're right—I have nothing to do with the house or anything in it. It's what makes me a better candidate than you to have possession of the keys to the attic."

"Why on earth are you so worried about me going into my own attic?"

"Why on earth are you so determined to get up there?"

Alexandra glared at her in silence. Beatrice met

her gaze until finally Alexandra snapped, "I want to find Mother's will, of course. For some reason, she seems to have kept a lot of old documents upstairs. I want to go through them. It's personal business."

Of course, not all of what was up in the attic was personal to Alexandra. Some of it—in fact a good deal of it—was personal to Holly. Beatrice wondered how Holly would feel about Alexandra discovering she was her half sister. She likely wouldn't want her to discover it by rummaging around in the attic— she'd probably want to have a conversation with her face-to-face.

"Once more, will you give me the key back?"

"Once more, no!"

"Then I'm going to have to insist that I go up in the attic with you whenever you go up there," Beatrice said heavily. "I want to make sure you don't destroy anything that might pertain to this case before the police are able to do their investigation."

Alexandra stared down her aquiline nose at her. "More about your *case*, right? I still say that the police are going to find that a terminally ill woman died of natural causes and that her lawyer died of a heart attack. But, sure—if you want to follow along on my trips to the attic, come along. I'm not going to come knocking on your door, though. You'll have to keep tabs on me, won't you?" She laughed unpleasantly.

Posy and Meadow joined Beatrice in the study after Alexandra had flounced out. "Want me to shadow her?" Meadow asked eagerly, once Beatrice had filled her in on their conversation. "I've always fancied the life of a private eye. Sneaking around and stuff."

The idea of Meadow managing to be quiet enough to follow people without being detected made Beatrice smile. "Thanks, Meadow. I don't think she's heading up there immediately, though. Besides, we can't watch her twenty-four hours a day. But we'll do our best."

Posy said slowly, "So are we thinking that Alexandra is behind these murders, then?" She shivered.

"I'm not completely convinced, no," said Beatrice. "Although she's definitely a top suspect."

"I'll say!" said Meadow. "She knew about the secret hiding place under the stairs . . . and there was the sleeping pill bottle. She knew about secret passageways, too, and it would have been easy as anything to kill Muriel and Colton and slip back to bed without being detected. Besides, she had a ton of motive—her mother was about to change her will in favor of Holly and a quilting foundation and who knows what else! She would have wanted to prevent her mother and Colton from coming up with a new will."

"You're forgetting one very important thing, Meadow," Beatrice replied. "Alexandra didn't know that Holly is her half sister. So there shouldn't have been any rush to prevent a new will from being written up."

"This foundation could have been huge, though," Meadow countered. "We don't know what Muriel was planning. Maybe Muriel was sick of Alexandra and decided to leave her a tiny amount as an insult and then leave the bulk of the estate to her foundation. That would certainly have provided Alexandra with a motive."

"I think you're stuck on Alexandra because you don't like her very much," said Beatrice.

"Sure, that plays into it, too," Meadow said with a shrug. "She's unpleasant. Maybe she's more than just unpleasant—maybe she's sort of wicked, too. And we don't *know* that Alexandra didn't know about Holly. Maybe she overheard Muriel and Holly talking— maybe she was eavesdropping on them. With all the secret passageways in this house, she could have been hiding out and listening to every word."

"There are other people with motives, too," reminded Beatrice. "Look at Winnie."

"Now there is one unhappy lady," said Posy, shaking her head sadly.

"It's like Dot was saying earlier," said Beatrice. "Winnie should learn to live and let live. But she couldn't forgive Muriel for stealing away the love of her life. She also appeared to blame her for her life of hard work, since she believes she'd have been living a much more comfortable life if she'd married her old beau. Winnie couldn't let it go and it ended up eating her up inside. That's a great motive. In Winnie's eyes, Muriel ruined her life."

"Poor Winnie," said Posy.

"Silly ninny," said Meadow. She thought a moment and said, "Holly could have almost the same motive, right? She was basically abandoned by her mother, who could have provided her with a very comfortable life. Instead, she was shuttled around to different foster homes. She could be vengeful, too, couldn't she? She could be bitter."

Beatrice nodded. "Holly could be. She sure was upset the night that Muriel revealed she was her mother. I thought she sounded mad, too. She had every right to be angry. And she certainly had the opportunity to commit the murders. Although I'd think she had even *more* motive to kill Alexandra—the other heir and potentially the *only* heir, if Muriel didn't get around to updating her will."

Posy said gently, "I know she's a suspect, but somehow I can't see Holly killing anyone. She seems like a wonderful person. Just because she got upset doesn't mean she'd commit murder."

"So what about Dot?" asked Meadow. "She's our last suspect, isn't she? Although I suppose she's a bit handicapped to have killed Colton. Muriel's death happened before Dot was injured, though."

"I don't think her sprained ankle knocks her out of the running as Colton's murderer," said Beatrice.

"But she was upstairs while everyone was having supper, wasn't she?" Posy knit her brows.

"True. But Colton did take his wineglass upstairs. Perhaps he left his room to visit the restroom and Dot slipped in and messed with his drink," said Beatrice.

"Remind me again why Dot would kill Muriel?" asked Meadow, squinting.

"Because she worked for Muriel for years, and Muriel, who as owner was highly involved with the mill, kept telling Dot that she would give her a raise when she got promoted to some important position. But Muriel knew she was going to close the mill right after she gave Dot the promotion."

"Ahh, right," said Meadow.

"So she double-crossed her," said Posy indignantly.

"She sure did. Just to be cheap," said Beatrice.

"It definitely sounds like a motive to me," said Meadow. "But I still say that Alexandra did it. Money is always the strongest motive of all."

At supper that night, Alexandra didn't do much to persuade Meadow that she wasn't capable of murder. She yelled at Miss Sissy again for giving the cat their tuna and picked at her canned lima beans like a three-year-old.

Then Alexandra jumped on Holly when she mildly proposed they bring real bedding, perhaps even mattresses, to the library for those who decided to sleep there. "What right do you have to rearrange this house?" she asked archly. "It's my house, and I should be the one who says if furniture gets rearranged."

Alexandra was completely shocked when Holly burst into tears. "What is this?" she asked Beatrice, gesturing to Holly.

Beatrice wasn't about to be the one to explain Holly's recent news, so she kept her lips pressed tightly shut.

"While I'm at it," said Alexandra, angry at Beatrice's determined silence, "I'm really sick of this charade of an investigation that you're putting on. Playing detective. Why don't you give it a break?"

Holly managed to say in a shaking voice, "Alexandra, leave Beatrice alone. It's me that you're angry with, so stop yelling at Beatrice. She's just trying to work things out and she's doing us all a favor." Holly took a deep breath. "What I'm upset about is that you and I are sisters and you know nothing about it."

"*What?*"

Alexandra appeared completely shocked and horrified at the revelation. "It isn't true—" She gasped.

Holly's eyes were sad. "It is true. And I'm very sorry."

Meadow gave an uncomfortable laugh. "Well, it's certainly not *your* fault, nor does it have anything to do with you, Holly."

"So that's why you're here," Alexandra snapped. "Did you learn how to quilt so that you could wiggle your way in to see my mother? Did you learn that she was deathly ill and you wanted to make sure to visit her, charm her, so that she'd change her will in your favor? What did you do for her while she was alive?"

"What did *you* do for her while she was alive?" Dot asked with a snort.

Alexandra narrowed her eyes.

Holly quickly said, "Alexandra, I don't want to

argue with you. You're right—I wasn't here for your mother . . . our mother. But I wish I had been. I wish I'd gotten to know her. I had no idea she was my mother until she told me our first night here. That's one thing I wish I had from her—time."

"And money," said Alexandra coldly. "This is all such a likely story. I bet you hired a detective to track down your birth mother. Then as soon as you found out she was someone with means, you learned how best to win her over. It must have been very easy to learn of her passion for quilting."

"But I've been quilting for decades!" Holly sputtered.

"So you say. Biding your time, most likely, until you hear that Mother is terminally ill. Then you realize you'd better make your move so that she can change her will before she passes away." Alexandra sneered.

"She sent me an invitation about the quilting foundation!" said Holly. "You heard her mention that she'd invited me."

Alexandra shrugged. "A coincidence. And a lucky one for you."

They all stared wide-eyed at Alexandra, at the pure viciousness and hatred dripping from her voice.

She met their gazes and said, "I've had enough of all of you. I'm going upstairs."

After helping clean up—which somehow Alexandra had yet again gotten out of—Beatrice decided she'd do the same. Her head was pounding from all the unanswered questions and from the heightened emotions over dinner. "I've got a terrible headache, y'all. I'm going to turn in."

"Sleeping upstairs?" asked Meadow.

"I think I need a more comfortable place to sleep tonight," said Beatrice. "Maybe I can relax more and get better-quality rest. Are you sleeping upstairs, Meadow?"

"No. If it's all the same to you, I think I'll sleep down with the fire again tonight. It feels chillier tonight somehow."

Great. All they needed was more cold. It was almost as if they were entering a second Ice Age.

Beatrice crawled into bed and fell asleep as soon as her head hit the pillow. Even when the others came upstairs to turn in, she didn't stir and continued her deep sleep.

Until there was a scratching on her door.

Chapter Eighteen

Beatrice froze in bed, her eyes open wide. Had she been dreaming? She lay completely still, listening. Then it came again—a definite scratching on her bedroom door. Was it a rat? The cat?

She sprang out of bed, stumbling toward the door in the dark. Beatrice yanked it open and strained her eyes to peer in both directions in the darkness. Her heart was pounding so hard she could barely think straight.

Beatrice walked down the hall toward Muriel's room and the attic stairs, but didn't see anyone. She'd wondered whether she'd been mistaken— maybe she'd actually heard Alexandra sneaking into the attic to go will hunting? She didn't see anyone, though, so she started down toward the other end of the hall. Beatrice squinted as she thought she spotted motion down at the other end of the hall. She hurried in that direction, calling out, but right as she was passing the stairs, arms reached out from no-where and pushed her diagonally onto the staircase. She cried out in horror as she tumbled down the stairs.

Beatrice hit the side of the staircase, running directly into the banister, where she was able to grab hold of the balusters for dear life.

Her fall must have made a tremendous crashing sound—soon everyone was awake and gaping at her from both upstairs and downstairs.

"Beatrice!" Posy gasped, rushing to her and gently putting a hand on her shoulder. "Are you all right?"

"Can you move everything?" Meadow asked urgently. "Any broken bones?"

"God forbid," said Alexandra in a sarcastic tone. "We'd have Dot and Beatrice fighting over the cane and walker."

Beatrice gingerly moved everything. It all hurt, but nothing hurt so bad that she thought it was broken or even sprained. "I don't think I've broken anything." She still felt that overwhelming horror at falling, though, and her heart still thumped so hard that her head was spinning. The headache had returned, too.

"What happened?" asked Posy.

"Did you take a wrong turn on the way to the restroom?" asked Meadow.

"I was *pushed*," Beatrice said grimly as she struggled slowly to her feet.

There was a murmur of consternation from the quilters.

Alexandra said sarcastically, "More drama, Beatrice? Did you have to fabricate a push just to prove that you still have a case?"

"I was *pushed*," Beatrice repeated through gritted teeth. "I heard a scratching sound at my door and came out to investigate."

"It was probably a rodent of some kind," Alexandra said with a shrug.

"Or the cat?" Holly said in a concerned voice.

"I think I might have spotted the cat at the end of the hall when I was walking past the staircase," Beatrice said. "But it definitely wasn't a cat that pushed me down the stairs." She shivered. Someone had tried to kill her. It wasn't just a small push to make a point. It was a strong shove that was intended to make her fall all the way down the very steep flight of stairs. And whoever had tried to kill her was standing in front of her right now.

"All right," said Meadow, bustling up to her. "Let me help you into the library, Beatrice. You're shivering with cold and shock and could use a glass of wine, too."

"By all means." Alexandra rolled her eyes. "Go ahead and deplete my wine collection."

They ignored her and Beatrice gingerly made her way down the stairs, holding on to Meadow's arm. Her legs were shaking so badly she thought they were going to buckle under her.

Meadow helped settle Beatrice in the most comfortable armchair in the library and Posy found a soft quilt to put over her legs.

"Red or white wine, Beatrice," Meadow called to her. "Never mind—let's do red. Supposed to be better for you."

Beatrice continued shivering, despite the warmth of the room. Miss Sissy came in and sat down in front of her, watching her with serious eyes. "I guess you didn't see who pushed me, did you?" Beatrice asked.

Miss Sissy shook her head. "I was sleeping. In here." She gestured toward the far wall of the room.

Typical. When Miss Sissy had the opportunity to witness a crime, she slept right through it.

"Wickedness," Miss Sissy muttered. "Eye for an eye."

Beatrice studied the old woman with narrowed eyes. "So you think these murders are all about revenge?"

Miss Sissy snorted scornfully. "'Course they are."

Meadow returned with a bottle of red wine and a large glass. "This looks good," she said, squinting vaguely at the label. "Or at least, I'm presuming it's good because it's here. If not, then you can do a taste test for another bottle."

Beatrice took the glass from her and drank three big gulps, without even tasting it. She sat back in her chair with a sigh. Meadow was waiting expectantly. "Oh. It's fine, Meadow. Thanks."

Posy said, "Beatrice, are you sure you're okay? Even a short fall on those stairs would hurt."

"I think I'm going to be very sore tomorrow morning and will have lots of bruises as souvenirs of my trip down the stairs. But besides that, I don't think there's anything really wrong with me. Of course, it just about gave me a heart attack. I still feel like my heart is beating at double its usual speed."

Meadow said, "I don't understand why someone would do something like that. What would killing you benefit anyone here?"

Beatrice shivered again and took another gulp of her wine. Meadow poured more in. "I think maybe I'm getting close to figuring out who's behind all this. That I'm scaring the murderer into wanting to get rid of me so that I can't report what I know to the police. Or maybe it's even personal—a vindictive shove. The murderer has got to be feeling pretty confident by now—she's killed two people and gotten away with it so far. Maybe she wants to make life easier by killing me, too."

Posy reached out and hugged Beatrice. "You look so bleak!"

Beatrice felt bleak. Despite what the murderer thought, she felt no closer to figuring out who the culprit was than she had been at the start of her investigation. Now the aches and pains of her tumble were starting to set in, she was hungry for a good meal, she was exhausted from nights of fright and sleeplessness, and she was bone cold from fear and the chill. What a night.

Miss Sissy studied her cannily. Slowly, she reached into the large pocket of her floral skirt and pulled out a butcher knife.

Everyone gasped and Meadow giggled nervously. "Here, Miss Sissy, what do you want with that? Let's put it away, okay?"

Miss Sissy was scornful. "Not for you! For Beatrice. To carry for protection."

Miss Sissy had tried protecting Beatrice before, in other cases she had investigated, with mixed results. Beatrice smiled at her. "Thanks, Miss Sissy, but I don't have a big pocket like you do. I'd have to carry it around in my hand, and that wouldn't work very well."

Miss Sissy studied her shrewdly, then reached into her other skirt pocket and pulled out a pocket-knife.

"Goodness! You're well armed, Miss Sissy," Beatrice said weakly. She reluctantly took the pocket-knife from her. The old woman bobbed her head in satisfaction.

"Now what?" asked Meadow.

Beatrice said, "Well, I'm definitely sleeping downstairs now. I'm done wandering around in the middle of the night, despite having Miss Sissy's weapon."

"I blame myself for this," Meadow said with a gusty sigh. "If I hadn't slept downstairs, it never would have happened. I'd have gone *with* you to chase the intruder. I'd have been George to your Nancy Drew."

"I see you as more of a Bess," said Posy, squinting thoughtfully at her.

"It's no one's fault but my own," said Beatrice

glumly. "I don't know what I was thinking, jumping out into that dark hallway, knowing we have a murderer on the loose."

"You were half asleep," said Meadow loyally.

Beatrice appreciated their efforts to cheer her up, but it wasn't doing any good.

When Beatrice woke up, she felt sore from head to toe. She was relieved to find that stretching seemed to help a little. Posy gave her two ibuprofen from her pocketbook.

Meadow entered the library with fruit cocktail and a guilty expression on her face.

"What's wrong, Meadow?" Posy asked.

"Oh, I just feel sort of bad," muttered Meadow. "I didn't want to hang out in the kitchen because Winnie is having some kind of breakdown and I couldn't handle it."

"A breakdown? Did something else happen?" Beatrice asked.

"No, nothing happened. Well, nothing happened that I know about, anyway. She's absolutely falling apart—you saw it coming. Seeing ghosts, acting so jumpy all the time. Winnie isn't handling the stress well. So she's in the kitchen crying over her bean salad." Meadow shrugged helplessly. "I tried to give her the fruit cocktail as sort of a consolation prize, but she waved me off. So she's stuck with the bean salad."

Posy and Beatrice glanced at each other. "I hate to

admit it, but I don't feel particularly inclined to try to comfort Winnie, either," said Posy. "Every time I talk with Winnie, it makes me feel anxious and stressed."

"She has a gift for drama," drawled Beatrice. "How about I go in the kitchen and just give her an ear? It might make her feel better and I might learn something at the same time."

"Are you sure you feel up to it?" Posy asked doubtfully. "Has that ibuprofen started kicking in yet?"

"I'm feeling fairly limber," said Beatrice, giving her a smile and being careful not to wince as she moved toward the kitchen. She pushed open the door and was stunned to see Alexandra with her hand on Winnie's shoulder. She was patting it in a way that was meant to be comforting, although Alexandra looked rather stiff doing so.

"You need to stop worrying, Winnie," Alexandra said. Her voice was peremptory, but Winnie responded to it. "There's no reason to be so upset. You'll sleep in the library with the others tonight, right? You're clearly getting no sleep at all upstairs and it's at nighttime when these incidents happen. If you sleep downstairs you'll be nice and warm and won't be by yourself. I don't know why you've been sleeping upstairs in the first place."

Winnie gave a small hiccup. "It's too uncomfortable on the floor. And anyway I don't know if I'd get any sleep with the others in the same room."

Alexandra pinched her mouth shut while she appeared to be making a decision. Then she bobbed her head in a short nod. "All right. What if we put some mattresses downstairs? Would you try it?"

Winnie's voice trembled. "But you said you didn't want to move things around the house."

"Well, when something isn't working, I can change my mind in response," said Alexandra briskly. She stiffened as Winnie reached out to hug her.

Beatrice, not wanting to embarrass Winnie, popped back out of sight until Winnie left the kitchen. Then she walked in, startling Alexandra, who was staring blankly into space.

"Sorry," said Beatrice.

Alexandra, quickly back to her normal self, rolled her eyes. "Sure you are. You were happy to eavesdrop, weren't you?"

"I didn't want to embarrass Winnie, that's all," Beatrice said mildly.

Alexandra shifted restlessly, tapping her fingers on the table. "What I wouldn't do for a cigarette," she whined.

Beatrice raised her eyebrows. "Oh, I didn't know you smoked."

"I do. But I haven't since I've been here, obviously. I stupidly didn't bring any with me. I thought it was only going to be a short visit at my mother's house, and I knew she didn't approve of them." She laughed harshly. "I sure am sorry about that now, though."

"Nicotine withdrawal couldn't have helped your

general disposition much," said Beatrice, more to herself than to Alexandra, but Alexandra grated out a laugh. "I did overhear a little of your conversation with Winnie. What you did was very nice."

Alexandra grunted. "It wasn't really. I still dislike Winnie, so I feel fake when I'm nice to her."

"But she needed some kind words. And perhaps a little firm redirecting, too, which you also provided. I've been concerned about Winnie's health lately and was wondering if she could handle the stress here."

"She'll be all right. She's still in better shape than that Miss Sissy of yours," Alexandra said with a snort. She hesitated, staring blankly out the window again. "As I said, I don't like Winnie. But I do feel sorry for her." She sat rigidly, as if regretting even mentioning her feelings. "Winnie is my mother's victim, the same as me. She trusted her to be a good friend and I trusted Muriel to be a good mother and we were both let down by her."

Beatrice nodded and opened her mouth to agree with Alexandra and coax her on, but the words were already spilling out of her.

"I can't cover for her," said Alexandra, almost to herself. "Just because I feel sorry for her, I can't pretend it didn't happen."

"Pretend what didn't happen?" asked Beatrice, sitting very still.

"Pretend I didn't spot her coming out of my mother's room the night she died," Alexandra said with a sigh. Then she fixed Beatrice with a stern expression. "Not that I'm buying your theory that Mother was murdered. But I was stepping out of my room late at night and saw Winnie hurrying out of Mother's room. I know I told you I heard them arguing, but I only said that so you'd focus your investigative zeal on Winnie. It wasn't actually an argument that I witnessed—it was Winnie coming out of Mother's room at a very late hour."

"Why didn't you say anything before now?" said Beatrice, still so exasperated at all the unforthcoming quilters.

"I didn't think Mother was murdered, but everyone else apparently did. I didn't want to throw suspicion on Winnie. She wasn't acting suspicious when I saw her." Alexandra gave a sardonic twist of her lips. "She just seemed angry or upset. There wasn't any argument as far as I know." Her eyes were brooding. "Beatrice, do you know why I've been so bound and determined to find a will in my favor?"

Beatrice raised her eyebrows. "I presume because you'd like the extra income."

"Well, there's that, of course. But mainly because I feel my mother owed me. She never acted like a real mother to me—she was never loving or nurturing. She rarely even looked me in the eye or listened to me. She didn't teach me much about loving others. I think she owed me. I really do."

"And she didn't owe Holly?" Beatrice asked carefully. "At least Muriel provided you with a roof over your head and a comfortable lifestyle and the opportunity to get to know her."

Alexandra gave that harsh laugh again. "The opportunity to get to know her? No. I never knew a thing about Muriel Starnes. But did she owe Holly?" She considered this, then said, grudgingly, "Probably."

"I wasn't doing anything!" Winnie gasped when Beatrice found a quiet moment with her in the library. "Nothing!" Winnie's bony fingers tensely gripped the hexagonal fabric of her quilting pattern. Then, suspiciously, she said, "Who told you I was in Muriel's room? It was Alexandra, wasn't it? She has it in for me! She was always jealous of my friendship with Muriel!"

Actually, Beatrice thought the opposite was probably true. She said, in a calming tone, "That doesn't really matter, does it? What matters is what you were doing in that room the night Muriel died. And why you've lied about it."

"I didn't lie," Winnie said bitterly. "I simply omitted any mention of it. That's because I knew it would be misinterpreted. I visited Muriel that night because I wanted to talk to her in private."

"What did you talk about?"

"I told her that her pitiful excuse for an apology wasn't good enough. The damage she caused was far too great to be expunged by an insincere apology." Winnie's cheeks blazed with color.

"What made you think it was insincere? Muriel

sounded sincere to me. Maybe it wasn't the best way to make an apology, but I think she meant it."

"Only because she was trying to dot her *I*'s and cross her *T*'s to make sure she was accepted through the pearly gates," Winnie snapped. "I don't think there was a genuine feeling of regret there at all. So I marched right into her room and told her what I thought of her and how I'd suffered through the years. I gave her a piece of my mind." Winnie seemed satisfied with her words.

"And she was obviously still alive at the end of your conversation?" Beatrice asked delicately.

Winnie glared at her. "Come on! She was alive and listening intently to my rant the whole time."

"What did Muriel say after you'd finished your . . . rant?"

"She didn't say anything. And not because she was dead," Winnie said defensively. "I think she was shocked that I would finally stand up for myself and tell her off."

"You didn't see or hear anyone when you left her room?"

"Not a soul. Wish I'd caught sight of whoever tattled on me. And, Beatrice—I've had about enough of your prying and poking around. Leave me out of it. If you keep pushing me—well, you'd better watch your step, that's all."

Following this rather threatening statement, Winnie squinted at something on the other side of the library. "What's that moving around over there?" She gasped. "Is it a rat?"

Beatrice quickly stood. "Oh. It's only the cat—you know, Miss Sissy's friend. What did she call it? Clarisse."

To Beatrice's amazement, the creature bounded across the library to settle in the chair next to Winnie, snuggling into the fabric. Winnie gave a surprised laugh and tentatively put a hand on the cat's back to rub it. "Clarisse."

"She seems to like you," Beatrice said with a grin, and was surprised to see Winnie blink rapidly as if fighting off tears. She cleared her throat. "I should be going." She wasn't sure that Winnie even heard her as she gingerly petted the cat. As Beatrice headed for the library door, she saw Miss Sissy peering in, intently watching Winnie with the cat.

Dot called from upstairs, "Can someone give me a hand? Think I accidentally wrenched my stupid ankle again." Frustration filled her voice.

"I'm on my way," said Beatrice, going upstairs.

"Are you sure?" asked Dot, frowning. "Aren't you feeling some aches and pains yourself?"

Beatrice shrugged, then offered her arm to Dot. "It could be worse. I was lucky. I took ibuprofen after I woke up this morning."

Beatrice did worry a moment, since Dot was particularly unsteady on her feet this morning—the thought of both of them tumbling down the stairs made her shiver.

She was relieved when they reached the bottom of the stairs. Dot must have been, too—Beatrice guessed she might not seem the steadiest herself.

"There now!" Dot said brightly. "Thanks for the helping hand, Beatrice. Now, on to breakfast!"

Beatrice watched frozen as Dot limped off to the kitchen.

She was favoring the wrong foot.

Chapter Nineteen

Beatrice's mind whirled. Was Dot lying about being hurt? She couldn't have also hurt the *other* ankle, could she?

If Dot really had never injured herself, it meant that the night of Colton's death she could have hurried downstairs, peered into the dining room for a chance to tamper with his drink, then run back upstairs again and gotten back in bed.

So she had the motive, means, and opportunity. And Alexandra claimed that Muriel had told everyone about the storage room under the stairs—Dot might have heard about it at a guild meeting or even at work.

What did they really know about Dot? She appeared cheerful and easygoing, but she hadn't been forthcoming about the fact that she'd worked for Muriel. When Beatrice had brought it up, Dot had acted dismissively, as if it was no big deal. But wouldn't that have been a good strategy to cover up a murder?

Beatrice glanced out the front window. The ice was showing some patchy melting in spots where the sun filtered through the trees. If she stepped carefully, she could probably walk around a bit to search for a cell phone signal. She went back upstairs to get her cell phone and coat, then made her way outside, walking cautiously down the porch stairs and into the driveway.

Beatrice realized she hadn't really taken notice of the other cars, having lost interest in them once she knew they were useless for escaping. Alexandra was the only one who had a brand-new expensive car. Winnie's was a well-maintained but much older model. And Holly's looked to be even older than Winnie's.

Beatrice couldn't even see Dot's car because she'd carefully placed a cover over it. The large tarp completely concealed the body of the vehicle underneath it.

With a quick glance around, Beatrice pulled off the cover to reveal the oldest car of the bunch. It had dents and nicks in the sides. Why would Dot bother to put a cover on a car like this?

Beatrice tried the doors, but they were locked. She bent to peer through the windows and caught her breath.

Dot was clearly living in her car.

There was an inflatable twin mattress taking up the entire backseat. It had a quilt for bedding and a pillow, too. Beatrice spotted stacks of clothing in the front seat and what appeared to be a plastic crate carrying a towel, soap, toothbrush, and toothpaste.

Obviously it would have seemed odd if Dot had brought those things inside—no one else had toothbrushes with them.

She'd covered the car to conceal the fact that she was living in there. Dot was a lot worse off than she'd let on—she'd become destitute and lost her home after being laid off. Beatrice realized, though, that she had no proof of Dot's guilt in the murders . . . just a strong gut feeling. Dot's room was very close to the stairs and Holly had slept downstairs last night. Dot was clearly lying about her ankle injury, using the injury as a smokescreen. And now she realized how much Dot had lost when Muriel had misled her and then laid her off. It all added up.

A wave of sadness swept over Beatrice as she carefully covered the car again. She felt more anxious than ever that they get out of there. She glanced around the yard and driveway. She could see that there was a watery layer underneath the ice. In a few spots where the sun filtered through the trees there were bare patches of grass showing through.

Beatrice took her phone out of her pocket. She could go carefully from bare spot to bare spot and check for a signal. She glanced around her, then decided to try the highest point of the large yard. Surely the higher you were, the better your chance of getting a cell phone signal.

Beatrice walked toward the edge of the yard, watching her cell phone signal bars as she went. It was a very delicate process, stepping carefully from grassy bare spot to grassy bare spot while checking her phone signal. And she was terrified that the phone was going to die at any second. She'd had it turned off for days, but knew there was hardly any battery left at this point.

Just as she was reaching the farthest, highest part of the yard, she was rewarded by the appearance of a signal bar on her phone's screen.

Beatrice froze, not wanting to disturb the fragile signal by moving forward or backward. Whom should she call? Meadow's police chief husband was still away. Piper was still in California. It needed to be either Posy's husband, Cork, or her minister friend, Wyatt. Considering the way her heart warmed at the thought of Wyatt, the decision was an easy one. She found his number on her phone and called it.

When his steady voice answered, Beatrice gave a sob of relief and quickly said, "Wyatt! I think my phone will die, so please listen. Meadow, Posy, Miss Sissy, and other women are here at Muriel Starnes's house—you know the one. The Victorian mansion on the mountain on the way out of Dappled Hills. But . . . there have been two murders. We're okay, but come with the police. I know who's responsible."

Wyatt started to answer, but Beatrice cut him off with a quick "Bye" and hung up. What if she needed to call out again or if they couldn't find the house for some reason? Best not to use up the remaining battery. She was about to turn off the phone when she heard a serious voice behind her say, "You know who's responsible, do you?"

Beatrice turned slowly around to see Dot standing behind her. And she was holding Alexandra's gun. And no cane at all.

Beatrice took a deep breath until she felt she could trust herself to speak without her voice shaking. "You don't want to do this, Dot."

"Don't I?" Dot's features were tense and her eyes were completely cold instead of infused with the warmth that was usually there. "I think I do. I think you're going to tell the police what you know—and you've got to know something, right? Since you were snooping around my car a few minutes ago."

"I was only trying to learn more about you," Beatrice said cautiously. "You haven't really talked much about yourself, and then I realized that looking at your car might be a good way to find out more."

"Except that's not really why you decided to poke around," said Dot, all trace of her usual jolliness absent from her voice. "I think there was something else. Come on. What gave me away?"

Beatrice remembered the knife that Miss Sissy had foisted on her. It wasn't much, but it was her only hope. Getting it out without Dot noticing would be tricky. Beatrice decided to keep Dot talking in the hopes that might distract her.

"I did notice a few minutes ago that you were limping on the wrong foot," Beatrice said. She slipped her hand a little closer to her pocket.

"Ohh," said Dot, glancing down at her ankles. "Did I switch over? How careless of me."

"So you weren't hurt at all when you fell?"

"Oh, I wouldn't say that," Dot said, shrugging carelessly. "It hurt when I fell down—my muscles were killing me the next day. But the fall didn't hurt my *ankle*, no."

"Yes," said Beatrice tightly. "I know all about sore muscles from falls. Your bedroom door is awfully close to the stairs—so easy for you to scratch at my door to wake me up and lure me into the hall, then dodge back into your room, coming back out again just in time to push me down the stairs."

"You were nosing around a little too much." Dot continued staring at Beatrice with those same cold eyes. "I had a feeling you were right on the brink of figuring everything out. Obviously, I was right."

Beatrice kept inching her hand closer to her slacks pocket. "Your 'injury' was the perfect cover for you. You pretended to be upstairs resting, when you were actually running downstairs to find a good opportunity to put the sleeping pills you'd swiped from Muriel's room into Colton's drink."

Dot gave a satisfied smile. "Yes, I was pretty smart there. I don't think y'all even considered for a minute that I wasn't upstairs."

"And this is all because you were peeved at Muriel for laying you off?" asked Beatrice, innocently hanging a finger on the pocket where the knife was hidden.

Dot's face darkened. "Not *peeved*. That makes me sound like I'm some kind of unreasonable, spoiled person. I was done wrong. Totally wrong. And my life fell apart because of it. I couldn't find work because I was competing with everybody I used to work with who were also unemployed. I kept searching for jobs, but employers didn't even bother to call me for an interview."

"Then you lost your house."

"Yes." Dot's eyes were sad. "And I loved that house, Beatrice. I'd poured all my heart and soul into making it the kind of place I wanted to come home to every day. Oh, it was nothing fancy—I decorated it mostly from thrift stores, but I put a lot of care into it. It was all just the way I wanted it. It was home. Then I lost it."

"You didn't have any family who would take you in?"

Dot snorted. "All I've got left of my family is a cousin on the other side of the country. I didn't want anybody to know, anyway, much less ask them for help. But I still had my car, so I set it up as my home away from home. I'd find different places to park so I could go to sleep. Lucky for me, the gym had a special when I bought my membership—buy six months, get six months free. I'm not one for working out—" Her voice turned jolly again as she patted her considerable belly with her free hand. "But a gym membership sure is useful when you're looking for a place to shower."

"I guess it was only Muriel you planned on killing," Beatrice said. "Then it sort of escalated from there." She could feel the top of the knife in her pocket.

"I wasn't originally planning on killing *anybody*," Dot said with a chortle. "It wasn't like I stole over here in the middle of the night to take my revenge. I was an invited guest of Muriel's. I was going to stay after everyone left to talk to Muriel one-on-one. I wanted her to know what had happened to me after she'd let me go. Who knew—maybe she'd take pity on me and find me a job somewhere or give me a little cash?"

"But no one left," Beatrice said quietly. "And your resentment against her grew."

"Because she told us all the real reason she'd brought us together—it wasn't the quilting foundation. It was to give that pathetic apology to everyone she thought she'd hurt. And *that* made me mad . . . the fact that she thought she could sweep her sins under the carpet like that at the eleventh hour. When the ice storm rolled in and we were trapped, it felt like the stars were lining up exactly right for me to get my revenge on Muriel."

"Did you plan on killing her when you went into her bedroom, then? Or were you still thinking you were going in to let Muriel know how much damage she'd done?"

"Damage?" Dot snorted. "It wasn't only *damage*.

It was total destruction and she was the one behind it. Maybe I thought it would be satisfying to give her a piece of my mind before I killed her, but she was sleeping so soundly when I walked in her room that I realized I could smother her and she wouldn't even wake up. It sure was going to make things a lot easier from my perspective just to let her keep sleeping instead of getting my two cents in. So that's what I did."

"Colton obviously figured things out. So he was next on your list."

Dot spread her hands out, still clutching the gun, although she appeared to have almost forgotten it was there. "Hey, I didn't come here wanting to murder Colton. But Colton just had to be a smart aleck and figure things out. Apparently, he'd had a tough time tracking me down when Muriel had asked him to get in touch with me. Imagine that," she said bitterly.

"How *would* he have found you if you were living in your car?"

"Oh, I was putting my gym's address down as a residence whenever I sent off a résumé or something. The gym was pretty cool about it. I guess he thought it was kind of weird, but that's where he sent me Muriel's invitation."

"Then, after Muriel died, he started thinking it over. Why would you use your gym's address to pick up your mail?"

"He snooped around in my car." Dot nodded.

"Sure enough, he put two and two together. He wasn't a stupid man."

"Did he come to talk to you about it?"

"He did. Before supper, actually. He came upstairs and knocked on the bedroom door to talk with me. Holly was downstairs helping to make supper, I think. Colton didn't come out and accuse me of murdering Muriel, but he said that he had his suspicions and would be keeping an eye on me. But I could tell he felt pretty sure about it."

"So you ground up those sleeping pills and ran downstairs and waited for your chance to put the powder in his wineglass."

"It was easy. I figured he'd have a glass of wine, and he did. You took him off to talk to him, which gave me plenty of opportunity to doctor his drink. Alexandra had wandered off without helping to clean up and the others were in and out, clearing the table and doing dishes. I waited until no one was there, then added the powder and stirred it in real quick. I remembered Muriel had told our quilt guild about the hidden spot under the stairs . . . I'd found it earlier, thinking it might come in handy. I put the pill bottle in there."

Beatrice closed her fingers around the knife and pulled it out of her pocket, opening it up quickly and holding it up in the air.

Dot stared at her in disbelief. "You bring a knife to a gunfight?" She let out a derisive chuckle. "I thought you were smarter than that, Beatrice."

Just then, Beatrice's phone rang loudly—a jangling, imperative ringtone that she'd never figured out how to disable. Dot jumped, eyes open wide at the unexpected sound, and Beatrice grabbed her one chance. She ran at Dot, pushing the stout woman to the ground.

The gun went flying out of Dot's hand, skidding on the icy ground. Dot cried out hoarsely, scrambling to get up, but slipping on the surface as she struggled to move.

Beatrice got a foothold in a melted area and bent down toward the gun, scrabbling in the melting ice to grab the weapon. Dot roared with anger behind her as she struggled, panting, to get to her feet.

Beatrice's arm burned as she stretched out for the gun. She pushed harder with her feet, scooting across the ice and mud. Finally she felt the cold metal with her fingers and she pulled the gun close, then scrambled to her feet and pointed the gun at Dot.

"You wouldn't use that," said Dot, eyes squinting appraisingly at her.

But there must have been a touch of steel in Beatrice's eyes, because, looking at her, Dot seemed to come to the realization that Beatrice would use it. Dot sank back down into the muddy slush, warily eyeing her.

Beatrice was too worried about the gun in her hand to try to fish her phone out and find the missed call. So she simply stood there shivering, holding the pistol in two shaking hands.

She'd never been so glad to hear Meadow's boom-
ing voice. "Beatrice Coleman! What in the Sam Hill
is going on here?"

Dot drawled, "I think Beatrice is holding a gun on
me, Meadow. That's what's going on."

Meadow stamped through the ice and slush, in
complete disregard to its treachery. She gaped at Beatrice. "Is Dot our murderer, Beatrice?"

"She certainly is," said Beatrice grimly.

"So what are we going to do with her?" asked
Meadow, staring at Dot in horror.

"I'm thinking we're going to stay like this until
we're rescued."

"Won't we freeze to death?"

"I don't think so," Beatrice said slowly. Her voice
was still shaking, so she took a deep, calming breath.
"You see, I got a signal on my phone here."

Meadow gasped. "Did you? In this very spot?"
She glanced around her as if on hallowed ground.
"Who'd you call?"

Beatrice cleared her throat. "Well, I was terrified I
was going to lose my signal so I called the first person who came to mind."

"Wyatt?" Meadow asked cannily. "How romantic
of you, Beatrice!"

Beatrice said in a brisk tone, "This is hardly the
time or place that, Meadow."

Dot shrugged, not looking at all concerned about
being held at gunpoint.

"Did he say anything about Boris? Oh, my poor
dog!"

"No, I didn't have time to chat, Meadow—the battery is nearly dead. I told him where we were and what had happened and that the police needed to come."

"And that she knew who was responsible," drawled Dot.

"I'm sure they're all already on their way," said Meadow. She shivered. "Hope they'll get on with it. I'm freezing!" She turned toward the house and brightened. "Here comes Posy! Maybe we can send her back for our coats." Meadow started inching toward Posy and the house.

"Have y'all seen Miss Sissy?" Posy called out.

Beatrice glanced her way for only a second, but that was all it took for Dot to lunge at her with both hands outstretched for the gun. Beatrice's hands tightened on it a moment too late, and it fell to the ground. They both dropped down to grab it as Meadow hurried back toward them.

Suddenly, Beatrice heard a guttural cry from behind a row of trees and bushes. "Wickedness!" And Miss Sissy popped out from behind several large azaleas, wielding Dot's cane, which she quickly used to whack at Dot's right arm, which was reaching for the gun.

Dot yelled in pain and snatched her arm back out of the way and backed up away from Miss Sissy as far as she could. Miss Sissy continued wildly hitting the ground in front of her with the cane. "Found her cane inside!" Miss Sissy shouted. "Lied! Evil!"

Beatrice quickly picked up the gun and backed off

slightly with it, keeping it trained on Dot. "Thank you for coming to investigate, Miss Sissy."

"No cane! Not hurt!" Miss Sissy continued.

Beatrice gave a shuddering sigh of relief at the sound of sirens—still far away, but getting closer.

Dot slumped on the ground, this time looking defeated.

Chapter Twenty

The police hadn't known exactly what to make of the scene they encountered when they finally made it up the steep mountainside driveway to the house. They'd had to leave their cruisers at the bottom of the drive and hurried up to the top on foot. Beatrice was more than happy to relinquish the gun, of course, but not until she felt the police had the situation well in hand.

Beatrice beamed at Wyatt, who was behind the police . . . with Noo-noo. The corgi was overjoyed to see her and Wyatt appeared fairly happy to see her himself.

Posy's husband, Cork, was close behind. For once, his usually grumpy face was creased with a smile at the sight of his wife.

Holly, Alexandra, and Winnie had come running out at the sound of the sirens and were amazed to see Dot in handcuffs. *"There's* my gun!" Alexandra had frowned. "I'd just been wondering where it was. I was about to go search Winnie's room again. I should have known it had been snatched . . . I'm not one to be careless with a gun."

Dot gave a derisive snort. Understandably, since she'd twice ended up with the gun in her possession.

Winnie was flushed with anger. "Dot? You were the one who planted the gun in my room? But why? Why did you do that to me?"

"Just trying to throw everyone off the scent, that's all." Dot shrugged. "Don't take it personally, Winnie."

The police had put Dot into the back of a police car before questioning everyone. The questioning took a long time and the police officers kept raising their eyebrows at the talk of bodies, sleeping pills, suspicious deaths, secret passageways, and hidden rooms. It did all sound fairly unbelievable, but after some preliminary investigating, they listened a lot more carefully to their story.

Everyone was glad when they were finally released. However, the police told them they would be in contact for further questioning.

"But how are we going to get out of here?" asked Meadow, hands on her hips. "We're really still in the same fix. The driveway is still too icy to drive down, particularly as steep as it is."

Wyatt said, "Cork and I will escort y'all down to the bottom of the driveway and take you home. The lower section of the driveway has gotten a little more sun and isn't as icy as the top part. I think we can hop from dry patch to dry patch. And we also brought a few ski poles to help us maintain our balance—I dropped them at the top of the driveway. We'll come back later for your cars. They'll have to get a crew to cut up those fallen trees that are blocking the driveway."

"What about Holly, Alexandra, and Winnie?" asked Posy, her forehead wrinkling with concern.

One of the police officers explained that they would escort the ladies home and they could retrieve their cars later after the ice had melted.

Meadow started walking down the driveway. "Boy, am I glad to get out of here!"

Amen, Beatrice thought.

Piper's voice was filled with relief when Beatrice called her on the way home from Muriel's house. "Mama, I was so worried! The only thing that kept me from being completely frantic was that I knew at least you'd be with Meadow and Posy."

"And Miss Sissy," reminded Beatrice dryly. She filled Piper in as quickly as she could.

"Where are you going now?" Piper asked with concern. "Do you need to run by the doctor's office?"

"I just want to go home," Beatrice replied. "It's amazing how much I've missed that little cottage."

It was a wonderful feeling when the car finally pulled into her driveway and she walked into the small stone cottage.

Noo-noo was overjoyed at being back home with Beatrice. "Cute little guy," Cork had admitted, in his grouchy voice. "Could tell he missed you, though." Cork had brought Noo-noo and Boris over to stay with him while Beatrice and Meadow had been gone. Apparently Boris hadn't been as good a guest as Noo-noo.

A week went by—a week full of catching up. She watered her parched houseplants, bought groceries, and worked her way through the mail and newspapers that Wyatt had thoughtfully collected for her while she'd been gone. Concerned friends from church and other quilters stopped by for a hug and a quick visit.

The police had questioned Beatrice a couple of times during the week, double-checking the timing of events and getting more details about what she'd discovered. When she'd tried to turn the tables and question the police, though, it hadn't gone as well. They wouldn't give her any information at all. She'd just have to wait for Dappled Hills police chief Ramsay to finally return from his trip and fill her in.

Which he finally did. Ramsay, with Meadow and their tremendous beast, Boris, in tow, knocked at her cottage door one morning. When Beatrice opened it, Meadow said, "Okay, Beatrice, let's dispense with the pleasantries and have a seat. Ramsay wouldn't tell me anything about what the police found out until he told you at the same time."

"Hate having to repeat myself," said Ramsay, quietly coming in and sitting down on Beatrice's ging-ham armchair.

"Can I get you an iced tea or—?" Beatrice offered.

"No!" Meadow said. "Sit down and let's hear what he's found out, Beatrice. He had coffee before he came over here."

Beatrice and Meadow settled down near Ramsay in the little living room. Boris promptly walked over to sit on Beatrice's feet and sprawled his upper half over her lap. Beatrice's Noo-noo decided that turn-about was fair play and leaned against Ramsay, who bent down to rub her tummy.

Ramsay cleared his throat, "First of all, Beatrice, you were right to assume these were murders. They were."

Beatrice nodded. "I'd thought they must be."

"Smothered and poisoned with an overdose of sleeping pills," Ramsay confirmed.

"The poor things," Meadow said with a gusty sigh.

"And Dot was responsible, I suppose?" asked Beatrice. "At least, she'd indicated to me that she was."

"Yes. She didn't even try to defend herself," Ramsay explained. "Didn't even ask for a lawyer. Just upped and confessed to both murders. Said she'd murdered Muriel Starnes out of revenge for past treatment and out of anger for the way Muriel seemed to think she could make everything magi-cally okay again with a blanket apology."

"And Colton for putting two and two together," said Beatrice.

"That's right. It was all pretty much the way you'd figured. The autopsy revealed that the number of sleeping pills in his system was enough to knock him out almost immediately. If it's any comfort, it would have been a fairly easy way to go."

Ramsay and Beatrice thought quietly on this for a few moments while Meadow wriggled impatiently. Finally, Meadow couldn't shush herself any longer. "What about the rest of the story? What about the will? And the other people who were stuck at the house with us? I want to know how everything ended up."

"That Colton was a cagey guy," Ramsay said with admiration. "For all the apparent talk of updating the will the night Muriel died, she obviously never got the chance. But Muriel did have Colton draw up a will only a few weeks earlier that included several new provisions. It was witnessed by Colton and Muriel's housekeeper, who she'd occasionally called to clean for her. Colton didn't say anything about the will to y'all, did he?"

Beatrice and Meadow looked at each other and shook their heads.

"So why would she want *another* will?" Beatrice asked.

Ramsay shrugged. "Maybe Muriel really did plan to include a quilting foundation in her will. At first, it could simply have been a ruse to get everyone over to her house for her apology, but then she might have warmed to the idea and decided to include it in an updated will."

"But then she died before they could make the changes," said Meadow. "Pooh."

"Where did you find the most recent will?" Beatrice asked. "Alexandra turned the house upside down searching for it. Although I don't think she ever really got the chance to search in the attic."

"Oh, the will wasn't in the house. It was at Colton's office. He had drawn it up at Muriel's house, since she was unwell at the time, and then taken it to his office to file it. It's all perfectly in order."

"So what'd it say?" Meadow asked impatiently.

"I think you'll be happy to hear that Holly ended up with the house," Ramsay said. "But Muriel wasn't totally awful to Alexandra—she gave her a very comfortable sum of money. Although I don't think Alexandra saw it that way. She appeared angry over it all."

"She certainly acted as if she thought she owned the house lock, stock, and barrel," said Beatrice. "She expected to be the sole heir."

"Until she found out about Holly," said Meadow with a snort. "Oh, I'm so glad to hear that Holly will inherit that house."

"And money for fixing it up, too," said Ramsay. "Which it desperately needs. With a few upgrades and with that nice view, the house will be a good nest egg for Holly with a nice resale. Muriel's estate was worth over a million dollars, and yet she pinched pennies and didn't keep up her home. She really was a miser."

"But there was no money for a quilting foundation mentioned?" asked Meadow, ever hopeful that perhaps Ramsay had just forgotten to mention this detail.

"No quilting foundation," said Ramsay. As Meadow's face fell, he added quickly, "But you'll be happy to hear that she did earmark a tidy sum to go to various area quilt guilds—Village Quilters included."

Meadow clapped her hands, startling Noo-noo, who jumped to her feet looking alarmed.

"Although there were some provisos on the money. I think it had to be used to promote quilting in the community and schools," Ramsay added in a cautionary tone.

"Oh, that's fine—that's what the whole foundation thing was supposed to do. So this is a onetime gift instead of an ongoing one, but we'll take it." Meadow had a big grin on her face.

"Was anyone else mentioned in the will?" asked Beatrice. "Anyone from the house, I mean."

"You mean Dot or Winnie?" Ramsay asked.

"Or even Colton," Meadow said with a shrug. "They were married once, after all."

"Not a thing for Colton. But she did earmark some money for both Winnie and Dot. Along with an apology. I guess she felt a mere apology would be inadequate and she wanted to at least give them some form of reparation. It's too bad that Dot won't be able to inherit anything from Muriel now—since she'd be profiting from a crime. Winnie, though, was delighted to hear about the money that Muriel willed her. Although she was even more delighted about the cat."

"What's that about the cat?" asked Meadow.

"Alexandra didn't want it and Holly is apparently mildly allergic. We naturally brought it to Miss Sissy, since she'd been so taken with it. But Miss Sissy insisted that we offer it to Winnie. I called Winnie from Miss Sissy's house, because I just couldn't see that sour old woman giving the cat a home, and I figured Miss Sissy would take it if no one else would. You could have knocked me down with a feather when Winnie said she'd take the cat in. Actually, she was delighted to."

"I think she's lonely," Beatrice sad. "And that loneliness has made her bitter."

"When I asked her about the cat," Ramsay said, "she actually burst into tears."

"The poor thing," tutted Meadow.

"Was Alexandra spitting fire when she heard she wasn't inheriting the house?" Beatrice asked.

Ramsay shook his head. "Nope. Guess she didn't want to acknowledge that her feelings might be hurt. At first, she had this expression like she'd been slapped in the face. But after that, she said in this snide tone that the house was a money pit, anyway. 'Good luck to Holly . . .' That kind of thing."

"Typical," Meadow said with a snort. "Sour grapes."

"That's very cynical of you," said Ramsay, eyebrows raised.

"I got to know Alexandra pretty well over the course of our ordeal," Meadow said. "I wasn't very impressed."

"Well, this tidbit might surprise you. While the men were hunting around for a will, they came across a box full of mementoes. It had photos of Alexandra, blue ribbons she'd won at field days, locks of her hair, pictures she'd drawn when she was a kid, the papers she'd made A's on . . ."

"You're right." Meadow gaped. "I *am* surprised."

"Me, too," said Beatrice, absently patting Boris, who was insistently laying his tremendous head in her lap. "Who'd have thought that Muriel was sentimental or maternal enough to create a keepsake box?"

"You're not the only ones," said Ramsay. "Alexandra appeared to be in a state of shock when the cops handed the box to her. Got kind of choked up, actually. She held it very carefully—cradling it, really."

"Sweet," said Meadow, although she still didn't appear particularly convinced about Alexandra's good side. "Now there's one person I'm a little concerned about. Someone I ended up really being rather fond of."

"Clearly not Alexandra," Ramsay said dryly.

"Nope. Dot. I liked her. She was blunt and funny and always in a good mood."

"When she wasn't killing people," Beatrice said.

"Right. So what's going to happen to Dot?" Meadow asked.

"Well, Dot's going to have to go to prison, naturally," Ramsay said.

"What! With no trial?" Meadow asked.

"Of course with a trial. But Dot plans on pleading guilty, apparently. If it makes you feel better, she was very pragmatic over the whole thing. She was very matter-of-fact when she said that at least she had a roof over her head and knew where her next meal was coming from."

"So, in a way, everything ended up all right in the end," Beatrice said.

"Well, except for Colton and Muriel," Meadow reminded her. "And Dot. Although Dot apparently has found a silver lining to her situation."

"Except for them. And I, for one, was delighted to get back to my cottage and my Noo-noo," said Beatrice, reaching down to her corgi, who had joined her by her side. She scratched behind her ears. Boris bumped her hand jealously with his head.

"Boris and Noo-noo don't seem any the worse for wear, do they?" said Meadow. "From all accounts, they loved being at Camp Cork."

Ramsay chuckled. "Cork was good to take them in for us. I somehow get the impression that Posy is usually the one who takes care of their dog. I heard him say that Noo-noo was very good, but he didn't seem to have anything positive to say about Boris's behavior."

Boris lifted his head and gazed sadly at Ramsay before laying it back down in Beatrice's lap.

"You know Cork loves Boris. Everyone loves Boris!" Meadow said stoutly. "He probably just forgot to mention how much he enjoyed his company because he got so busy, you know. Taking care of the dogs and searching for Posy and us and trying to get extra help to fill in at his wine store."

Ramsay glanced at Beatrice's wall clock and stood up. "Hate to say it, but I've got to head over to the police station. Don't you have things you've got to do, too, Meadow?"

Boris leaped up at the realization that a walk back home was in order. He loped over to join Ramsay as he headed to the door.

Meadow made a face. "I suppose so. Laundry and cleaning, I think. I'm in no hurry. I'll hang out with Beatrice for a while and keep her company."

Beatrice stifled a sigh. Ramsay winked at her.

As Ramsay was opening the front door, he stopped. "You're about to have more company, Beatrice. Pastor Wyatt is pulling into your driveway."

Beatrice's heart leaped and she carefully calmed herself down. "Really?" she asked, feigning indifference. "That's nice of him."

She apparently wasn't fooling Meadow, who rolled her eyes. She stood up behind Ramsay and peered outside, pushing Boris aside. "I think he's got a box of restorative chocolates, Beatrice! And a bag of treats for Noo-noo!"

Beatrice smiled and said sedately, "Very good of him to do that."

Meadow nodded. "Sometimes being at home is the best thing of all." She grinned at Beatrice. "But the next time you want to take a quilt trip with me, just say the word. There's this quilt show in Georgia . . ."

Ramsay and Beatrice both groaned simultaneously.

Quilting Tips

Save time by cutting all your fabric for a project at once so that you can pick up a project whenever you have a few minutes to work on it.

Color wheels are helpful tools when you're trying to experiment with different color combinations.

Small hammers make good seam flatteners.

Try doing a sample block for a quilt to decide whether you want to make a whole quilt with the same blocks.

Fabric swaps among friends can be a good way both to get rid of unwanted fabric and to get new fabric for projects. Or use some of your leftover blocks to make pillows or miniature quilts.

Cork bulletin boards provide excellent places to hang and evaluate blocks, pin up ideas for future projects, and easily find patterns and instructions.

Recipes

Although Beatrice and her friends were stuck with canned food and no electricity, here are recipes for some of Meadow's favorite comfort foods that she wished they *did* have with them.

Chicken and Broccoli Casserole

Salt and pepper to taste
3 chicken breasts
2 chicken thighs
1 package frozen chopped broccoli, cooked
1 can cream of chicken soup
½ cup chicken broth
6 T mayonnaise
¾ t lemon juice
1 t curry powder
2 cups seasoned stuffing
¼ cup butter

Preheat oven to 350 degrees. Salt and pepper chicken as desired and boil until cooked. Debone chicken and cut into bite-sized pieces. Cover a 3-quart casserole dish with cooking spray and place cooked chicken on the bottom. Cover with the cooked broccoli. Mix the chicken soup with half a cup of chicken broth, the mayonnaise, lemon juice, and curry powder. Spoon mixture on top of broccoli. Sprinkle the stuffing over the top. Melt the butter and drizzle on top of the stuffing. Bake at 350 degrees for 25 minutes.

Spinach Bake

1 6-oz package corn muffin mix
2 eggs, beaten
8 oz sour cream
2 10-oz packages frozen chopped spinach
½ cup melted margarine
½ cup grated cheddar or Monterey Jack cheese

Preheat oven to 350 degrees. Cover a 9-by-13 casserole dish with cooking spray. Combine all the ingredients and bake at 350 degrees for 30 minutes.

Chili con Carne

6 T butter
6 medium onions, sliced
3 lbs ground round
3 20-oz cans tomatoes
1 6-oz can tomato paste
1 cup ale or beer
1 T salt
½ t hot sauce
2 T chili powder (or more, to taste)
2 12-oz cans whole kernel corn

Melt the butter in a large saucepan. Add the onions
and cook until softened. Add the beef to the pan and
cook until browned. Add the remaining ingredients,
except for the corn. Cover the saucepan and simmer
for 45 minutes. Add the cans of corn and simmer for
15 more minutes.

Banana Nut Bread

3 very ripe bananas, mashed
¼ lb butter
1 cup sugar
2 eggs
2 cups flour
1 t baking soda
½ cup finely chopped pecans

Whip bananas until light. Cream the butter and sugar together and add the eggs. Sift flour and baking soda and add to egg mixture. Combine with the pecans and the bananas. Spoon into a greased loaf pan and bake at 350 degrees for one hour.

Read on for another Southern Quilting
Mystery by Elizabeth Craig
SHEAR TROUBLE
Available now from Obsidian.

"The funny thing, Beatrice," said Meadow, beaming through her red-framed glasses, "is that all this time I never knew that Boris was a genius."

Beatrice looked doubtfully down at the aforementioned Boris. The massive animal of mixed bloodlines was grinning at her with his tongue lolling out. He actually looked rather slow. And this was the same dog who strong-armed his way into her kitchen on a regular basis and upset her canisters while searching for food. "How did you come to that conclusion, Meadow? I mean, I'm sure Boris is *smart*, but I wouldn't have said he was more clever than . . . well, Noo-noo." She looked with satisfaction at her own dog, a well-behaved, alert corgi.

"He's just so incredibly intuitive and communicative. Lately, he's put his paw on my leg whenever he wants to tell me something. I've been amazed." Meadow looked wonderingly at the huge animal's tremendous paws. Boris yawned. "Yesterday morning I had a real absentminded episode. I put eggs on the stove to boil and then something distracted me. . . . I don't now remember what it was. Anyway, I walked outside to get the newspaper. While I was outside, I saw weeds were really making inroads into my flower bed. So I pulled weeds for a bit."

Beatrice took a bite of her shortbread cookie. She was used to Meadow's meandering stories and had confidence that her friend would eventually come to her point.

"Out of the blue, Boris bolted out the door. I swear, I don't even know how he opened it. Do you think he turned the handle?"

Beatrice didn't.

"Anyway, he galloped outside, giving me this incredibly intelligent pleading look. I get goose bumps whenever I remember it." Meadow thrust out her arm for Beatrice to view the indisputable truth. "He put his paw on my shoulder—that's because I was stooped over, weeding—clearly telling me to come inside. He gave a few sharp barks and ran to the front door. I tell you, Beatrice, I started running. Sure enough, the pot was already blazing when I went in, so I sprayed my kitchen extinguisher on it and put it out. Boris saved the day!" Meadow choked up at this last bit and pulled a tissue out of her purse, blowing her nose loudly.

Noo-noo looked concerned, and Beatrice reached over to rub the dog's head. "That's a very scary story, Meadow. Thank goodness that Boris paid such close attention. I'd hate for this gorgeous barn to burn down." Beatrice gazed around her. The old barn had been turned into a beautiful home. Skylights in the cathedral-like ceiling lit the large, open living area, illuminating vibrantly colored quilts hanging from the walls.

Meadow reached over to refill Beatrice's iced tea

before she could protest. Meadow took her hostessing duties seriously, but Beatrice was wondering if she'd need to make a pit stop by the powder room before she and Noo-noo walked home. Before she knew it, Meadow had put another couple of shortbread cookies on the china plate in front of her. "Meadow!" she groaned.

"Oh, please. Like you need to worry about calories. I've never seen a fitter sixtysomething-year-old than you. Platinum blond hair, carelessly stylish buttondown, and capri-length khakis." Meadow snorted. "How did I end up with the big bones and crazy hair? The least you can do is eat a few cookies with me in sympathy."

"I'm afraid my hair is white, not platinum. I'm not as fit as you're giving me credit for. And your hair isn't crazy at all. I've always thought your braid suited you." It was a long gray braid, which did suit Meadow to a T.

Meadow said, "Hey, how is your quilt coming along?" Her eyes were wide and innocent, but Beatrice knew that this was a dead-serious follow-up.

"Oh, I figured I'd finish it the night before the quilt show. There's still plenty of time," said Beatrice in a studiously careless voice. Meadow gasped, choking a bit on cookie crumbs, and Beatrice chided, "Meadow! It's all finished, of course. You know how I am about meeting deadlines." She reached down and gave Boris a distracted pat as he laid his mighty genius head on her lap to look lovingly at her shortbread cookie.

Meadow flashed her a relieved look as she reached

for her drink to wash down the cookie. She said, "Well, thank goodness. I only wish that everyone else in the guild had your work ethic. This show might be featuring a bunch of unfinished quilts from the Village Quilters." She frowned thoughtfully. "Do you think we can spin that somehow? Promote it as high art? 'The Process of Quilting,' or some such thing?"

"I don't think so, no." Somehow, Beatrice didn't think a modern-art deconstructed-quilt exhibit was going to go over well in tiny Dappled Hills. "Are you sure that everyone is running so far behind? That doesn't sound like Savannah, for instance."

Meadow cleared her throat. "Well, Savannah has been busy doing other things lately."

"That sounds ominous," said Beatrice, slowly. "Are you talking about her little borrowing problem?" Savannah, who looked like a prim and proper, buttoned-up old maid, was a complete kleptomaniac.

"Let's just say she's kept her sister busy lately," said Meadow with a sigh. "I happened to be in the quilt shop when Georgia came in to return a thimble that Savannah had swiped. Sometimes she goes through spells with it, you know. Just be sure to nail down your stuff when it's your turn to host a guild meeting."

"Okay. Well, I can understand the two of them being a little behind then. But Miss Sissy? She's up all night with insomnia. You can't tell me that she hasn't finished her quilt. What else does she have to do?" Miss Sissy was the oldest member of the guild. She'd become a bit demented and was fairly arthritic, but she could still produce the best needlework of anyone in the state.

"Who knows?" said Meadow gloomily. "Whatever she's doing, it's not quilting. At least not on the quilt that's supposed to be in the show."

"And Piper?" asked Beatrice. "Surely my own daughter is enough like me to meet her deadline with lots of time to spare."

"I think Piper and my son have been spending a lot of time talking on the phone together lately," said Meadow. This, at least, put a smile back on her face. "Ah, they're really a lovely couple, aren't they? I can tell that Ash is just wild about Piper."

It was a pity that Ash lived all the way over on the other side of the country. Beatrice was both happy for her daughter and sorry that she was in a relationship that might eventually result in a move. Piper had only recently returned from a long visit in California to see Ash.

"So Piper isn't done either?" This *was* looking bad for the quilt show. "I wonder how the Cut-Ups are doing with their quilts," said Beatrice. The Cut-Ups and the Village Quilters had a friendly rivalry with one another. Friendly *most* of the time, anyway.

Now Meadow's face looked even glummer. "I'm sure they're completely done, as usual."

"Well, why don't we set up some sort of bee?" asked Beatrice. "You know the Village Quilters love to socialize—maybe that would be the best way to keep everybody from procrastinating and finish their quilts."

Meadow brightened. "Great idea, Beatrice! Maybe Posy will let us use the Patchwork Cottage's conference room. We could set up a bunch of long tables, run some extension cords, and everyone would have plenty of space to spread out."

"A retreat," said Beatrice, nodding. "A quilting retreat. We could all bring some food—that'll lure them in if the quilting doesn't."

"Do you think Posy will go for it?" asked Meadow. "The shop has been so busy lately and it seems like she's always on the go."

Beatrice could tell Meadow would keep stewing over this issue until it was addressed. "Tell you what. Why don't we head over to Posy's shop and find out right now? We can ask her about the retreat and I can pick up a few things for the new quilt I'm working on. Can Noo-noo visit with Boris while we run the errand?"

Meadow beamed at her. "Boris will *love* it!" she said as she snatched her keys off the kitchen counter.

Noo-noo apparently didn't share the sentiment and stared reproachfully at Beatrice as she and Meadow left.

Beatrice felt a smile pull at the corners of her mouth as soon as she entered Posy's shop. The Patchwork Cottage made her feel a bit more relaxed, a little more mindful. Posy always had soft music playing in the store, usually by local artists. The large room was a visual feast for the eyes with bolts of fabric and lovely finished quilts on display everywhere—even draped over antique sewing machines and old washstands. Gingham curtains hung in the windows. Posy had made the shop as welcoming and friendly as she was herself.

Beatrice and Meadow waited a moment while Posy was finishing up with a customer. Meadow elbowed Beatrice. "Looks like Miss Sissy has taken up residence in her usual spot."

Beatrice glanced over at the sitting section to see the cronelike old woman sleeping on the sofa. As if somehow feeling their gaze, she abruptly awakened, glaring around the store and muttering, "Poppycock! Poppycock!" She spotted Beatrice and Meadow looking at her and brandished an arthritic fist at them.

"Looks like she's in rare form today," murmured Beatrice.

Posy quickly walked over and greeted them, and they filled her in on their idea for the quilting retreat. "Oh, I think that's a marvelous idea!" said Posy, twinkling at Meadow and Beatrice. She was a tiny, bespectacled woman with a gentle smile. "Believe it or not, the store has been so busy that I haven't finished my own quilt yet."

Meadow said to Beatrice, "See? This is what I'm talking about. Even Posy can't get a quilt finished."

"Can we do it Friday night?" asked Posy. "You know the shop closes early on Fridays, and that would give us a little time to catch up before the quilt show. We can put long tables in the storeroom and extension cords for all the tables."

"May I come, too?" asked a voice behind them, and they turned around to see an attractive woman who looked to be in her late fifties, although she had a remarkably unlined face. "Sorry for listening in. But I'm way, wayyyy behind on my quilt for the show,"

Posy quickly said, "Oh, Beatrice. This is Phyllis Stitt—she's a member of the Cut-Ups guild. I don't know if y'all have met."

Beatrice and Phyllis shook hands. Phyllis gave her a solid handshake.

"Do you mind, Posy?" asked Phyllis again. "It would really help me out."

Meadow looked a bit scandalized. "But it's a guild meeting for the Village Quilters!"

Miss Sissy wandered up from the sitting area and glared at Phyllis. "Village Quilters!" she repeated in a low growl.

"Pooh," said Phyllis, waving away Meadow's objections with a sweep of her hand and completely ignoring Miss Sissy. "We're not talking about industrial espionage or uncovering state secrets here. Quilting is quilting, right? I've gotten behind because things have been completely awful at the Cut-Ups lately. In fact, Meadow, I was planning on giving you a call and talking with you about it. I might be a refugee from the guild."

"Whatever do you mean?" asked another voice

behind them. This one was a good deal colder in tone. Beatrice turned to see Martha Helmsley standing nearby. Martha was also in the Cut-Ups and was their most elegant member, with her loosely upswept red hair, pearls, and tasteful designer clothes in various neutral hues. She was usually fairly reserved when she spoke, but this time her tone was downright frosty.

Phyllis colored slightly at being overheard, but raised her chin up and said, "You heard me, Martha. The Cut-Ups hasn't exactly been a fun group for me lately. I don't get the warm fuzzies when I go to the meetings anymore. Don't act like you don't know what I'm talking about, either. You're the one responsible for the rest of the group giving me the cold shoulder."

"That's ridiculous," snapped Martha. "You're imagining things. And I'm sorry to hear," she added in a censorious voice, "that you're behind on your quilt. You certainly shouldn't be." She stalked away to shop for fabrics.

"See what I mean?" asked Phyllis in a shaky voice. "So what do you think, Posy? You'd really be helping me out?"

"No room! No room!" snarled Miss Sissy. Beatrice decided she sounded very much like one of the demented guests from the mad tea party in *Alice in Wonderland*.

Posy, whose blue eyes had anxiously watched the standoff between Martha and Phyllis, said quickly,

"Actually, I was just counting tables in my head. I'm sure we have room for you at the retreat."

"But, for heaven's sake, don't tell anyone else!" said Meadow in her loud whisper, which could likely be heard by passersby on the street outside.

"Thanks so much," said Phyllis, giving Posy and Meadow and even a startled Beatrice hugs. "I'll be here Friday evening."

"Let's make it five o'clock," said Posy.

"Remember to bring food," Meadow called out as Phyllis started walking toward the door. "We have to have lots of sustenance for this kind of thing."

The door chimed as Phyllis left the shop. "That was interesting," murmured Beatrice.

"Those Cut-Ups with their silly melodramas," said Meadow with a sniff. "It's good to belong to a grown-up guild." She froze as Martha Helmsley gave her an unfriendly stare. "That is . . . well . . . oops. I have foot-in-mouth disease. Sorry about that, Martha."

Beatrice could barely see Martha's tense face over the huge pile she was holding. She held yards of several different patterns of fabrics—enough material for several quilts—and quilt batting, to boot. Posy quickly rang her up and Beatrice raised her eyebrows at the final total for the purchase.

"Thanks so much, Posy," said Martha smoothly. "You always have everything I need here."

"Thanks for being one of my best customers," said Posy brightly.

"Before I go," said Martha carelessly, "I wanted to see if I could join you ladies on Friday evening, too."

"Oh!" said Posy, startled. She looked helplessly over at Meadow and Beatrice for direction.

"No room! No room!" Miss Sissy repeated aggressively.

Meadow gave a ferocious frown, putting her hands on her wide hips. "I thought you told Phyllis that you were done with your quilt."

"No," said Martha, "I said that *Phyllis* should be done with her quilt. She procrastinates. I, on the other hand, have been incredibly busy. I only have a little ways to go, but this would give me a deadline for finishing my project." She looked expectantly at Posy over the bags of fabric still sitting on the checkout counter in front of her.

Posy nervously fingered the beagle pin on her fluffy blue cardigan. "I'm sure I can find a spot for you at the retreat, Martha. I'd love to have you come."

Martha rewarded her with a smile. "Thanks so much, Posy. See you ladies on Friday," she added coolly to Beatrice and Meadow.

"Now, why on earth would she want to come to your retreat when clearly she and Phyllis don't get along?" asked Beatrice.

"Isn't it obvious?" asked Meadow. "To get on her nerves, of course."

"Dangerrr," crooned Miss Sissy, right on cue.